He Went With

Christopher Columbus

He Went With
Christopher Columbus

LOUISE ANDREWS KENT

ILLUSTRATED BY
PAUL QUINN

Living Book Press

Publisher's Note

He Went With Christopher Columbus was written over 80 years ago and tells the story of a young man accompanying Christopher Columbus on his adventures around the world.

An excellent storyteller, Louise Andrews Kent provides the reader with the opportunity to experience a different time and place through the eyes of the main character, including the social customs, religious beliefs, and racial relations. Taking place over 500 years ago, many parts of life are foreign and sometimes offensive to us now, including specific customs, practices, beliefs, and words. To maintain and provide historical accuracy and to allow a true representation of this time period the words used and the customs and attitudes described have not been removed or edited.

This edition published 2022
by Living Book Press

ISBN: 978-1-922919-09-0 (hardcover)
         978-1-922919-08-3 (softcover)

A catalogue record for this book is available from the National Library of Australia

CONTENTS

1.	Book and Tree	1
2.	Matador	11
3.	Good-Bye, England	20
4.	Stone from a Sling	37
5.	Hunt for a Thief	60
6.	A Table is Set	75
7.	Ocean Sea	85
8.	Birds Fly West	96
9.	Men From Heaven	110
10.	Christmas Eve	125
11.	Present for Gonzalo	141
12.	Green Valley	149
13.	Esteban Sees a Procession	157
14.	Silence on *Española*	170
15.	Battle of Gourds and Reeds	177
16.	Dance, Caonabo!	190
17.	Lizard Man	200
18.	Esteban is Amused	211
19.	Valley of Pigs	224
20.	Shave and Haircut	238
21.	Chains	252
22.	Green Garden	264
23.	Portrait of a Gentleman	271
24.	Safe Harbor	282

TO J. A. J. JR

After you moved out of your room it looked pretty empty—no model planes, no skiing posters, no harmonicas—so I moved in with my junk. I piled stacks of books about Columbus all over your bed and on the chest and on top of the red filing cabinet. I crammed the wardrobe full of papers (some of which I found again when I wanted them) and then I sat down to write.

The result is this book. I am amazed at how neat and handsome it looks. It doesn't say all I'd like to say about Columbus, but I hope people who read it may go on and read some of the books I studied. Since I finished writing my story, Professor Morison of Harvard has come back from sailing over the route that Columbus followed. I'm glad to hear that he thinks Columbus was a great navigator. Every now and then I would read a book that said Columbus was only a landlubber who happened to be lucky. I couldn't see how that could be true, and it's interesting to have someone who really knows what he is talking about travel where Columbus went and see what he was up against. I have tried in my book to tell about some of his difficulties. Probably no one has ever told them all—or ever will.

I got some advice that helped me very much from Miss Alice Bache Gould who has worked in Spain on documents about Columbus and his companions and who knows more about them than anyone else. I know she kept me from making one or two mistakes, and I am very grateful to her. If I made others, it is my fault. People do make them: even Columbus thought he'd got to India. We are still calling the original inhabitants of this part of the world Indians as a result of that mistake.

It isn't necessary to tell all that Columbus went through to show that he was a great man—one of the men who change the world simply because they have an idea and won't let any amount of discouragement keep them from carrying it through.

I expect your reading is mostly larger and heavier books than this now, but as long as this one was written in your room, I thought I'd dedicate it to you. Now that I have cleared up the room so that it no longer looks as if the hurricane had struck it, it is ready for you any time.

A visit will please us all, especially

Yours sincerely,

LOUISE ANDREWS KENT

BROOKLINE, *April* 1, 1940

CHAPTER 1

BOOK AND TREE

HIGH up in a beech tree Peter Aubrey was reading his new book. On the green lawn below, his two uncles, the Englishman and the Spaniard, walked up and down. Don Diego's black velvet and Sir Henry Tallard's crimson cloth caught Peter's eye as they passed below his hiding place, but he did not look after them.

He did not listen to their talk either, though his ear caught his own name. He did not care what they said. He wanted only to be left alone with his book, to hide from his cousins, Gwen Tallard and Esteban Medina-Barrios, to hear only the rustle and swish of the beech leaves and the blackbird whistling in the hawthorn.

Peter was rather like a blackbird himself. His clothes were black, so was the straight hair that hung over his forehead, so were the eyes that followed Marco Polo's story...

'I will pass hence to the land of the Indies where I, Marco Polo, dwelt a long time, and now I will begin with the island of Cipango. The people of this country are fair and of good manners though they worship idols. There is in this island a King frank and free, and he has great plenty of gold. He has a marvellous palace all covered with gold plate. The windows and pillars of this palace are all of gold. Also there are precious stones in great plenty...'

'It must be a fine sight,' Peter thought.

He shut the book and looked out through the beech leaves over the pleasant English country, almost hoping for a moment to see that shining palace standing among strange trees. Instead he saw fields where sheep slept in the shadow of the oaks, green hedges with their new branches gently waving in the summer sun, white clouds drifting lazily high up in the air, the blue and silver river slipping quietly towards the sea.

The sea itself—the road to Cipango—was hiding under a soft haze. Not even a gleam showed where it was. The mist hid the harbor, too, and his father's warehouses and the masts of his ships.

Peter thought, not with pleasure but with the dull ache that always came with this knowledge: 'They are my ships now.'

It was still hard to believe that his father was dead. Don Diego had brought the news less than a month ago. Don Luis de Medina-Barrios—known in England as Lord Aubrey—had been killed near the walls of Granada by a Moorish arrow.

Don Luis had come to England with King Henry the Seventh and had fought for the King at Bosworth Field against the humpbacked Richard the Third—the man who had had his nephews, boys no older than Peter, murdered in the Tower. King Henry had given his Spanish friend the estate over which Peter was now looking. Melcote was its name. The King had knighted Don Luis on the field of Bosworth and later had made him a baron. English tongues had changed his Spanish name to Louis Aubrey. Names were easily changed in those days. Until Don Diego had come back from Spain bringing the news that Louis Aubrey had died there. Peter had almost forgotten that his own name was Pedro de Medina-Barrios in Spain, though in England it was Peter Aubrey.

'He spends too much time with his nose in a book,' Henry Tallard said in his big voice.

Don Diego made some answer, but as usual he spoke so softly that even if Peter had tried to listen he could not have heard the words. Besides, he did not care what they were. It was Don Diego who had brought him Messer Marco Polo's book. It was in Latin, a printed book, not written by hand. His uncle had put it in the chest that he had brought back from Spain, the chest that contained Peter's father's clothes. Louis Aubrey's sword was in it, and the suit of crimson velvet that he wore to court when the King had made him Baron Aubrey. Peter had not unpacked the chest. He had locked it and put the key under a book on the shelf near his bed. The only thing he had taken out was the copy of Marco Polo.

His Uncle Diego, Peter thought, might say what he liked as long as he gave him books like this. Perhaps when they went to London to see the lawyer, his uncle would take him to Master Caxton's press and let him buy a book there. Master Caxton was dead now. He had printed books in English, stories of knights and gentle deeds. They were easier for Peter to read than Spanish or Latin, though the chaplain, Father Patrick, had taught him both. Peter's father had promised, if he did well in his Latin, to buy him a book Master Caxton had printed, by a man named Geoffrey Chaucer. *The Canterbury Tales,* it was called. Only now his father—

It was better not to think about his father now.

Peter opened his book and read on...

'In the midst of that hall is a cistern of fine gold that will hold ten hogsheads, which is always kept full of good drink. At dinner out of the cistern they draw, with pots of gold, wine to serve the great Khan. And everyone that sits at the table has a cup of gold. When the great Khan drinks all the musicians that are in the hall play on their instruments...'

Henry Tallard said: 'We have been waiting for you, Hubert. Can you show us some sport?'

Peter looked down through the leaves. He saw Hubert the Falconer's sandy red head, the scarlet sleeves under his black coat, his gloved left hand, the hooded falcon on his wrist.

The three men went out of the garden through the great gate. It was Peter's chance to get to his own room without being seen. His cousins had hunted for him there already— he had seen them open the leaded casement and look out. He wrapped his book in his silk handkerchief and, carefully holding it under one arm, climbed higher in the tree to be sure Esteban and Gwen were nowhere in sight.

He could look down now into the courts and over the roofs of the new house his father had built. The tiles shone in the sun like small red shields. The new rusty pink brick walls with the pattern of dull blue brick running through them showed smooth and clean. The heavy oak doors, bolted and strapped with iron, stood open. So did the casement windows with their panes of painted glass. Not everyone had glass, especially painted glass, in his windows, but Lord Aubrey's house had everything that was of the newest fashion: floors of wide oak boards laid as tightly as the sides of a ship, oaken panels on the wall carved to look like folded linen, ceilings of carved wood and plaster brightened with touches of gold.

The garden seemed to be sleeping in the afternoon sun. Tom the Jester lay curled up asleep under a red rosebush. His yellow leg was twisted over his green one. His yellow arm was over his face and the green one under his head. He moved a little, and Peter could hear the bells on his clothes tinkle.

Father Patrick had said his prayers and now he, too, was dozing. His small brown book had slipped into the folds of his brown robe. He was smiling happily at something he was dreaming about. Two stableboys were asleep on a pile of straw in the yard. Even the red cattle outside in the field were only half awake.

It was so still that Peter could hear bees buzzing in the roses, a lamb in the field crying for its mother, and—suddenly—the squeaking twitter of frightened birds. He saw the falcon sail high above the trees, then dive so swiftly that he could hardly follow her flight. He could almost feel the rush of air past his cheek, hear it sing through the feathers, see the swooping shadow close above him, feel the clutch of the terrible claws.

Peter hated cruelty. Gwen Tallard had often laughed at him for turning such a strange color under his dark skin because a bear was baited or a bird torn to pieces. She had laughed when he had got the scar on his right arm—those five lumpy tooth—marks—where the deer hound had bitten him. Peter had snatched away a kitten that the dog had been shaking in his fierce jaws. Hubert had burned the wounds with a red-hot nail. Peter could not sleep that night and his arm ached for many days. The kitten, however, was chasing her tail spryly the next morning.

Even now, when there was a storm coming, his arm would

ache. It did now as he climbed down the tree. He only tucked his book under it tightly, swung by his left hand from a branch high above the ground, landed as lightly as the kitten could. She was a cat now, a handsome striped creature the color of Meg Sutherland's hair. Peter had named the cat Rusty Maggie—as a compliment to Meg, he said. Meg did not thank him for it...

No one was in sight as he slipped from the shade of the beech to the clump of dark yews near the house. Hidden behind them was a small door, so cleverly made to look like the rest of the brick wall that even Peter could not see where the joints were. He was the only one who knew about it now. His father had told him the secret. There was a ram's head carved in stone on the wall. The ram had a collar from which a stone ring hung among carved leaves and flowers.

Peter found the ring, pulled at it gently. A piece of the wall opened. He slid through, shutting the door behind him. It closed with a click that only a very sharp ear could have heard. He moved quietly through the cool darkness. His soft shoes made no sound on the stone steps. There were four of them, then a level place. He was back of the Great Hall now. He ran his left hand along the wall until he found the flap of canvas back of the peephole. He raised the flap, stood on his tiptoes, and looked into the Hall.

His mother was sitting in the carved chair that Lord Aubrey had brought from Spain. It was the first time that Peter had seen her since the news of his father's death had come. She had shut herself into her rooms. No one had seen her but Dame Butts, once her nurse, now the housekeeper, and Father Patrick.

She looked very white and ill. Her face was nearly as pale as the white linen around it. Her hands looked white and thinner than ever against her black dress. She was holding the right one out now towards Meg Sutherland.

'I dropped my needle, Meg,' she said in her low, clear voice. 'Can you find it for me, Sweet? I am so clumsy today.'

All the ladies were working on the big tapestry for the west wall of the room. Usually they talked and sang while they worked, but today they made their stitches of blue and green and rose in silence. They were working as if the tapestry must be finished that afternoon, though it had been years in the making and there was another winter's work still to be done. Louis Aubrey would never see it now.

Meg Sutherland knelt down hunting for the lost needle. Her rusty red hair, Peter thought, looked ugly against a crimson patch that was a king's robe on the tapestry. Her dress was the same old dress that Peter had often seen her wear. It had been chosen, not to look well with her hair. and freckles and bright hazel eyes, but because brownish-greenish yellow was a practical color. It had been pale blue when it belonged to Gwen. Dame Butts had dyed it.

'Poor Meg!' Peter thought. 'Hunting needles instead of riding!'

Meg found the needle and stood up. She moved quickly and easily. Peter had noticed that before. She was pleasanter to watch when she was running or riding than Gwen Tallard was, though Gwen was known as a beauty as far as Chelmsford and Meg was not known, even in their own village, except as a poor girl from the north somewhere, that Lady Aubrey had taken in out of charity. The Tallard family had property up north, near Lincoln, some said. Meg's father was a Scottish knight. That was why, people in the village thought, she was so wild and strange. Climbed trees like a boy, she did. Stole

Master Peter's clothes and rode a young colt bareback. Ran away to go fishing, too. Dame Butts had no end of trouble with her.

The good wives of Upper Melcote clicked their tongues over such doings. They did not stop when Hubert the Falconer said that if a girl rode a colt bareback she was wise to leave her petticoats at home. A girl, they said, should be happy at home, sewing or learning to make venison pasty and oaten cake. There was no one who understood curing hams and bacon better than Dame Butts. Meg ought to be glad to know how, and also to learn about turning a cheese so it would ripen properly.

Meg's lack of interest in these secrets was a pity. Even worse, the village considered, was her way of going about with her hair uncovered. And such hair! The color of a bay horse in the sunshine, only curly! A girl of fourteen ought to wear folds of linen over her hair and under her chin and a cap of velvet on top of the linen. Even Gwen Tallard, whose hair was like ripe corn, real English hair, kept it covered now with fine linen and velvet. Well, anyway, mostly covered. Gwen was always a lady. It was a pity Meg was not more like her.

Peter wished he could open the door in the panelling and go in to see his mother, but naturally he could not, since it was a secret, even from her. She was moving her needle now, but slowly, as if stitching hurt her. Meg was yawning. She tried to hide the yawn, but Dame Butts saw it and twitched her bushy gray eyebrows. Meg swallowed the yawn, took a piece of blue wool, licked the end of it, and tried to push it through the eye of her needle.

It went through the third time she tried. Instead of beginning on the leaf she was shading, Meg began to yawn again. Dame Butts did not see her this time, but the yawn stopped suddenly, became a strange sound: half gasp, half squeak.

'What is it, Meggie?'

Meg was staring, Peter realized, straight at the peep hole, straight into his eyes.

He dropped the flap.

His mother's voice said: 'What is it, Meggie? Did you prick yourself?'

'No, my lady,' Meg said. 'I fear I was falling asleep. I—I dreamed the eyes in the portrait—in his portrait moved.'

'I wish they could,' Lady Aubrey said gently, and Meg gasped: 'Oh, my lady, I should not have spoken of him.'

'I am glad you did, Meg. Now that I am stronger I see that— as Father Patrick said—I was wrong to shut myself away from you all, and not to speak of this sorrow. It was shutting my dear lord away from me. I am glad that you spoke of him, and that his picture hangs there, showing how he looked when the King first named him Baron Aubrey. And now, sing to us, my sweetheart. Your voice always makes our needles fly faster.'

Meg's voice—it made Peter think of the blackbird in the pink hawthorn—began an old Scottish ballad. He did not stop to hear it, but went quietly to the stair that led to his own room.

CHAPTER 2

MATADOR

THINGS might have been different if Peter had not climbed to his tower room just then. Still, he thought afterward, he would probably have fought with Esteban sooner or later in any case. The growing dislike between them had begun years ago on Esteban's first visit when Peter had tried, vainly, of course, to rescue the puppy Esteban was teasing.

Esteban was not really hurting the puppy, he said, quickly moving away from Peter's blundering rush and then upsetting him by a neatly placed foot. Besides, it was only a mongrel anyway. Try not to be a silly fool, he said.

Lord Aubrey had come into the garden just then. It was the only time Peter had ever seen him angry. The things he said both in English and Spanish ought to have made Esteban ashamed, but he only looked at his uncle out of his narrow gray eyes with the usual scornful twist of his upper lip. It was five years ago, but Esteban had not changed. He had the same cool stare, the same sneering look, the same way of raising his

11

right shoulder as he walked, and of moving his left hand palm down, thumb up, to show his contempt for anything.

He was tall for his sixteen years. He had fought outside Granada. He knew famous people: his distant cousins the Dukes of Medina-Sidonia and of Medina-Celi, Alonso Ojeda, the King and Queen themselves. He told stories about them all in his drawling way. The stories all made Esteban seem very grand and the grand people very small.

King Ferdinand was a little man, Esteban said. Stingy, too. He would rub his hands together and say: 'Come to dinner today, Don Diego, and bring your son. We are going to have a fowl for dinner.' The fowl was generally a rooster, one that had been fond of walking. All Esteban got would be the neck.

Queen Isabella, Esteban said in his patronizing drawl, was a fine woman, only a little crazy. Now that she had finished chasing the Moors out of Granada—she rode into battle in full armor instead of staying in her tent where she belonged—she was planning to conquer Cathay and make a Christian of the great Khan.

She listened to the talk of a crazy man who followed the Court wherever it went, Esteban said. The man's name was Christopher something—Colombo, Colon, Columbus. People called him all three.

'He thinks the world is round,' Esteban had drawled. 'He is going to reach the East where Kublai Khan is by sailing west. Moonstruck—that's what he is!'

'But the world *is* round,' Peter said. 'Everyone knows that. The Greeks knew it hundreds of years ago. Have you never stood on the deck of a ship and seen another ship vanish over the horizon, hull first, until you could see only the banner flying at her mainmast? That is because the world is a round ball.'

Esteban only laughed.

'I'll lend you my book, *The Image of the World*. You can read it for yourself,' Peter said.

'Reading is only for women and priests,' Esteban said with that sneering twist of his lip.

They had not fought that day. Peter had bitten his tongue and walked off. After all, Esteban was his guest.

'I won't,' he thought, opening the panel into his own room, 'fight with him even when he calls me "Peter, Lord Aubrey, Second Baron Aubrey of Melcote in Essex," in that hateful voice. Let him sneer.'

He put his book on the shelf with the others and walked to the window. He could look down on Melcote again, but there was no drowsiness now. Everyone was moving in one direction—the stableboys, Tom the Jester, the kitchenmaids, men from the farms, girls from the dairy. Even the shepherd had waked up, had left his dog to care for the sheep, and was running towards the walled green field beyond the barns.

Peter could look into the field. What he saw sent him swinging out his window to the gate between his tower and his mother's. He ran along the narrow path above the gate, balancing himself with an outstretched hand; found the window ledge and the two projecting bricks that were his footholds on the other tower; threw himself across empty space to the tough branch of a young elm; slid down the trunk without noticing either that his new black hose were scraped through or that his knees were raw and bleeding.

He ran panting towards the paddock, not seeing the courts and passages and gardens through which he ran, but only the picture of the green field with Minotaur, his young bull, plunging through it; Esteban with the sun flashing on his

Swinging out his window

sword; the figures flapping pieces of scarlet cloth; Gwen standing on the wall clapping her hands.

He heard a voice as he ran gasping: 'Minotaur! Minotaur!' and knew suddenly that it was his own voice. Then he shut his lips firmly. He needed all his breath if he was going to be in time.

He did not remember that Minotaur was a valuable piece of property. He remembered only that his father had given him the little red calf for his own; that Lord Aubrey himself had fed him, shown Peter how to take care of him; that Minotaur was as trusting and friendly as a young dog. And now—

Peter turned the corner of the barn, scrambled over a five-barred gate, and jumped into the paddock. He was in time.

Minotaur was still making headlong, blundering

'Now, Esteban, now!'

rushes for the scarlet cloth that one of the village boys waved at him. His hoofs slipped on a muddy place in the grass. He almost fell as the boy stepped aside. The other boy dashed in waving his cloth and the bull turned towards him, but stood for a moment pawing the ground and making a rumbling noise in his throat. His red sides were dark with sweat. He shook his hornless head in a way that was more puzzled than fierce.

'Now, Esteban, now!' Gwen Tallard shrieked from her place on the wall. In the bustle of people climbing on the wall to see the sport, she had not seen Peter's entrance. Neither had Esteban nor the village boys. Their backs were towards him.

Peter never forgot that picture: Gwen in her blue-and-gold dress against the blue sky, the hot gold of her hair just showing under her headdress of deeper blue; Bill Turley and Jack Smith in their suits of Lincoln green, flapping with their dirty red fists the fine scarlet cloth that Bill's father had woven; Esteban's tall figure in black and silver, his sword partly covered by a black cape lined with scarlet; Minotaur with foam on his velvet muzzle, his soft eyes turned red and angry.

Peter heard Tom the Jester laugh.

'Oh! Oh! La—la—la! There'll be dancing on the green. Merriment we'll have. Yes, and mirth. Melcote and Merry England. George and the Dragon. Or is it Peter and the Bull? This sun dazzles my poor eyes.'

The Jester was on the wall near the gate, swinging his long green-and-yellow legs. No one but Peter paid any attention to his high, cackling voice.

'Quiet, Tom,' Peter said, and the Jester answered sensibly enough: 'Right, my lord. I only thought to stop it. If you need a leg to trip up that prancing cockatrice, I've two that are long enough.'

Peter said, 'Stay where you are, Tom.'

He walked a little way under the wall on which Gwen Tallard was standing, turned suddenly, crossed the trampled grass, and stopped close behind the pawing, snorting bull.

There was silence around the field. Grooms and serving-maids stopped guffawing and giggling. Gwen's pink cheeks flushed pinker. The Jester yawned, stretched himself along the wall, and pretended to go to sleep, all except for one watchful green eye. Jack Smith and Bill Turley tried to stuff bunches of scarlet cloth under their green jerkins.

Only Esteban stood his ground. He still held his sword pointed at Minotaur, still kept his easy balance like a cat ready to jump forward, back, or to the side.

'A very good afternoon to you, Peter, Lord Aubrey, Second

Baron Aubrey of Melcote in Essex,' he said in his silky voice. 'Can your humble servant persuade you to a little sport?'

'Yes,' Peter said quietly. 'Look out for yourself, Don Esteban Medina-Barrios.'

He felt his voice tremble, but it was steady as he spoke to the bull: 'Minotaur, old boy, we're going to get a drink.'

At the familiar voice Minotaur stopped pawing and turned his head.

'Open the gate, Bill, and be quick about it,' Peter said. 'Come, Minotaur, water.'

He put out his hand for the bull's swinging tail. For three years now Peter had driven Minotaur, guiding him by his tail, to the river for his evening drink. Could he do it now—or would the bull, angry for the first time, turn and trample him?

The tail swung, lashing the air like a strong whip. Peter seized the end firmly, gently.

'Water, Minotaur,' he repeated, and felt the tail tighten in his hand.

The gate was open. The bull made a headlong plunge for it. They passed so close to Esteban that the cape over his sword waved in the rush of air.

'Wait for me, Don Esteban,' Peter said.

The words spun past the young matador's ear. He only gave that hunch of his shoulder, spread out his left hand, palm down, thumb up, in his gesture of contempt. He was leaning easily against the wall, looking up at Gwen Tallard, when Peter, having watered the bull and stabled him, came back into the paddock.

'Now for the sermon,' Esteban yawned. 'We are to hear, I suppose, about kindness to cats, delicacy to dogs, benevolence to bulls. Unless—just for once—you could leave preaching to the chaplain.'

Peter's answer was to hit his cousin on the mouth.

It was not a dignified, knightly affair, that fight. Somehow, he never knew exactly how, Peter got Esteban's sword away from him and pitched it over the wall. It may be, as Esteban said afterward, that Peter's first blow jolted Esteban's elbow against a sharp point of rock and that he dropped the sword. He had several good explanations of how he—who had fought the Moors at Granada—was disarmed by a barehanded boy younger and smaller than himself. In any case the fight from then on became a scuffle in which feet, nails, fists, and teeth were all useful. It stopped only because Gwen's screams brought her father, Don Diego, and the falconer.

Hubert and Sir Henry Tallard pulled the boys apart. Don Diego only stood and smiled gently at Esteban's black eye and Peter's bleeding nose.

'English sport,' he murmured. 'My brother called it manliness, I believe. And was there not something about raw beef for eyes closed in this manly pastime? Bleed on this, nephew,' he added, holding out a square of fine white silk towards Peter. 'Share it with your cousin. Otherwise I have fears for his new doublet. And we Medina-Barrios are poor people.'

Peter used his own handkerchief. His uncle's voice slid along like the water past Minotaur's drinking place. Peter hardly listened. He knew vaguely that Don Diego was telling for the tenth time how the Medina-Barrios had given men and money, had made themselves poor to help drive the Moors from Spain, and that the sovereigns had given them nothing in return.

'But—fortunes of war, fortunes of war,' the smooth voice went on. 'Patience! Shake the dice well! It may be our turn some day. In the meantime, my son, you must learn to take affronts more calmly. Beggars, you know, cannot afford pride. You can scarcely expect your host to ask your pardon.'

Peter heard this.

'He should not have tried to kill my bull,' he said stubbornly.

Esteban laughed.

'I had no idea of killing the fat sluggard. I told Mistress Gwendolen that I would touch him with my sword's point at the place where in Spain I have killed a bull—a Spanish bull with courage, fire and horns. You would not have found a flea bite on his coward's coat, my Lord Aubrey.'

His lip was puffed and swollen. There were scratches on his face. His tight eye was closing rapidly. Yet he kept his air of dignity that always made Peter feel awkward, clumsy.

Peter's nose had stopped bleeding now. He put away the handkerchief and said curtly: 'Since you are my guest I will forget what you have said and what you have done. Jack Smith, fetch Don Esteban his sword. You will find it, I think, among the cabbages.'

He bowed stiffly and went out through the gate.

The Jester raised his head and murmured: 'Oh! La-la! Merry! We must all be merry!'

Peter heard Gwen Tallard's laugh. It seemed to follow him; seemed to grow louder as he went farther away.

CHAPTER 3

GOOD-BYE, ENGLAND

MEG SUTHERLAND met him in the great court. 'Peter,' she said, 'you're hurt! What happened?'

He told her briefly.

Meg groaned: 'The only fight for weeks and I'm not there! And Gwen on the wall—this is a hard world. While outside there's blood and battle, I sit indoors singing about knightly deeds and twanging my lute!'

'And a very good thing,' Peter said crossly. 'If all girls stayed inside and played the lute, the world would be the better for it.'

'Oh, Peter—you're not going to be like all the rest! "Meg, be a lady. Cross your feet when you sit down and be sure your skirt covers your ankles. Fold your hands in your lap. No, the other way, so that your rings show. Buttermilk will bleach your freckles. Keep out of the sun. Here's a cap in the French style to keep your hair smooth. Cover it, child. No one will know it's red." Shall I have to hear it from you too, Peter?'

Peter laughed. He could not help it. Meg had given such a lifelike imitation of Dame Butts that he could see the stout housekeeper shaking a fat white forefinger and hear her panting out her advice to girls.

'Forgive me if I spoke crossly,' he said. 'I'll go wash the blood off my face.'

At last he was alone in his room. He unlocked his father's chest and lifted the carved lid. He would feel better, he thought, if he could touch something of his father's. He knelt beside the chest and looked into it. The crimson velvet tunic with the gold embroidery on its full skirt and sleeves lay on top of the pile of clothes. The old-fashioned pointed shoes were there too. So were the crimson hose and the low-crowned velvet cap with the brim nicked at the left side. Peter lifted them out carefully. It was the sword he wanted to see again. It was there, under a cloak of brown cloth: an old cloak that Peter remembered well. He took out the sword and held it towards the light.

He seemed to hear his father's voice say: 'Be patient, my son. Be courteous. Be kind. Courage is not a thing by itself. It is part of courtesy and patience. Anger is easy...'

'I will remember,' Peter said.

He put the sword back into the chest and laid the other things carefully over it. He had just put the key back on the shelf when he heard a knock at the door.

'Lady Aubrey wishes to see you in the Great Hall, my lord,' said his mother's page.

It was Dick Carpenter from across the county, with whom he had often sailed boats on the river. Dick watched Peter while he washed his face and smoothed his black hair. Dick had a way of raising his light eyebrows and puckering his mouth when he knew something that Peter did not know. He did both now.

'What makes you look like a cat that has eaten a robin?'

Peter asked, but Dick only straightened his eyebrows and said: 'Nothing, my lord. Nothing.'

'He thinks I am going to be scolded,' Peter thought. 'No doubt he is right.'

He followed Dick's neat figure. Dick was getting to be the perfect type of lady's page. He swung the heavy door of the Hall open, made a fine bow, said in his high, clear voice: 'My Lord Aubrey, my lady,' shut the door behind Peter, and walked off with loud steps to show that he was not listening.

Lady Aubrey was still sitting in the big chair. Peter wished he could have seen her alone, but both his uncles were there. Don Diego was sitting on a low stool beside her. He looked sympathetic and sad. Her brother, Sir Henry Tallard, was stamping up and down with his big head lowered and his big red hands behind him.

Peter knelt beside his mother's chair, took his mother's hand and kissed it. She smiled and touched his bruised cheek, but she did not speak of the fight. Her smile had more sadness than amusement in it.

'Your uncles would like to talk to you, Peter,' she said, and sank back against the red-and-gold leather looking white and tired. No one said anything for a moment, and she added: 'Tell him, Henry, what his father wished.'

Peter got to his feet and stood beside the chair with one hand on the back of it.

Sir Henry stopped his pacing. His big voice echoed through the big room and seemed to lose itself in the carved timbers of the roof.

'Your father wished you to carry on the trade with Spain, Peter. "There's no use leaving it to hired people," he said, and he was right. There's a ship of his—of yours—leaving next week for Spain with a cargo of our Melcote cloth. For—what's the name of the place—Palos?'

Don Diego nodded and Henry Tallard went on: 'Your Uncle Diego and I both feel that you had better sail to Palos. We'll go first to London. See Master Studley, the lawyer. He and I are your guardians and in charge of your English property; Don Diego of your Spanish estates. We both wish you to learn all you can about your affairs.'

He paused, and Peter said, trying not to choke over the words: 'Very well, sir. Whatever my father wished, I will try to learn.'

'Good lad!'

Henry Tallard clapped Peter on the shoulder. There were bruises on it. Peter had hard work not to shrink away from the kindly hand.

He said: 'Thank you, Uncle,' bowed, and started towards the door.

'Not so fast. There's—there's something else.'

Peter thought Don Diego looked amused as Sir Henry stumbled over the words, but perhaps it was only the Spaniard's usual half-smile.

'Your father,' Henry Tallard began. 'That is, your mother—that is, we all—you had better tell him, Elinor.'

Lady Aubrey said gently: 'It's about your marriage, Peter. Your betrothal to Gwendolen should take place, we think, before you make your voyage. That is, your Uncle Henry and I think so. Your Uncle Diego feels that it is not yet necessary.'

Peter was glad that she kept on talking. It gave him time to steady his voice before he asked, 'Was this my father's wish?'

'Yes, Peter. In his will he gives your Uncle Henry the right to arrange your marriage and suggests that Gwendolen should be your wife. He had always hoped so.'

'And—and you wish it too, Mother?'

'Yes. It would make me happy. My only brother's only child. A girl so good and beautiful. But if, Peter, as your Uncle Diego suggests, you might rather marry in Spain... He has a daughter... We will not force you... It can wait—your betrothal—till your return.'

Peter saw his Uncle Diego lean forward in his chair and almost stop smiling. Peter remembered—he could not have told why—the shadow of the hawk above the frightened bird that afternoon. For a moment it was as if he himself were standing in the edge of that shadow, feeling something moving towards him, not knowing what it was.

Then he thought: 'I may go to Spain with you, Uncle Diego, but I will not marry your daughter who looks like Esteban in her portrait. That would be worse than Gwen.' The shadow

Uncle Diego stopped smiling

seemed to pass as he said aloud: 'Whatever you wish, Mother, and you, Uncle Henry. It may as well be before I sail.'

It gave him pleasure, as he bowed and left the Hall, to see that his Uncle Diego had most certainly stopped smiling.

He thought at first, as he started for London that next morning, that it was Gwen waving to him from the window of the South Tower. Then the sun brightened and he saw that it was only Meg. He might have known Gwen would not be waving out of a window at dawn.

He waved to Meg and forgot her. He wished he could forget Gwen too, but he kept seeing her on the wall and hearing her call: 'Now, Esteban, now!' He could not keep anger out of his mind whenever he thought of it. Why couldn't it be Esteban who was going to be Gwen's husband? He was sure Don Diego had planned it, and Esteban too.

Still, Peter supposed, he would have to marry someone, and it might as well be Gwen since his father had wished it. And it displeased Esteban—that was something. Peter did not care especially to annoy Don Diego. After all, he had given Peter the book of Marco Polo's *Travels* and had promised to buy him more books in London. On the whole he had been pleasant about the fight, although he had, as usual, talked tiresomely about the Medina-Barrios. Peter had no sense of belonging to that family. He felt English—as English as the poppies coming up among the young corn, as English as the sturdy oaks of Epping Forest under which they rode, as English as Master Caxton's little shop.

He had died the year before, but the shop was still there in Westminster near the Abbey. A shield with a red bar down the middle hung over the door. The sign of the Red Pale, the

The sign of the Red Pale

printer called it. Peter would have spent all his time there if he could, watching the type being set and the sheets come out of the press.

Master Caxton was not only a printer, his successor, Wynken de Worde said; he made translations of books in other tongues. It was harder work than printing, Wynken de Worde said.

"'I became a printer,' I have often heard my master say, "because I was lazy. For years I copied books with this very hand. My pen was worn, my hand weary, my eyes dim with much looking at white paper. So I began printing instead of writing, and now people can come to the Red Pale and get their books at once, as many as they like, and cheap too, without making these old eyes and fingers ache.

"'Yes, printing is easy," he would say, "but now it is my brain that troubles me. How am I to put the Latin of Virgil into good English? We do not know what good English is! Our tongue has changed much since I was born. It is different in different towns. I know a man of Sheffield who stopped in a seacoast town and asked a farmer's wife for supper. He would like eggs, he said.

"'She did not understand; said he must be French by his talk. At last his servant said: 'My master means *eyren*,' and then she understood and boiled some eggs for him. Now, which should a man write—*eggs* or *eyren*?" It is still hard to tell,' Wynken de Worde added, rubbing ink off his fingers.

'They taste the same in any language—if they're fresh,' Henry Tallard said with his jolly laugh. 'Come, Peter. Come away or you will make beggars of us all.'

Don Diego bought *The Canterbury Tales* for Peter. Sir Henry gave him Malory's *Morte d' Arthur*. With his own money Peter bought Caxton's own translation of *Cicero*, but he said there was still something more he wanted.

Henry Tallard pretended to groan and said again that they would be beggars. 'What is it this time?' he grumbled.

'Since I am to sail to Spain—a map so I can learn where I am going.'

'For that,' Master Wynken de Worde said, rubbing his inky fingers again, this time on his forehead where they left some dark smears, 'for that you must go to a chart-maker. Walk down this street to the tavern. Turn right, then left. On the third house you will see a sign with a dove. Ask for Master Bartholomew Columbus.'

'I have had enough of shops,' Sir Henry said. 'I will go and pray in the Abbey awhile.'

'I will go with you,' Don Diego said. 'We will wait for you there, Peter.'

The chart-maker's shop was in a dark house in a dark, narrow street. There was no glass in the window. A man sat beside it drawing a map, quickly copying the lines of an irregular seacoast from a finished map spread out in front of him.

Peter could hear the scratch of the quill as it moved over the paper. The man had a fierce, proud face. His nose was like a falcon's beak. His long chin looked longer because of the pointed beard that covered it. It was a stiff black beard that seemed to stab the air as he raised his head.

He threw down his quill, began to cut a new one, looked up and saw Peter.

'You wished something, sir,' he said politely enough, but without smiling.

He had strange piercing gray eyes.

Peter said: 'A map of Spain if you please. Are you Master Columbus? Master Wynken de Worde sent me.'

'Yes. They call me Columbus here. In Spain—Colon. In Italy—Colombo.'

'I—why, I heard those names spoken yesterday of a man in Spain who wishes to sail west to Cathay.'

'My brother!' Bartholomew Columbus said quickly. 'Have you news of him? Have the Spanish King and Queen given him the ships he needs?'

'I think not,' Peter answered. 'From what my cousin said, who has come lately from Spain, I think he is still waiting.'

The chart-maker sighed impatiently.

'Kings are all alike. Your King here will spend more on one

tomb of bronze and stone than it would cost to send a ship to Cathay. First he was hot to do it. See, here is the globe I made to show him how we would sail west to Cipango—'.

'Where the roofs are all of gold,' Peter murmured.

'Yes. In one voyage we would more than pay for the ships. And after that—spices, silk, gold, pearls—all we could carry!'

'Why does he refuse?'

'He does not. He says neither yes nor no. One day he is all for sending the ships. The next it would cost too much. Cost too much—a new route to Cathay! And I sit here, drawing charts so other men may sail the seas!'

'Try another king.'

'They are all the same, I tell you. In Portugal they gave my brother no answer, but they got his charts and secretly sent out ships to find the way. The cowards came back saying there was no end to the Ocean Sea. Then my brother went to Spain. There the King and Queen encouraged him, but they say he asks too much for his services. As for your King, I daresay he would like to get my globe from me and then send out his own captains. But Christopher and I have learned our lesson. I show the globe, but it never goes out of my hands.'

Bartholomew Columbus covered the globe with a cloth. He took a map from the pile and held it out to Peter.

'Here you are. Portugal and Spain. For what port do you sail?'.

'Palos.'

'It is here.' The map-maker touched it with a strong ink-stained finger. 'There are good ships and sailors there. As good as any on the Ocean Sea. Will you go to the Court?'

He had a sharp way of asking questions, but something about his face made Peter answer willingly: 'Perhaps. After our business is done. My uncle has affairs to settle.'

'You may see my brother. Say this for me. I expect my answer from the English King soon. If it is no, I try France. If fortune is still against me I take what service I can find. The Portuguese have a new king. I will try him, although, as I said, they are all alike. One thing is certain. I shall not sit here drawing charts forever. To be a signpost, telling everyone where to go, never going myself, I find strangely wearisome.'

He gave a short bark of a laugh. Peter paid for the chart and walked back through the gray streets to the gray Abbey of Westminster. In that dim, shadowy church he wandered for a while, read the words cut on old stones, stared up at Henry the Fifth's saddle on the beam above his tomb, looked at the King's sleeping figure in his silver armor, at other figures in bronze that shone like gold.

At last he found his way into the Lady Chapel. There was some talk that the King was planning to rebuild it. Peter found his uncles talking to a thin-faced, long nosed, poorly dressed man who seemed to have some ideas about building. Peter wondered why his Uncle Henry listened so politely. He had often heard Sir Henry say that his old Norman Castle was good enough for him. He wouldn't give a yard of his thick stone wall for a mile of this new flimsy stuff. As for a lot of carved wood with gilding on it, and griffins and wyverns and dragons chipped out of good stones—well, it might be all very pretty, but when your neighbors made you a visit with pikes and arrows and mangonels, and cannon, why what you wanted was a wide moat, a drawbridge, good thick walls with narrow loopholes. These brick walls stuck full of painted glass—a nice thing to keep out cannon balls!

'I'm an old man. I like old ways,' Sir Henry would say, pulling at his square golden beard that was beginning to be streaked with silver. He did not say so today. He stood crumpling his velvet cap in his strong fingers and listening to the thin man with the quick, smiling eyes.

These eyes saw Peter before his uncles did, and their owner said: 'Another visitor. I hope you approve of our design for a new chapel, sir.'

He had a paper in his hand. It had a picture on it showing how the chapel would look with its new roof and windows. It was a wonderful drawing. Peter looked at it, feeling as if he could step into it, while Henry Tallard said: 'It is my sister's son, sire. Louis Aubrey's boy. You were speaking of him just now.'

Then Peter realized that the shabbily dressed man was the King. He knelt down and the King said: 'We are glad to see you, my Lord Aubrey.'

He borrowed Don Diego's sword, touched Peter lightly on the shoulder with it, and said: 'Stand up, Peter, Baron Aubrey of Melcote. We have not forgotten your father's services. To show you that we remember his loyalty we confirm you in his rights and honors with our own hand.'

He gave the sword back to Don Diego and added with his sly, twinkling smile: 'But not with our own sword, being too poor to wear one. It gives the beggars a wrong idea. Now, dressed as I am, I can walk from the Tower to the Abbey and none will ask me for a penny. Indeed they are more likely to offer me one. Was that what you were going to say, Lord Aubrey?'

Peter, who had been thinking of something not very different, said with some stammering that he, being a country boy, did not know how it was in London, but that he could say that down at Melcote people did not have many pennies, but there were swords at least at His Majesty's disposal. Also roast beef and cabbages and good brown ale and cheese. Country fare, but plenty of it. And a bed of live goose feathers that Dame Butts said was fit for a king—though no king had used it yet.

'Why, that is well spoken,' King Henry said. 'I may try it some night.'

His architect, a swaggering handsome man, far better dressed and more important-looking than the King, now appeared. Peter and his two uncles were dismissed with a quiet nod of the head that somehow suggested royalty and power. As he left the chapel Peter heard that magnificent peacock of a man, Torrigiani, asking pardon for not having certain drawings ready as meekly as Peter might explain to Father Patrick why he had not finished his Latin verses. The great man was the one in the patched gown.

On the way to Melcote Don Diego said: 'I suppose when your King has filled his treasure chests till they burst the hinges, he will buy himself a new robe.'

'He looks like a king in the old one, I think,' Peter said.

Don Diego was all smiles at once. He did not, he said, mean to offend Peter. Peter felt it was he, not his uncle, who had been rude.

About his betrothal Peter remembered afterward very little. His thoughts were all on Spain. He had not been there since he was a small boy. He could not remember much about the country, but he could see clearly how Queen Isabella looked riding through Seville on a chestnut mule. She looked, Peter remembered, as beautiful as a lady of King Arthur's Court. She was all dressed in soft blue and white. Her eyes were a softer blue than the sky, and the band of hair that showed under her headdress was the color of Meg's...

He was studying his map of Spain when they called him to come into the Great Hall. Master Studley, the plump, pink-faced lawyer, had finished drawing up the papers. Peter remembered signing them, and that as he put out his hand the sleeve fell away from his wrist and showed the tooth marks just above it.

Master Studley said: 'I remember when Hubert burned those marks for you, and how you bit almost through your tongue and never made a sound. I thought, "Studley, you'll be proud to serve that young man, some day." And so I am, my lord.'

His mother looked pale and sad. Meg looked strange with her bright hair for once properly covered and wearing an old dress of Gwen's. The strange headdress or Gwen's outgrown finery—or something—made Meg seem cross and uneasy. He thought she might even have been crying. Perhaps Dame Butts had been scolding her. He had no time to find out for his ship sailed at dawn. There was hardly any darkness that night, only a long silvery twilight, dim enough to make the moon like a great plate of gold as he rode to the harbor.

He could not think, when he was on the ship tossing on the channel in a choppy sea, what it was that Gwen had worn. It was some light color—pale blue or rose, not like Meg's ugly purple that set your teeth on edge. Gwen could wear that color. She looked beautiful in anything, so no doubt she had at the betrothal. Beside her he himself in his black suit must have looked as cheerful as a raven.

Still, the bruise on his cheek had faded out. Even in the flickering candlelight in the chapel Peter had noticed that Esteban's eye was still in the green-and-yellow stage. It would have looked better, Peter thought, if Esteban had not worn his crimson velvet with the yellow-satin trimmings.

'And in this sea,' Peter thought, 'he would look green all over.'

One of the sailors had told Peter that, on the voyage from Spain to England, the young Spanish gentleman had never left his bunk, and that he had groaned every time anyone offered him food and said: 'Land—is there no land yet?'

'But you, Master Peter—that is, my lord—you are a regular dolphin. Father Neptune, he's put his mark on you surely.'

'Oh, this is only the channel,' Peter said.

'Only the channel! The channel can do what she likes! You face the channel with the tide running against the wind, same as now, and you're an English sailor. Yes, *sir!*'

Peter flushed with pride under his dark skin. It was pleasant to stand on the deck of his own ship in the wind, to feel that he was master of both ship and sea.

'You'd maybe like to steer her a bit later,' the Captain said to him at dinner. Peter did, and the Captain spoke well of Peter's seamanship.

Melcote seemed very far away. He wondered some times about Minotaur. Peter had warned the grooms and the farm hands never to let Esteban go near the bull. He had even spoken to Tom the Jester about Minotaur.

Tom had only laughed and said: 'Wise men keep their treasures under lock and key. Fools know enough to keep what they wish to keep in their own pockets. You are not a fool, my lord.'

There was little satisfaction in this remark, or in Meg's. When he asked her to visit Minotaur in his paddock, to take him apples when they were ripe, to be sure the men did not forget to give him water, she only said crossly: 'Don't worry about Minotaur. *He'll* be all right. He can bellow when he's unhappy, trample people if he's angry, defend himself.'

He had not paid much attention to that speech, but now the words came back to him and he wondered what—if anything—she had meant. Was there some danger at Melcote? He did not like vague warnings. People ought to say things straight out or else be silent.

Had Father Patrick meant anything when he said: 'Do not stay away too long, my son. We need you here.' He had taken hold of Peter's wrist just where the five tooth marks scarred it, and Peter thought he had meant to say something more. His Uncle Diego had come up to them just then, smiling, and the priest had smiled too and added: 'Come back so that I can beat more Latin into that thick head of yours, my lord. There were five mistakes in your last verses. That scar healed well,' he said, and moved off.

It was strange that his mother had spoken of the scar, too; or perhaps it was natural that people noticed it, since his new loose sleeves showed the purple welts.

'The mark is like the track of a dog's foot,' she had said. 'I never saw that before. Had you noticed that, Meg?'

Meg spoke gently, as she always did to Lady Aubrey.

'Yes, I have seen it,' she said.

She had her lute in her hand.

'Sing to us, Meg,' Lady Aubrey said. 'I can sleep a little now—I think.'

She was in her bed with the embroidered curtains that her own fingers had worked. Her face was almost as pale as the linen of the pillows behind her. There was as much silver as gold in her hair.

'She has grown old in these last months,' Peter thought. He said aloud: 'Shall I stay in England, Mother? I can go later.'

She smiled and shook her head, saying: 'No. Your father would wish you to go.'

She kept her fingers on his scarred wrist until her hand grew limp and let his fall. Meg's voice grew softer and softer. She hardly moved the strings of the lute. Peter left the room softly, still hearing as he went the faint breath of the old tune.

Before he went he stole back once more. The room was dark. She was still asleep. He did not see her again.

CHAPTER 4

STONE FROM A SLING

THE little trading vessel was called the *Speedfast*. She was a good sailor, but even the fastest ship cannot move in a thick fog and without wind. Off the coast of Portugal the fog was like wet wool and the sails hung limp. The vessel rolled on gray, greasy waves. It was so quiet in the fog that sailors lowered their voices so as not to break the silence. Moisture dripped off everything. Sometimes Peter thought he could hear the drops falling.

He spent much of his time in the forecastle or amid ships with a young Spanish sailor called Martin Alzate. Peter liked to practise his Spanish with Martin, who was kind and courteous about mistakes, never laughing at Peter's English accent but gently suggesting corrections. Martin was a little older than Peter. He was a thin, dark boy about Peter's height, but so much stronger and so much more skillful about everything that had to do with a ship that Peter felt ashamed. Martin went up ropes and masts like a cat. He always seemed to be balancing on one foot in some dizzy place.

He had a mouthful of very white teeth, and these always flashed out in a smile against his dark face when he was in some especially dangerous spot.

'Boy's half monkey! Come down off there, you ape,' the master would say, and Martin would swing himself by his hard brown arms and land with bent knees, his bare feet touching the slippery, rolling deck at just the right moment.

Don Diego, if he had known about it, would doubtless have disapproved of young Lord Aubrey's friendliness with Martin Alzate, but Don Diego spent most of his time in his cabin. He was not seasick, he often said, but he felt the motion a little, particularly when the boat was becalmed. He lay in his bunk a good deal. He did not seem to need amusement. When Peter went in to see his uncle, he generally found Don Diego lying with his hands behind his head, smiling a little, apparently at his own thoughts. He never seemed weary of the bare cabin.

His servant, Gonzalo Palma, a flat-nosed, pale man who always seemed to be looking just over your shoulder with his round green eyes, was often in the cabin. He was, Peter thought, the ugliest man he had ever seen. Gonzalo had a high bulging forehead and above it, standing straight up, a bush of frizzy black hair. His ears were long and pointed and stood out from his head. He kept Don Diego's handsome chin beautifully shaved, but his own chin and cheeks were shadowed by a half-grown beard. He was a short, square-shouldered man, but his arms were so long that his hands seemed to hang below his knees.

Peter had never seen him smile, seldom heard him speak, but as there were often two voices in his uncle's cabin, one of them with a high-pitched, squeaky laugh, certainly not Don Diego's, Gonzalo was probably better company than he looked.

Peter wondered sometimes what his uncle and Gonzalo found so amusing, but as Peter was no listener at doors—indeed he always took pains to make his approach to his own cabin next door a noisy one—he never found out.

One thing he did learn was that Gonzalo was a native of the island of Mallorca. Martin told him so. It was after the fog lifted. The *Speedfast* was ploughing through a choppy sea before a strong breeze. They were not far from the coast of Spain. There were gulls skimming over the dark-blue water near the ship.

Martin Alzate had a sling in his hand. It was made of two long thongs of leather threaded through a wide piece of leather with a hole in it. It was an innocent looking weapon, but when Martin slipped one of his brown fingers through the loop at the end of one thong, balanced a stone in the wide piece of leather, whirled the sling around his head, suddenly letting go the other thong, the stone travelled fast and far. He did not hit any gulls, however.

The thong would snap like a whiplash, the stone would whiz through the wind like—Peter said—ten arrows leaving ten bowstrings, but it only plopped harmlessly into the water, leaving the gulls still banking, swooping, gliding.

'Good, you missed him!' Peter would say, and Martin would flash his cheerful grin and whang another harmless stone into the water.

'I'll get Gonzalo Palma to knock one down,' Martin said at last, rolling up the sling and dropping it with his few remaining stones into a small canvas bag.

'Could *he* hit one?' Peter asked.

He had seen Gonzalo do nothing more active than sharpen a razor or balance a bowl of hot soup on a tray.

Martin said: 'Well, he ought to be able to. He comes from one of the Isles of Slingers—Mallorca. Have you not seen how Phoenician he looks?'

'I thought he looked like a frog,' Peter said. 'Of course I know Phoenicians came to those islands, but that was thousands of years ago. They've had time to change their looks.'

Martin Alzate smiled and said: 'Well, they can still sling stones. I was there once. I got my sling there.'

Not many minutes later Gonzalo appeared on deck. Martin offered him the sling, but the Mallorcan shook his ugly head. He did not know how to use it, he said, in the high squeak that came so strangely from his big mouth.

The call came just then for Martin to go to the galley to get the kettle of salt beef and cabbage for the crew's dinner. He put the sling into a bag with his stones and skipped off, followed more slowly by Gonzalo, who would carry a tray full of more delicate food to his master. He would, Peter suspected, eat most of it himself. His uncle seldom ate anything but some dry bread with a little Spanish wine, but the dishes were scraped clean when they went back to the galley.

When Martin came back with the kettle of beef and cabbage, he no longer had the bag of stones hanging from his wrist. Peter supposed Martin had found it in his way and had put it into his bunk. That was his answer when Martin asked that evening if Peter had seen the bag.

'I put it down—I cannot think where. I have searched everywhere, but no bag. And I *know* I could hit a gull now,' Martin said.

'Then I am glad you have lost it,' Peter said, smiling.

The disappearance of the sling did not seem important at the time. Neither did the paper that had blown out of Don

Diego's cabin one day when the breeze freshened suddenly. It had brought the paper to Peter's feet. As he picked it up he could not help seeing that it was a list of the income from the Melcote estate. As this was his business, Peter read on.

Two things struck him as odd. In several cases the rents were not the correct ones. Peter knew them from having helped his father with the estate accounts. The rent from the gristmill at Melcote-under-Lyme was wrong. The profits from the trade in wool and woollen cloth were only an estimate.

Don Diego's business was with Peter's Spanish property, but of course Henry Tallard might have told him about the Melcote estate. Only—wouldn't he have given the figures correctly? And—the second point—would he have added figures about his own property? It was unlike Sir Henry to give that information to anyone. Yet there was a string of figures about his affairs.

Peter only glanced at them. Someone had pried into the Tallard estate along with his own, but he did not intend to take advantage of anyone's spying. He tore the paper into small scraps, went to the side of the ship, and let them flutter off into the air. They whirled and twisted for a while, then sank slowly and were caught at last in the crest of a wave. They were soon lost from sight in the tumbling water.

It amused Peter to see Gonzalo Palma hunting for something in the passage to Don Diego's cabin. As Gonzalo did not ask Peter if he had seen the paper, Peter decided his uncle did not wish Peter to know of its existence.

'So,' Peter said to himself, 'it would be a piece of Spanish courtesy not to speak of it. No Spaniard embarrasses another by knowing what he is not supposed to know.'

Like the lost sling, his uncle's interest in Tallard and Melcote did not seem important. Almost everyone, Father Patrick used to say, would like to know how much money anyone else has, but men of gentle birth did not show their curiosity. Money, he said, was only important when you had none.

'And to a fat old teacher with a good dinner under his belt, a good sleep ahead of him, a good pupil to listen to him when he's awake, it is not important even then.'

Father Patrick had smiled and thumped Peter's shoulder. He had a hand like a sirloin of beef and never remembered how heavy it was. He had added, 'The lesson for today is over. Good-bye, my lord. If you hear a dragon snoring in the rose garden, do not disturb him—it will be your teacher.'

Thinking of Father Patrick in his old brown robe waddling off to the rose garden, Peter felt suddenly homesick for Melcote. He had forgotten the feeling, though, in learning to swim. That was the day after he had found the paper. The ship was becalmed again. It was a hot day. The water was like green glass. Peter had happened to say to his uncle that he could not swim. He could not remember afterward how their talk had turned on swimming, but he remembered Don Diego saying with a yawn that Peter must learn. Gonzalo, who had taught Esteban, should teach Peter. He had a good method—his own invention.

'I have nothing to use,' Gonzalo grumbled, but Don Diego said he could easily fix something. 'Sailors have fish poles, haven't they?' he said.

Gonzalo's invention turned out to be a canvas belt fastened tightly around the pupil's chest. One end of a strong rope was fastened to the band. The other end was attached to a long pole.

'He will hold you up,' Don Diego explained, 'until you have confidence in the water. Swimming is only thinking you can swim. Gradually it will be the water that holds you, not the pole, and you will be swimming yourself.'

Peter was too long and thin to be a natural swimmer, but Gonzalo's invention gave him confidence, just as his uncle had said, and all that hot morning he spent going in and out of the warm water, splashing, pushing with his arms, kicking himself along with his feet. It was not till afternoon that the accident happened.

The loop on the canvas belt to which the rope was fastened suddenly gave way. Peter's head went down. His feet went up. He splashed his way to the surface only to go down again. He gasped, swallowed water. Now he could not breathe. He struggled, hitting out wildly with arms and legs because he must, must get back to Melcote.

He saw it suddenly through the gray-green twilight: saw the rose-red towers and Meg on a chestnut horse the color of her hair coming through the gate; saw his mother looking up from her embroidery at his father's portrait; heard a strange noise that was partly Father Patrick snoring, partly Minotaur bellowing, partly Tom's bells jingling.

Then someone grabbed his hair. He struck blindly at whoever it was, but he was hauled into a boat just the same. They carried him dripping, choking, and shivering up the side of the ship.

It was Martin Alzate who had dived and caught Peter's hair just in time, Martin who had kept his friend afloat until the boat could be lowered.

Don Diego, who, hearing the shouting, had actually left his cabin and come on deck, spoke with great kindness to Martin and offered him a gold piece. Martin refused it, and without much Spanish courtesy.

'Why should I let him drown?' he asked, scowling and

pushing his wet black hair out of his eyes. 'I would not let a cat drown. Keep your money, Señor. I am no hero. I like to swim.'

Don Diego shrugged his shoulders, tossed the gold piece and another besides to the cook, and said with his pleasant smile: 'Serve out wine to the crew, then, and let them drink Lord Aubrey's health. We must celebrate this happy day. Come, my dear Peter, you must get dry. We must not have you ill when we land in Spain.'

There were no more swimming lessons. The sail maker who had made the belt was scolded by Gonzalo for not having sewn the loop firmly. He took the reproof quietly, but that night after he had drunk Peter's health a few times, he was heard shouting that he could sew stronger than any Spaniard that ever touched canvas, and offering to fight any two of the Spanish sailors to prove it.

He went to sleep, Martin told Peter the next day, still muttering something about canvas and linen thread and that he had sewn the belt strong enough so you could sling a young ox in it—let alone my Lord Aubrey, who was only skin and bones...

It was hotter than ever the next day. Peter found his suit of black Melcote cloth far too hot and heavy. He put on instead clothes he bought from the ship's chest: a loosely woven shirt and breeches of coarse brown linen, a red sailor's cap to keep his black hair out of his eyes. It was growing long, as long as Martin's. In fact, now that they were dressed alike, there was little difference unless you looked closely between Martin Alzate, deck boy of the *Speedfast*, and Lord Aubrey of Melcote.

Peter tried to be as much like Martin as he could. He admired Martin more and more. He would not offer his friend money for saving his life, but he was determined to find out something he

Martin kept his friend afloat

could do for him. He stayed with Martin all day, helping him clean the decks, watching the glasses through which the running sand marked the time, turning them at the right moment, singing with Martin when he called the men on deck. Since some of the sailors were Spanish—the Captain was Spanish, though he had been much in England—they sang the calls both in Spanish and English. Peter helped Martin, too, when he went to get food for his mess. Instead of joining his uncle for dinner Peter ate salt pork and biscuit with the sailors that day.

The swimming accident might not have been Gonzalo's fault, but Peter felt a dislike to being anywhere near the Mallorcan. He had a particular distaste for the feeling that Gonzalo would be standing behind him at dinner. It was a foolish feeling, he knew. He tried to forget it in helping Martin, but his scalp was still sore where Martin had yanked him by the hair. There were still scrapes and bruises on his legs and ribs from his having been dragged hastily into the boat. With these reminders it was hard to forget his accident and Gonzalo.

There were more gulls than ever mewing and screaming around them that evening. The sun had blazed down into the sea, leaving behind a sky full of fiery feathers. Below them, as if it were rising out of the sea, was a cloud city with towers, domes, and flat-roofed houses. It stood out so sharply blue against hot gold that it looked more solid and real than the Spanish coast. It was near now but it seemed to melt into the pale Eastern sky.

'Do you think,' Peter asked his friend, 'that there is really land to the west? Could what we see there be the shadow of some city of the Indies? I have heard that from the Canary Islands they see land on a certain day each year, always in the same place.'

'Where is it the other days, then?' Martin asked with a smile. 'Floating around to cheat poor sailormen? No, I do not believe anyone has ever seen land to the west. Why we cannot even see Palos yet, and I know we are not far from it. We shall go over the bar of Saltes with the morning tide. I heard the Captain say so. No, my lord—'.

'Don't call me "my lord." My name is Peter—'

'Well—Peter, then—that city is only clouds, but—'

'I knew it was only clouds really.'

'But'—Martin went on—'if you wish to find land in the west you must go with Cristobal Colon—Columbus, you would call him, I suppose.'

Peter said with a start: 'That's the third time.'

'The third time—?'

'That I have heard his name. Do you know him, Martin?'

'Yes.'

'Is he a madman as my uncle says?

'Because he thinks he can reach the Indies by sailing west? He has good company in his madness, then. There are good sea captains and shipowners in Palos—Martin Alonso Pinzon for one—who think he is right. Father Perez at the convent—a man who knows geography and the stars, the wisest man in Palos—thinks the plan sensible. So does Doctor Hernandez, another man of good sense. I would believe them sooner than fools who talk of strange monsters and seas of pitch. I've sailed the seas,' Martin said importantly, 'six years. It might be amusing if there were monsters in the sea, but there's nothing in it but water.'

'How old were you when you went to sea?'

'Eleven. I ran away.'

'Are you sorry or glad?'

'Don't call me "my lord"'

'I hardly know. When a voyage is long I begin to think how I might have a house with an orange tree close to the wall. There'd be a cow and hens and a gray mule. I'd sit in the shade of the orange tree. If I felt thirsty I would just reach up and pick an orange. Or I'd have a drink of new milk from the cow. On feast days there'd be a fowl to stew for dinner. When I heard the hens cackle I'd find the eggs all hot and smooth and my wife would bake a cake.'

'Your wife?'

'If you have a house, you must have a wife,' Martin said. 'She cooks while you sit under the tree. I would buy her a red dress and a white veil and she could ride to church on the mule.' He chuckled and added: 'But when I go ashore and have to milk cows and feed mules and chase hens out of the garden, then I think how fine it is at sea. So I go to sea again. But when I have a wife—then I will stay at home. If you have a wife, you must have a house.'

Peter laughed.

'And so on, around and around,' he said; but he thought, 'Martin shall have his house and his orange tree some day.' Then he said aloud: 'But we were talking about Columbus. Where did you see him?'

'I had gone to the convent of La Rabida to light candles for a friend of mine who was lost at sea. When I came out there was a tall man walking down the road. He was shabby and dusty, but he looked strong. He was carrying a little boy in his arms, a little boy with red-gold hair. The man's own hair was white, but there were some red streaks in it. His eyes were clear blue gray. They seemed to look through me and see something I could not. He asked me if this were the convent. He did not speak our Castilian Spanish quite as we do, yet he had a fine way of speaking and a grave, deep voice.'

It had grown dark on the ship. Martin had been sitting on a coil of rope. Peter had been leaning against the rail. It reached above his waist and had a smoothly polished top. They changed places now. Martin strolled out from behind the mainsail, strolled across the deck, flung one leg over the rail as if he were straddling that gray mule he had wished for. Peter, after a moment or two, lay down so that he could watch the stars.

Martin went on telling about Christopher Columbus: how he had asked Father Perez, in that deep voice that was not like a beggar's voice at all, but like some great nobleman's, like a king's, perhaps—because the higher a man is the more gently he speaks—had asked for a little bread and water for his son.

The boy was asleep. His hair was like a gold halo. It made Martin think of Saint Christopher carrying the Christ Child across the river.

Perhaps Father Perez thought the same thing. He took the man into the refectory. He sent Martin to milk a goat. When Martin came back with the milk—it took him some time, because the goat did not know him—Columbus was saying: 'Because no king will accept the kingdom I can give, I go begging my bread.'

Still he did not sound like a beggar. There was no whine in his voice. It was only sad and deep and made you feel strange under your ribs, the way the notes of a great bell do. Father Perez asked quietly what kingdom he meant. Columbus dipped his finger in the goat's milk and drew on the table, showing how he would reach the Indies by sailing west. There were millions of people there who knew nothing about Christ. The great Khan in Cathay had sent to the Pope long ago asking for teachers for his people, but none had been sent. The journey eastward by land was too dangerous. To the west there were no savage tribes, only a little water. All that was needed was three small ships—and faith. Did not our Lord feed hundreds of people with a few loaves of bread, some small fishes—and faith?

There was gold in those countries. The roofs shone with it. Spices and silks, too, and pearls. From the trade in these things would come money, money enough to win back the Holy Sepulchre from the Moslems. People laughed at him for believing that he—one man—could win back the place where Christ was buried, but is not everything worth doing one man's work?

Father Perez did not laugh. He brought maps and the two men studied them. The small boy slept in the corner on his father's cloak. Martin curled up under the table and slept, too. After a while they woke him up and sent for Garcia Hernandez, the doctor, and for Captain Martin Alonso Pinzon.

This Pinzon was the great man of Palos, Martin Alzate said. For more years than anyone can think the Pinzons had been shipbuilders, shipowners, captains, traders of sardines and slaves and wool. Martin Alonso was a little man with a big red face and a loud voice. He always knew more than anyone else.

'Oh, yes,' he said, when he saw a map that the great geographer Toscanelli had sent to Columbus, 'I saw one like that—only better drawn—in the Pope's library. Yes, no doubt we could sail west to the Indies, but it would take a year.'

Then Columbus gave reasons for the world's being smaller than Captain Pinzon thought. They were fine reasons, no doubt, for the names of great men beginning with King Solomon were mixed with them, but Martin Alzate went to sleep again and did not hear them all. The next time they woke him up, they sent him for a sailor named Rodriguez. When he came back with the sailor, Father Perez was finishing a letter to Queen Isabella. He had once been her father confessor and he felt sure the Queen would listen to what he said.

He was right. The Queen sent and asked Perez himself to come to Court. The monk hired a mule from a farmer named Cabezudo, spread his brown robe over the mule's brown back, and jogged off. It was two weeks before he came back. Columbus spent those weeks copying his map of the world. Martin Alzate used to go to the convent every day.

'I hoped he would take me with him when he sailed for Cathay,' Martin said. 'I hoped he would notice me, but his eyes were always on his map or on the sea. He never seemed to know me, though I had trudged on all those errands. He spoke courteously—as he did to everyone—but his thoughts were far away.'

Yet although his thoughts wandered—perhaps across the tossing sea that thunders so close to La Rabida, perhaps following Father Perez to the Queen's tent outside Granada's walls—his hand was always steady on the paper. His son—Diego was the boy's name—and Martin would watch those clever fingers draw pictures on the map of cities and churches. He would show by pictures or tell in writing what the countries produced. Along the coast of Africa he drew ostrich plumes, cotton, sugar-cane. Near the Cape Verde Islands he wrote: 'Wheat grows here, but it never ripens because many grasshoppers eat it while it is green.' There was a picture he made showing the earth like a sphere. In Cathay he wrote: '*Here he lives.*'

'Who is it he meant, do you think?' Martin asked Peter.

'He meant the great Khan,' Peter said.

He felt a shiver run through him. It was as if, like Marco

Polo, he found himself kneeling before the King of Kings, the Lord of the Indies and of its treasure of gold and pearls.

'What happened when Father Perez came back?' he asked.

'He brought money to Columbus from the Queen and a command to go to Granada. She said she would give him three ships—when the city fell.'

'The city has fallen.' Peter was silent a moment thinking of his father killed by a poisoned arrow just before Granada fell. Then he asked: 'Did he get his ships?'

'I do not know. Days and days went by. We heard nothing. My money was gone. The *Speedfast* needed a deck boy. So—here we are, my lord.'

'Don't call me "my lord," I said.'

'Peter, then. I wish I could have sailed with him. He said once, "The names of those who sail with me—for I shall sail—will be known as long as ships toss on the sea." I would like my name to be remembered with his, even though he does not know it.'

'Perhaps it will be,' Peter said. 'Shall I tell you what it is like in the palace of the Khan?'

'Please.'

Peter told him. Martin was still straddling the rail of the *Speedfast*. The breeze had freshened and the ship was skimming over the dark water. Peter still lay on the deck and watched the clouds scurrying across the stars. Martin's figure was a light spot against the dark sky.

'Perhaps we'll go some day, you and I,' Martin said. 'Perhaps we'll see those tigers that bow down and those cups that move by magic.'

'I will get a ship and you shall be captain of it,' Peter said.

Martin said: 'I'd rather be a deck boy, if it would be like today. This is the best day I ever had.'

He was silent after that. Peter was too, for just how long he never knew. He may have dozed a little before the sound cut through the wind and the creaking of the ship.

It was like the lash of a whip, like the twang of a bow string, like the buzz of an angry swarm of bees.

The sound was followed by a splash. Peter started up rubbing his eyes. The rail where Martin had perched was empty.

In a hoarse voice that he did not know was his own Peter shouted: 'Man overboard! Starboard side!'

In the confusion that followed—the tramping of feet, the shouted orders, the shifting of sails, the lowering of the boat in the darkness—he was thrust out of the way. He was no use, he knew. He could not swim. Any one of the sailors could handle a boat better than he. He leaned over the bulwark, staring desperately down into the black water.

'Martin can swim,' he kept saying over and over to himself. 'He'll keep up till they find him.'

The boat was in the water now. It followed the path the ship had left. A man in the bow held up a lantern and gave orders to the steersman. Peter's eyes followed the light, its broken pattern on the dark sea, the bearded face of the man who held it, then his back at first darker than the sky, then only a shadow with a faint light behind it, at last the whole boat only a dim shape in the tumbled water. It was all like some nightmare in which he could neither see nor speak.

Suddenly he heard his own name.

It was Gonzalo Palma speaking. His high-pitched voice rang out above the shouts of the sailors.

'I fear it is my Lord Aubrey, Captain. I can find him nowhere.'

Peter's thoughts came slowly, stupidly.

'What—makes—him—say that? He has not looked,' he

thought, and crawled, hardly knowing why he did so, under a lowered sail.

He heard Don Diego's voice. It had lost its calmness. It was rough and trembling as he said: 'A reward, Captain. Ten thousand *maravedis* to the man who saves Lord Aubrey. Tell them to hurry, Captain.'

'They are doing all they can,' the Captain said. 'Are you sure it was Lord Aubrey, sir?'

'I saw him sitting on the rail just after sunset'—it was Gonzalo speaking. 'Oh, if I had only warned him! The boat was going quietly then, but it began to pitch just now, and alas, he has an unsteady head! I was waiting on my master and did not think. If I had only spoken!'

Peter had heard enough. The sling—Gonzalo had taken it the other day. The stone he had thrown had been meant not for Martin, but for Peter. Gonzalo had seen Peter on the rail, but he had not seen Peter and Martin change places. The Mallorcan had waited until it was dark enough so that he himself would not be seen—he had on dark clothes. Martin and Peter had stopped talking. Gonzalo thought Peter was alone. Martin's figure and face would have been light enough to make a good target, even though it was dark enough so that Gonzalo would not see that it was not Peter on the rail. If Gonzalo had missed he would have hidden the sling and tried something else.

He had already tried drowning. There was that strap that came unsewn so conveniently. Peter saw it all, including the paper on which his uncle had calculated the value of Melcote and Tallard. His uncle—who always smiled so kindly and spoke so gently and brought him books... His uncle, who was his heir...

Peter's brain was working fast enough now. He heard the Captain order the rowers back to the ship.

'It's no use, sir; they'll never find him now. The sea is rising. I cannot put my men in danger out there longer,' the Captain said to Don Diego. 'It's a sad thing, but it's the luck of the sea. He was a fine young fellow, Lord Aubrey. A pity he could not swim. He must have sunk like a stone. He would have made a good master—it is a pity.'

'We hope you will remain in our service,' Don Diego said. 'He and his father would have wished it, I know.'

'Thank you, Señor—my lord.'

So it had begun. The Captain accepted naturally and easily the fact that it was Don Diego who was now the owner of Melcote and the Aubrey ships. Everyone knew that Don Diego was the heir. How easy it was!

For a moment Peter thought he would walk out of the tumbled folds of the sail and say: 'But I'm not dead, Uncle Diego.'

Something stopped him. What would his uncle do then? Knowing that Peter suspected him and Gonzalo, he would be desperate. And when they were in Spain together... Should Peter go secretly and tell the Captain he was still alive? He did not feel sure about the Captain. Peter had liked him, but he was a Spaniard too. He might be in the plot. He had accepted Don Diego very promptly as master of the ship.

'No,' he decided. 'I will wait; hide until we reach Palos at dawn. After my uncle and Gonzalo go ashore, I will try the Captain, or the Mate. He's English. I must hide. Where? I forgot. I must be Martin. If I am drowned, Martin is alive. There's his watch to keep. I will keep it.'

He choked down the sob that rose in his throat.

'It won't help Martin for them to kill me too,' he thought,

pulling his cap over his face and wrapping himself in Martin's cloak. It was still lying by the coil of rope where he had left it.

It was almost time for Martin's watch at the hour-glass. The English boy who was standing there was half asleep.

Peter said softly: 'Wake up, Billy. It's Martin. Your sand is almost gone. Time for your call.'

Billy yawned and stretched.

'Too sleepy to sing... hoarse, too... I have a cold... wish,... never gone... sea.'

'Go then to bed,' Peter said, copying as best he could Martin's Spanish way of speaking and keeping beyond the circle of light from the lantern. 'I will sing both, your call and mine.'

'You will? Good fellow! Always said... Martin... good fellow...'

Billy stumbled off. There was still a little sand to run

A good hour's gone.

before it was time to turn the glass. Peter stood watching it. It glistened in the light of the lantern near it as it trickled, grain by grain, to the heap below. In three minutes... two minutes... one minute, he must sing the call for the watch.

He was shivering as the last grain fell. His voice stuck in his throat. After a second, a second like an hour, he began the call.

> *A good hour's gone.*
> *A better one's coming.*
> *Down goes the sand*
> *And more is flowing.*
> *It will flow on, God willing.*
>
> *One. Two. Fair breeze for you!*
> *Ho, at the bow,*
> *Do you watch? Do you watch?*
> *One! Two!*

The man at the bow sang out to show he was awake.

Peter's voice grew stronger as he sang. It was clear and firm as he began the call for the watch to come on deck.

> *On deck, on deck, good sailors.*
> *God bless your watch and keep you!*
> *My lord the Captain calls you*
> *To watch: the hour is come.*
> *On deck! On deck! On deck!*

He sang it again in Spanish. The sailors came yawning from their bunks in the forecastle. Their sleep had been shortened by the accident. They were too sleepy to notice anything strange about the figure by the hourglass in Alzate's cloak.

Peter kept his lantern trimmed and filled with oil. He

watched the sand running and turned the glass at the right moment. He did it all as if he were still walking in a nightmare. He had been doing so ever since he heard the noise of the sling.

He tried not to think of Martin, but his mind kept going back to that evening. Could he have found him if he had gone in the boat? Peter did not think he could have. If he had not called when he heard the splash, the boat would not have been lowered so quickly. Gonzalo and Don Diego must have been worried for fear there would be a rescue, but with the darkness, with Martin stunned by the stone, sinking without even trying to swim, there was never any chance for him.

'I did all I could. It wasn't enough, but it was all I could do, but this night is not over—for you, Gonzalo Palma. I am not dead, Uncle Diego. Some day...'

'Talking in your sleep, Alzate?' asked the helmsman. 'Watch your glass.'

'I thank you, Señor,' Peter said.

He turned the glass and began his call again.

> *A good hour is gone.*
> *A better one coming...*

'Yes,' he thought. 'This is your good hour, Uncle Diego. Mine will come later.'

How much later he never guessed as the *Speedfast* slipped on towards Palos through the darkness.

CHAPTER 5

HUNT FOR A THIEF

THE watch was over before dawn. It was still dark when Peter stole towards his own cabin in the after castle. When he had reached it, he realized he had made the journey for nothing. He could not take the money that belonged to him. If he did, Martin Alzate, the deck boy, would be chased as a thief. He needed only a little money, he thought; only enough for a day or two in case his uncle did not leave Palos at once—enough to pay for a lodging and a little food.

'Never mind,' he thought. 'I will do without.'

He took only one thing, the little picture of his mother in its circle of pearls and carved gold. He had always worn it around his neck since it had come home to him from Granada. It was attached to the same fine gold chain by which it had hung around Louis Aubrey's neck when his portrait was painted in his crimson velvet. Peter had slipped it into the pocket of his black suit when he changed to his sailor's clothes. He took it out now, put the chain around his neck, and slid the picture down under his shirt. He felt sure that if his uncle remembered it at all he would only think that it was at the bottom of the Atlantic.

A board creaked under his foot as he started to go. He stood still, listening. From his uncle's cabin came the sound of someone turning over in his bunk, first one way, then the other. That must be Don Diego, because, above the noises of the ship, Peter could hear Gonzalo's whining snore.

Don Diego might be restless, but Gonzalo the slinger slept peacefully after his evening's work.

Peter tiptoed out. He was in Martin's bunk when the ship crossed the Bar of Saltes with the tide. He slept a little, but when the *Speedfast* came alongside the pier at Palos, he was awake. Before he had left his watch he had asked the mate for permission to go ashore early.

'I have vowed to go early to the Church of Saint George and light a candle for a friend,' he said.

'Who is it speaking? It's so black I can't see. Oh Alzate. Yes. You may go, but be back here to help unload or you'll get no pay.'

'Yes, Señor.'

No one paid attention to the figure of the deck boy going off into the morning mist. Neither had anyone noticed what the deck boy saw at the stern of the *Speedfast*.

There was a carved ornament with the arms of the House of Aubrey at the stern. Peter stopped for a last look at it. In spite of the mist that still hung around the docks he could see the shield with the red band cutting across it, the golden sheep on the green field above, the silver anchor on blue below. Underneath, on a carved ribbon of scarlet was the motto: 'Nunquam Dormio.'

'Nunquam Dormio—I never sleep,' Peter thought. 'No, Uncle Diego. No, Gonzalo Palma. I will never sleep until this score is settled.'

It was then that he saw the bag. It had caught by its cord on the carved scrollwork around the shield. It was hanging so close to the pier that Peter had to lean only a little way across the green water to reach it. Gonzalo must have dropped it over when he heard the boy he had struck with the stone fall into the water. The stones were still in it. Peter could feel them through the canvas. He thrust his hand in. The sling was there too.

It was all he had—the bag, and the picture around his neck, and the few silver and copper coins that he had found wrapped in a handkerchief under Martin's mattress—as he walked off into Spain.

He bought bread with the copper coins and put it into the bag with the stones. He was still too sick at heart over Martin's death, too angry with his uncle, too afraid of what Don Diego might do, to be able to eat. He knew, though, that sometime he would need food, so the safest time to get it was while his uncle was still asleep. He must not risk being seen later in the day anywhere in Palos. The silver coins he gave to the priest at the Church of Saint George. He saw his candles lighted on the altar, and knelt there for a long time praying for Martin.

He would have gone out to the convent at La Rabida, but he found that it was some distance outside the town, and he must watch the *Speedfast* so that he might see when Don Diego and Gonzalo left it for their journey to Seville. He had decided that as soon as he saw them go, he would return to the *Speedfast* and tell the Captain what had happened.

'It was only fear last night that made me think he might be helping my uncle. My father trusted him. I will trust him too,' he thought.

He would tell the Captain to sail at once for England. Never mind the cargo. The tide was already ebbing. They could move down the river towards the Bar of Saltes, wait in the lee of the island till it was safe to cross the bar. There was not much breeze, but what there was would help them.

Then when Uncle Diego came to England to take possession of Melcote he and that precious rogue Gonzalo—who would most certainly be with him—could be seized for murder on an English ship. Master Studley, the lawyer, would help. That would be better than trying to have his uncle and Gonzalo arrested here in Spain, where all the advantage would be on their side.

'I am weak. He is strong, but patience makes weak people strong in the end, Father Patrick says,' Peter thought.

He had been following a dusty road that led out of the town between pine woods. There was a scrubby, rocky pasture—a little higher than the land around it and more open—around the next bend. Cattle were feeding there among bushes with red and yellow flowers on them. Peter climbed the rough slope and sat down on a rock half hidden by bushes. From it he could look back at the town and the harbor.

He could see the *Speedfast* and the crew unloading the heavy bales of cloth woven at Melcote. It would take a long time to move them all, he knew.

He watched the moving figures. The deck boys were scrubbing the decks. The sun was blazing hot now as it shone on the wet wood and on the rippled silver of the river Tinto. Yellow sand was hot in the sunshine near the mouth of the Tinto. Beyond it was another gleaming silver ribbon that was the river Odiel. The two rivers met and made an estuary. It was green and smooth this morning except where the light breeze ruffled it for a moment. Saltes Island split the estuary in two and the green water slid around it. The Bar of Saltes took the green water of the estuary and the dark blue water of the Atlantic and beat them to foam.

There were no houses on this lonely road, but Peter could see a long way off the white walls of the convent half hidden by twisting pines. He thought of Martin trotting back and forth through the dust on those errands for Christopher Columbus.

Had he got his ships—the man who wanted to sail west to the Indies? There were three ships lying across the river from the *Speedfast*. One was much larger, one about the same size, one even smaller than the English ship. Men were rolling water casks towards the larger one. The middle-sized one lay so near in shore that now that the tide was going out she was lying on the sand. Men were caulking her sides. When the breeze blew, Peter could smell the hot pitch and hear the thump of the mallets as the men pounded oakum into the seams. They worked slowly. No one near any of the three ships moved so quickly as the *Speedfast's* crew.

In the pines near the road crows were talking. The sun was growing hotter and hotter. Peter slipped into the shadow of a rock. He could still see the *Speedfast*. There was no sign of his uncle on deck.

'Still sleeping,' Peter thought, yawning.

The moving figures and the river began to run together before his eyes. The noise of the crows and the breeze in the pines and the slow thuds of the caulkers' mallets ran together in his ears.

He shut his eyes—just for a minute...

Some hours later a young heifer walked over and looked at the red cap in the shadow of the rock. Another followed her and then another. The whole herd, in fact, inspected Peter. They

The Speedfast had gone

decided that he was not good to eat, so they ate around him, munching the short grass with a sound like the tearing of silk.

At last a young bull calf boldly nipped a tuft of grass close to Peter's cheek.

He woke suddenly, saying: 'Minotaur, old boy, is that you?'

The cattle galloped off with a great pounding of hoofs and stood in a semicircle watching Peter as he stretched and rubbed his eyes. It took him a stretch or two before he knew he was not in the paddock at Melcote with Minotaur's soft muzzle against his cheek.

Then the whole of the last two days rushed into his mind. He jumped up and looked towards the river.

The *Speedfast* had gone.

It did no good to run back along the road to the docks. The

answer from a sailor who was half asleep in the shadow of the wall was what Peter had feared.

Yes, the English ship had unloaded her cargo, put it in the hands of an agent, had gone down the river with the tide. Yes, that sail far out on the ocean, hardly larger than a gull, might be the English sail. An hour ago there had been enough water to cross the bar. The breeze was strong now—the ship had gone on wings... No, the owner had not come ashore. Señor Nunez, the agent, had gone on board to do the business. The owner was ill, the sailors said. It seemed some relative of his had died on the voyage and the shock had been so great that this nobleman, Don Diego Medina-Barrios—or Lord Aubrey, as the English sailors called him—had never left his bunk. He must be a very soft-hearted man. Still, it must be pleasant to lie down between smooth linen sheets all day, although it was true that the air was fresher out here in the shade.

The sailor leaned back against the wall and got ready to go on with his sleeping. He seemed to regard it as a serious business. He said he hoped no more English ships would come in that week and disturb him. Everyone in Palos, he said, was in too great a hurry lately.

There was that stranger Señor Cristobal Colon. If he wanted to sail west and hunt for floating islands, all right, but why such haste? Surely if the land had been there a thousand years, it would keep a few weeks. So why all this rushing around in the hot sun?

'Are those Señor Colon's ships?' Peter asked.

The sailor said they were, and went to sleep again. Not knowing what else to do, Peter sat down and watched the caulkers. Now that the tide was high they were working from boats anchored near the ships. They did not seem to be hurrying.

'They're not more than half doing it,' Peter thought.

He remembered how the hammers and mallets had swung in the shipyard near Melcote. It made him feel lonely and frightened. What should he do? What could he do?

He had no money. No one would believe him if he said he was Lord Aubrey. Still less if he said he belonged to the Medina-Barrios family. Why should they believe him? If the agent Nunez knew anything about the Aubreys, he knew that Louis, Lord Aubrey, had been killed at Granada, that his heir, Peter, had just been drowned. He was not likely to believe a boy in the clothes of a deckhand who claimed to be Lord Aubrey.

'Yet I must,' Peter thought, choking down a strange feeling in his throat. 'I must get back to England. I must get back and tell my mother I am not drowned.'

He spoke to the dozing sailor.

'Tell me, are there ships sailing soon for England?' he said.

The sailor took being disturbed good-naturedly.

'Someone else in a hurry,' he drawled. 'No, young sir. English ships are as scarce as mermaids. But if you want a bunk for a voyage, why not ship with the foreigner?'

'With Señor Columbus—Colon, I mean? Why do you not do so?'

'He is a stranger. We do not know him here in Palos. If I sign it will be with Martin Alonso Pinzon or with his brother Vicente. But I will not sign with anyone till the caulking is done. I have no taste for pitch. Soap, now, I enjoy. I might sign as a barber.'

He chuckled lazily and added, 'Have you eaten today?'

'No,' Peter said. 'I have some bread, but I am not hungry.'

'He has bread and he is not hungry,' murmured the sailor. 'Now I, Juan de Niebo, have no bread and I am hungry. But that is the way of the world. Ah, well! I can always tie my sash a little tighter.'

'You do not need to,' Peter said.

He took the bread out of his bag, broke it in two pieces, and gave the larger one to the sailor.

'A thousand thanks! This courtesy shall be remembered. When I bring back from the Indies enough gold to make myself a crown and shoes and a belt and perhaps a quart of pearls for a necklace, you shall not be forgotten. They say you pick up gold in the streets there. Hard on the back, stooping, but I, Juan de Niebo, will bestir myself to the extent of gathering a few bags. Tell me your name so I shall remember to bring you some trifle. An emerald the size of a goose egg, say. Or diamonds, small ones, no larger than a walnut, to hang in your ears. Your name, young sir.'

Juan de Niebo's drawling speech had given Peter time to think.

'Martin Alzate,' he said quietly.

'A Spanish name—yet I thought you had an English twist to your tongue.'

'I have been in England some time.'

'Well, no matter if you have a certain flatness in speaking our Castilian. Even if you do speak with the lips merely instead of with the eyes, shoulders, and elbows—still it was excellent bread.'

'Take the rest of it,' Peter said. 'Really I am not hungry.'

'No, you will be hungry sometime. And since I am not at present in position to give you the jewels of which I spoke, I will do you a good turn instead. Do you know a man like an angry frog, with hair that goes *so* and ears that stick out *thus?*'

'Yes,' Peter said, trying his best to keep his voice from trembling.

'Well, he is looking for a young man named Martin Alzate.'

'*Is* looking? Did he not sail on the English ship?'

'He did not. He said to Señor Nunez that he would stay behind, partly on some business about the cargo, partly to catch this young thief. That, I grieve to say, is what he called you—not that I believe it,' Juan de Niebo added. 'If you are a thief, you have very little to show for it, that is sure. Furthermore, if you had stolen from someone on the English ship, you would scarcely come here looking for it.'

'I am not a thief,' Peter said, 'but this man is my enemy—no matter why. The story is a long one. I must go where he will not find me.'

'He is looking for you on the road to La Rabida now.' Juan de Niebo pointed down the road over which Peter had just come. 'Look there.'

A party of men on mules was just disappearing around a curve in the road. Through the rising dust Peter could see that the fat one on the gray mule was indeed Gonzalo.

'I must go,' he said.

'Yes, and have everyone tell him where you have gone! The man fishing at the end of the dock is the one who told him you had gone into the village. He saw you outside the church and described you—even to that scar on your wrist.'

Peter could not help the gasp that he gave. So Gonzalo knew that it was Martin who had been drowned! Through the beating of the blood in his ears he listened dizzily while Juan cautioned: 'Someone else in the town no doubt told him you had gone towards La Rabida. You were lucky that you came back while he was eating and that no one saw you. Now, Señor Breadgiver, I have a plan. We will doze a few minutes—there is time: plenty of time if he goes all the way to the convent to ask for you; some time even if by bad luck he meets someone on the road who has seen you lately. So we sleep a little, with one eye open—one of mine. Then you will wake up, yawn, stretch, pick up your bag, walk a little way down the dock.

'Then I shall wake and call out: "Where are you going, young Martin?" You will say: "To Seville." Then I will give you some good advice for your journey—advice costs nothing—and you will start along that road there. When you get to the fork, you will see three warehouses. The back door of the third one is open. You cannot see it from here. The goods from the English ship are there. They will not be touched for a week. Señor Nunez has gone away on business. I heard him say so. And it is the last place they will look for you. Hide there—only be sure no one sees you go in. Spend a little time first in loitering. Sit down and eat your bread if anyone is looking at you. If anyone meets you, ask him questions about the road to Seville. When I think what you are to do next, I will come to you, but this thinking has made me sleepy. So we will take our nap. Understand?'

'Yes—and I—I cannot thank you enough.'

'It is nothing,' Juan de Niebo said, and leaned back against the wall.

Quarter of an hour later Peter felt a sharp nudge in his ribs.

Juan, without seeming to wake up, muttered: 'Your friend has turned back. He must have met someone on the road who saw you. Get up. But do not seem to hurry.'

Peter got up. He did not look towards the road to La Rabida, but out of the corner of his eye he could see that there was dust rising on it.

He walked slowly along the dock, whistling.

Juan's voice called: 'Hey, there, young Martin, where are you going?'

'To Seville, where the oranges come from. You've heard of Seville, I suppose, young fellow,' Peter called back.

'I heard of Seville before you knew an orange from a cabbage, you impertinent young imp. You boys sail six weeks across the water and you know everything. The chicken was hatched that morning. "Mother," it said to the hen, "do you know how to peck your way out of an egg?"—I've heard of Seville—yes! And when you get there, go to the house of Sebastian de Zurla, who is the husband of my sister, two streets beyond the cathedral, and tell them to give you a night's lodging. Say I sent you. I, Juan de Niebo.'

Juan went on for a moment sending messages to this imaginary sister and her three daughters. Plain girls, but such cooks. Such olla podrida they made! Such honey cakes! What matter if they were cross-eyed, especially the eldest? At last he waved his hand and Peter called good-bye. The fisherman never looked up from his fishing, but Peter felt sure he must have heard the word Seville.

It was hard not to hurry towards the third warehouse, but Peter walked along at an even pace as if he were starting a long journey. Luckily he met no one. Every one was sleeping at this time in the afternoon. The caulkers had put down their mallets and were sleeping. Or perhaps they had never really been awake!

The door was open as Juan had said. Peter leaned against the wall beside it for a while to be sure he was not seen. There was no one in sight—only that cloud of dust on the road to La Rabida.

Peter slipped into the cool darkness of the warehouse. He could see nothing for a moment, but his nose told him that the Melcote cloth was there. Then he began to see the bales.

He dragged some together, his hands shaking as he did so, made himself a sort of hut of them in the darkest corner, and lay down in it to wait.

It seemed like hours before he heard the feet of the mules on the road outside. Perhaps it was really only time enough for half the sand to run through a glass. To follow Peter's trail had not taken Gonzalo long, but judging from the angry sound of his squeaking voice he had not enjoyed the hunt. Peter lay still, with his own heartbeats sounding so loud in his ears that it seemed as if they must be heard outside.

However, the mules went past. There was loud talk down at the dock. Peter could not hear the words, but he could hear the party come back with Gonzalo cursing and beating his mule. Apparently the mule stopped just outside the warehouse, but after what sounded like kicks as well as thumps the whole party moved on again along the Seville road. The sound of hoofs in the soft dust and the tinkle of bells grew fainter and fainter.

The rest of that day, that night, all the next day Peter stayed in the warehouse. Juan visited him the first night and brought him water. The second day he brought him a piece of smoked sausage and some bread. Peter had long since finished his own bread. Danger makes people hungry after a time. His grief for Martin, his anger with Don Diego, his fear of Gonzalo, his anxiety for his mother had all joined in a grim determination to stay alive. Getting back to Melcote at any especial time became unimportant. The great thing was to get somewhere out of Palos before Gonzalo came back from Seville.

'He will surely go there,' Juan said. 'That gives you time. He had business in Seville: he told me so on the dock. The fisherman and I were both very obliging about telling him where you were going. He asked the fisherman first because

I was asleep—as usual. Then they woke me up. It is hard if a man cannot get a good sleep, even in the daytime, but I woke up after they had shaken and slapped me a little. At first I was pretty stupid, but I told them at last about what a fine boy you were, how you had missed your ship because you were praying in the church, and that you had gone to Seville.'

Juan grinned. He had a long, thin face with a nose that twisted one way and a mouth that twisted the other. He gave his mouth an extra twist and went on: 'Also I told them a great deal more than I ever told you about that sister of mine and her three plain daughters. I suggested that Gonzalo might marry the best-looking one—though the one that squints is the best cook.'

'I thought they were all cross-eyed,' Peter said.

'So they are. But one of them squints besides. I told him just how to reach their house. If he does he will be a cleverer man than Captain Colon! For whether the Indies are ever reached, I promise you no one will ever find Sebastian de Zurla's daughters. It is a pity—when you think what pancakes that oldest one makes! Here, take more sausage. There's cheese, too.'

'I must not eat all your food.'

'Think nothing of it. I can get more.' Juan clinked coins grandly in a pouch he had and chuckled: 'Do not worry—I came honestly by the coins, and the money too. It takes brains to be a thief. I am too stupid and lazy. I signed with Martin Alonso Pinzon just now. They have finished the caulking after a fashion. I asked both him and Vicente Yanez Pinzon if they needed a deck boy, but they are taking all their cousins and nephews and godsons—Martin Alonso is godfather to half Palos—so there is no room.'

'I must get back to England,' Peter said.

'Then you must fly or swim. Why not sign with Captain Colon? Being a stranger he has more trouble getting a crew. Even when the King and Queen said that anyone who enlisted would be free of certain crimes, people still hung back. There's a man who killed the town crier—Bartholomew Torres his name is. It was a fair fight. I saw it. The town crier struck first, and after calling some names that did no credit to our Castilian courtesy. Well, they threw Bartholomew into prison. Three of his friends—Alfonso Claviga, Juan de Moguer, and Pero Izquierdo—rescued him.

'They've been in hiding ever since, but now they have come out and this evening they signed with Captain Colon. They are the only ones, though. The other prisoners seem to prefer prison. There's no accounting for tastes. I have seen a man sit all day reading!'

Peter laughed. Now that he had eaten he felt better than he had for days.

'I like to read,' he said, 'but not in prison.'

'Then you had better sign with Captain Colon, for when your friend finds there is no such person as Sebastian de Zurla he is going to hunt for you again here, and you cannot hide forever. Something makes him very anxious to find you and he has gone up and down in Palos, Huelva, and Moguer saying you are a thief.'

'What shall I do, then?'

'We must leave here now while it is dark. You must spend the rest of the night in the Church of Saint George. The Captain will set table there in the morning'.

Peter did not know what Juan meant by 'set table,' but he did not ask what it meant—Martin would have known, he felt sure. He said nothing, but followed Juan out into the starlight.

CHAPTER 6

A TABLE IS SET

THE big candles that he had lighted for Martin had nearly burned down. Peter knelt a long time near the altar. After a while—he had said all the prayers he knew and was thinking about Martin—a man came in and knelt beside him.

He was a tall man. On his knees with his white head bowed he looked, Peter thought, like a mountain with snow on it. There was something strong and calm about his face. It might have been the face of a monk except for its being so sunburned. The lines at the corners of the closed eyes were the lines that come to sailors and farmers, people who spend their time squinting in the bright sun.

Yet he was too handsomely dressed for either a sailor or a farmer. Even the captain of a ship would not have a coat of such splendid deep crimson stuff, nor such finely woven linen. His shoes were of crimson Cordoba leather, shoes too delicate for walking. They looked new, as everything did that he wore. Even the scabbard of the short sword that he wore at his side looked new. The hat he had dropped on the ground was of crimson and black silk, a hat fine enough for Don Diego. And Don Diego himself had no rosary so beautiful as the one of amber and silver, the beads of which slipped so quickly through the man's strong fingers.

When Peter began to think about his uncle, he stood up. He knew it was not right to mix his feeling about Don Diego with his prayers. He walked towards the door of the church.

'Will it never be morning?' he thought.

To his surprise it was morning already. He walked a little way breathing in the fresh air. The river fog had not yet burned off, but it was growing thin and the sun was showing through it like a hot cherry. Men were filling water casks from the spring farther down the hill. Peter turned quickly back to the church. He remembered his danger—his two dangers. He might be recognized as the boy Gonzalo Palma was hunting for, the thief Martin Alzate. Or, someone else who remembered Martin might say: 'This is not Martin Alzate. He is a liar as well as a thief. Throw him into prison till Gonzalo comes.'

He hurried back to the church. There was a table in the porch now. Behind it was the man he had seen inside. He was taking money out of a velvet pouch and laying it in piles on the table.

This was 'setting table,' Peter realized, and the man who was doing it could only be that Captain Colon or Columbus—no longer shabby and begging his bread, but in command of three ships, ready to pay out shining new coins, new like everything else about him, to men who would sign for the voyage to the Indies.

'To Cathay,' Peter thought with a little shiver running up his back. 'To Cipango with its tiled roofs of gold, to India, where naked men wear necklaces of emeralds.'

The man looked up at last from his piles of money. The clear blue-gray eyes of which Martin had spoken looked straight into Peter's dark ones, and for the first time Peter heard the voice that he was never to forget.

'Are you for the Indies, young man?'

The words were ordinary enough. The voice was not. It had authority and kindness in its deep tones, and something else as well. Peter had no words for just what this other thing was. He knew only that there was something mysterious and exciting about it. Like the thought of Cathay, it made a shiver prick along his spine. There was music in it, too, like the voice of the big bell in the church at Melcote.

Columbus was smiling now. He picked up two silver coins and clinked them together. His hands had red gold hairs on the backs of them. They shone in the sunlight.

'Don't be afraid,' he said. 'There are no sea monsters out there'—he nodded his white head towards the west. 'Only water and clean wind and land. All good things for a sailor. And—who knows?—fame, perhaps. To be the first that ever crossed the Ocean Sea. People will remember your name a long time.'

'I am not afraid, Señor, but—'

'"But" is a word I have heard much these last years,' Christopher Columbus said. The smile left his lips. His voice softened and deepened. He seemed to be speaking to himself rather than to Peter. '"Yes," they said, "it would be fine to reach the Indies, *but* the world is flat... Oh, yes, now I remember. Scholars have written for a thousand years that it is round, *but* no one has tried it... yes, it might be well to try it before someone else does, *but* we are too busy just now... Only wait. A week. A month. A year. Seven years. Let them go by while your hair goes white...

'"Now, Señor Colon, we are ready to try your scheme, *but* we have no money. I would pledge my jewels"—yes, she said that, our gracious lady—"*But*," says the treasurer, "they are pledged already, Your Majesty." He advances the money himself, that treasurer. He was once a Jew. Do not tell me Jews are not generous. They are wise, intelligent, good to the poor, *but* they are driving them out of Spain. A bad thing. No country can live without brains...'

He was silent a moment, and then began clinking the coins again.

'After a while,' he went on, 'they said: "The money is here now, *but* we can get no ships. Next, the ships are ready, *but* there are no crews. Now, there are crews for two ships, *but* the third still needs men. Some sailors. A deck boy or two. It would be a pity if we failed to reach the Indies because a deck boy says "but," would it not?'

Columbus smiled again and the lines deepened around his eyes.

'It wasn't that kind of "but,"' Peter said.

'I thought I knew all the kinds. Which is this?'

'This was—that I would like to sign, *but* I am not greatly skilled, Señor Captain, and until my friend comes, I have no one to speak for me. And he knows very little about me.'

Columbus threw back his white head and laughed.

'A very good "but"! The best I have heard. I will give you one in exchange. I do not know much about you either, *but* I like your looks. You remind me a little of a young lad who once helped me—I forget his name—*but* that does not matter. I recommend you myself. Can you sing the calls?... Good. Sign the roll. That's it. You write clearly. Most sailors make only their marks. Here's half your wages. Put the coins into that pouch of yours and keep them safe. Do not waste them here. Save them to spend in Cathay.'

Steps—quick steps—came up behind Peter.

Juan de Niebo, out of breath, said hurriedly: 'I speak for this young man, Señor Captain. Sailor since his cradle. Strong as a cat. Voice like a nightingale. Sweeps a deck as a peacock does the ground. Serves out food—roughest weather—never drops a crumb. In short'—here Juan looked over his shoulder—'a remarkable boy. And lucky. Brings luck, I promise.'

'He does indeed sound remarkable,' Columbus said gravely. 'Part cat, part nightingale, part peacock. Perhaps somewhat too splendid for a mere deck boy, *but*'—here his light eyes gleamed—'I am glad he brings good luck—for he has already signed the roll of the ship *Santa Maria*.'

'Then,' Juan said, wiping the sweat off his forehead, 'shall I take him to the ship, Señor? He may be needed.'

'Yes, to sweep with that peacock's tail! Be off, both of you!'

Two sailors lounged up to the table. Columbus turned towards them.

'Run! Quick!' Juan whispered. 'Gonzalo turned back before he reached Seville. Be here—two minutes!'

They slipped into an alley. Juan twisted and turned down a narrow path back of houses and shops. Peter followed at his heels.

'Stop at this corner,' Juan panted. 'Keep in the shadow. I will stick my head around and see where he is. Ah—there he comes, looking like the frog that tried to be an ox, only this frog is purple in the face. Hear how he thumps his mule? Rub—a—dub! Rub—a dub! That's a fine mule. Goes by jerks. Ha! He nearly pitched Gonzalo off. Try again, mule! You'll land him in the Captain's lap next!'

Gonzalo Palma's mule had indeed a sudden way of starting and stopping. It plunged squealing now for a few yards and halted in front of the church porch, kicking out its hind legs with much ringing of silver bells and harsh words in Gonzalo's voice.

Columbus, who had been talking with the two sailors, finished writing their names on his roll opposite the roughly drawn crosses they had made.

Then he looked up from his writing and said gravely: 'You seem in haste, Señor. Are you for the Indies? We sail soon, but you are in time.'

Gonzalo gave one of his squeaking laughs.

'No, *I* am not mad,' he said contemptuously. '*I* have no desire to sail downhill into a sea of flames and never be able to sail back! I have no taste for sea monsters either.'

'Your ideas of geography are interesting, Señor,' Columbus said, 'but not exactly new to me. Since I can interest you in neither fame nor gold—you have a soul above both, I suppose—perhaps you will tell me in what way I can serve you.'

'You can tell me if a young scamp, a runaway coward and thief, who calls himself Martin Alzate has joined your precious crew of thieves, lunatics, and murderers.'

Columbus's naturally ruddy face flushed a shade redder. He stood up suddenly, sending the silver coins jingling to the stones at his feet.

'There are no thieves, murderers, nor lunatics in my crew,' he said. 'And no cowards either. As for young Martin Alzate, deck boy on the *Santa Maria*, he is especially protected from any charges you may make against him by the Royal Command of Their Majesties King Ferdinand and Queen Isabella. I will read it to you with pleasure, and afterward it will be equally pleasant to pull you off that mule and kick you across the Square.'

'What is he saying?' Peter whispered.

"I cannot hear,' Juan said. 'But he looks seven feet high and his eyes are like blue lightning. Gonzalo is trying to make the mule back and the mule is trying to take Gonzalo into the church. Not a bad plan either. It might stop the Captain from throwing Gonzalo into the well. I hope he won't—imagine the water! Now the Captain is reading from a paper. I thought he was going to kill Gonzalo, but it seems he is not. A pity!'

Columbus read Gonzalo the order from the King and Queen freeing those who signed for the voyages from punishment for any crimes they had committed.

'The only sailors who have taken advantage of the mercy of our sovereigns are some hot-headed young men who rescued a fellow sailor of theirs from unjust imprisonment. Here they come now across the Square. As for young Alzate, there is no evidence that he is a thief, but if he were, our gracious Queen pardoned him when he signed this roll.'

Columbus tapped his fingers on the roll.

'This is filled now. Every name on it will be known forever: written in letters of gold. Not as cowards, but as bold men who crossed an unknown ocean to help carry the light of Our Lord Jesus Christ into dark places, and to win new lands for our Queen. Bold men,' he repeated, 'and some of us have the faults of bold men. We are not always patient. I hope I can control my own temper.'

He turned and spoke to the men who had crossed the Square.

'Alfonso Claviga, Juan de Moguer, Pero Izquierdo—I had promised this gentleman to kick him down the street, but I have thought better of it. Instead, I ask you to escort him. Do not pull him off his mule and throw him into the river unless he calls any of you rude names. I feel sure he did not intend to when he spoke just now. So we will be patient and forgiving. Please see that he gets out of my sight. I shall be sorry indeed if anything happens to him.'

'Let me look,' Peter said. 'What is going on?'

'Take one good look and then we must go. You should be on your ship, not lounging around here.'

Juan stepped back after having given this good advice. Peter took his place.

What Peter saw was Gonzalo hurrying the mule out of the Square with three sunburned, strong young men running beside him. Gonzalo did not seem to be enjoying their company. He swore at his two servants, ordering them to fight the sailors, but the servants prudently kept out of the way. Neither of them seemed anxious to be thrown into the river.

'I think he will not come back soon,' Peter chuckled. 'I would not care to meet the Captain when he is angry.'

'Then—as I said before—you had better report to the *Santa Maria* and I to the *Pinta*. I am to shave the crew before they go out to La Rabida to Mass. If I am late, Martin Alonso will be angry, and that is like taking in sail in a tempest.'

'I did not know you were really a barber,' Peter said.

'Nor did I,' Juan said with his twisted grin. 'But I have shaved my own chin and I suppose I can shave others. All you do is to grab the man by the nose and talk loud enough so no one hears him grunt when you cut him. They needed a barber—I signed—I am a barber!'

They hurried down to the banks of the Tinto. By taking a short cut they arrived on the deck of the *Santa Maria* just in time to see Gonzalo being pushed off his mule into the river. The tide was low, the water warm and shallow. Yet Gonzalo did not seem to like his bath. He came out covered with mud and weeds and saying bad words.

Alfonso Claviga and Pero Izquierdo kindly helped him back on the mule. Juan de Moguer stood by and politely gave him good advice.

It was never wise to call names, he said. Gonzalo's mother should have taught him that. They were sorry they had been obliged to give him a bath, but perhaps it would do him good. A mud bath, Juan de Moguer said, was recommended by some very wise doctors. How would Gonzalo like some more mud in his mouth? He—Juan de Moguer—had never heard such language. Well, the land was a wicked place! He hoped their Captain would not by any chance come along and hear what Gonzalo was saying.

The three sailors all kept their grave and courteous faces until Gonzalo had disappeared. Then they sat down and laughed with their heads between their knees and punched each other in the ribs and laughed some more. At last they were so weak from laughing that they lay down on the ground and rolled over, gasping for breath. Now and then one would stop laughing, but then another would gasp out 'Frog in the river,' or 'Mud bath,' and they would begin all over again.

Peter could hear them from the deck of the *Santa Maria*. The tide was coming in slowly around her, but she was still resting on a mudbank. The caulkers were still working on her shoreward side, putting pitch into a seam that had not been properly done before. Their faces were sulky. They worked slowly, although the man in command splashed through the soupy water pointing out places where the seams were not tight.

'Do you want the whole Atlantic in the hold? Do you want to be drowned?' shouted the overseer.

Peter heard a man grumble: 'We'll be drowned anyway—what difference does it make?' and give a listless tap of his mallet.

The slow, uneven beat of the mallets on the side of the ship was the thing Peter always remembered about those first hours on the *Santa Maria*—that and the smell of mud, the blisters on his hands, the ache in his back.

The caulkers might be lazy, but at least the new deck boy scrubbed and swept as if reaching the Indies depended on how clean that deck was.

Chapter 7

OCEAN SEA

IN THE half—light before dawn of the third of August, 1492, the tide rose around the three small ships in the river Tinto. The wind rose, too, and set the banners at the mastheads. All three ships flew the flag of King Ferdinand and Queen Isabella with its green cross and the letters F and I. The *Santa Maria*'s own flag was black with a picture of Christ on the Cross. There was the brilliant royal banner, too, with the arms of Castille and of Aragon. On the new sails, as they filled, scarlet crosses could be seen in the growing light.

The evening before Columbus had marched his crews and their officers down the dusty road to La Rabida, and there Father Perez had said Mass and prayed for their safe return.

'Remember,' he had said solemnly, 'that from your Captain to the youngest ship's boy'—'That's me,' Peter thought—'you are carrying Christ to far countries. It is a noble task. There is glory for those who perform it. Only be steadfast, be faithful, be brave. Go now in peace, my children. Where glory waits.'

The men had gone back to their ships for the night in a brave mood, but it was hard for them to hear at dawn the sobbing and wailing of the women of Palos and Moguer and Huelva.

Yet, Peter thought, it was harder almost to know that in that

85

crowd of weeping women, no one thought of him; no hands waved to him; no voices called: 'Come back. Come back safe!'

He was glad when he heard the anchor ropes creak and when at last Columbus, in a great voice that rang out above the noise of the crowd, called from the high poop where he was standing: 'In the name of God—Let go!'

The sails filled. The ships moved over the green water, cut the ripples that played over it like schools of silver fish, slid down the river towards the Bar of Saltes.

The figures on shore became only a dark mass with pinkish dots. Then the whole mass faded into the brown and green and gray of the harbor shore. The voices they heard now were the voices of sea gulls. The whisper of the smooth waters of the estuary was lost in the rush and roar of the tide dashing over the Bar. Now the foam broke against the bows and boiled away under the ships, lifting them for a moment like horses jumping over a wall. The blue Atlantic took them with a gurgle of welcome. The voyage had begun.

Peter wondered how Columbus felt as the first salt splash of the Ocean Sea struck the bow of the *Santa Maria*. Whatever the Captain felt he kept to himself. He stood for a long time on the poop looking westward with those clear eyes that were brilliantly blue today, not gray at all. He never looked back towards Spain. At last he went to his cabin, took a new quill, and tried it on a scrap of paper in the words he always wrote when trying a pen—'Jesus and Mary be with us on our way'— and began to write. He had promised the King and Queen to write an account of his voyage. He started it that first day.

'In the name of Our Lord, Jesus Christ. Whereas, most Christian, most high, most excellent, and most powerful princes, King and Queen of Spain, and of the islands of the sea: In the year 1492 after Your Highnesses had ended the war in the City of Granada, where, on the second day of January, I saw the royal banners Your Highnesses had placed by force of arms on the towers of the Alhambra, and also beheld the Moorish King come out of the city gate and kiss the royal hands of Your Majesties... ,' he began, and went on to tell of his plans for finding the Indies and the great Khan and carrying the Christian faith to Cathay.

'And you ordered that I should not go by land to the east, but by a voyage to the west, by which course we do not know that anyone has yet passed. Your Highnesses bestowed great favors upon me, saying that when I had reached the Indies I might call myself "Don," appointing me High Admiral of the Ocean Sea, and Viceroy and Governor of all islands and mainland I should discover and gain. Also that my eldest son should succeed me and so on for generations.

'I departed therefore to Palos, a seaport, where I armed three ships and sailed, well furnished with provisions and seamen, on Friday, the third of August of the same year 1492, half an hour before sunrise, and set my course for the Canary Islands. I shall thence steer and navigate for the Indies and accomplish what Your Highnesses have commanded.

'I intend to write during this voyage all that I may see and do, both by day and night. Also I propose to make a chart showing the water and lands of the Ocean Sea. It will be necessary that I shall forget sleep and attend closely to navigation night and day, which will be a great labor.'

There was a strong sea breeze that first day. They went, as Columbus wrote in his journal, 'sixty miles—that is fifteen leagues—to the southward before sun set.' Later they sailed a little west of south—the course for the Canary Islands.

On the sixth of August the rudder of the *Pinta* broke. This ship was under Martin Alonso Pinzon's command, but her owner was Cristobal Quintero. Quintero had from the first been surly about obeying the King and Queen's command that the *Pinta* should be used for the voyage. He had caused much delay in getting her ready. On the *Santa Maria* it was rumored that Quintero had bribed his friend Gomez Rascon to damage the rudder so that Captain Pinzon would have to turn back to Spain.

That was not Martin Alonso Pinzon's style at all. He was, as Columbus wrote, a man of courage and understanding. Although the *Pinta* rolled helplessly for three days in a heavy sea, the rudder was patched up and they came at last to Teneriffe, one of the Canaries. There they repaired the rudder and recalled the *Pinta's* sides. She had already started to leak. It was no wonder, Peter thought.

The evening of the day they left Teneriffe was the first time Peter had any talk with Pedro de Salcedo. This solemn, curly-headed, pink-cheeked, roly-poly boy was Columbus's servant. He had often passed Peter while Peter was standing at the hourglass watching the red sand trickle through, but neither had spoken to the other.

They had looked each other over like two strange dogs. Peter decided that Pedro was too grand to speak to a deck boy. He called Pedro in his mind a conceited puppy. There was something rather puppy-like about Pedro's large, solemn eyes, and about his black hair that was as curly as a spaniel's, and about his way of opening his mouth and panting and showing the tip of a pink tongue when he was in a hurry, and about his way of walking. Especially about his way of walking.

It took him a long time to get used to the motion of the ship.

His feet seemed to get in his own way. Once, as he went from galley to cabin with a bowl of soup, he stumbled and spilled the hot liquid. When that happened, he tried harder than ever to look dignified.

Looking dignified with hot bean soup running into his sleeves was not Pedro's strong point.

Peter had hard work not to smile. He scowled at the flowing sand and pretended he had not seen any thing. Pedro's wrists were still red when Peter saw them that evening.

Columbus had come down from his cabin in the aftercastle and was walking on the deck amidships. It was the only place on the ship where there was room for anything of a walk. Columbus paced it with a long, swinging stride that covered the small open space in a short time. Behind him, trying hard to keep up, trotted Pedro de Salcedo. He had his master's cloak over his arm.

Columbus had sent the boy for the cloak, but now he had forgotten it. He had a small book in his hand. The light was fading, but he kept his eyes on the book, avoiding coils of rope and groups of seamen without seeming to see them. Sometimes he looked up at the sky or back at the high dark mass of Teneriffe, but he spoke to no one.

The men on the deck had been telling stories, throwing dice, laughing, wrestling. Now, as the tall figure passed them, they fell silent. Some of them grinned behind their hands as Pedro went by. No matter how Pedro held the cloak, it seemed to find some way to get between his feet. At last, as a wave higher than the others sent the *Santa Maria*'s starboard rail high up against the darkening sky, Pedro tripped over the cloak, slipped down the sloping deck, and landed at Columbus's feet. By that time Pedro was well tangled up in the cloak.

He fought his way out of it and stood up, very red in the face, and gasping: 'Pardon, pardon, my Lord the Admiral, I tripped!'

'So I see,' Columbus said gently. 'An accident. I had to learn to walk a ship's deck once myself. I was younger than you, scarcely twelve, but I learned—after a spill or two. When you have been at sea as long as I have, you will find that a deck is easier to your feet than the streets of the city—or the floors of palaces.'

He took his cloak, flung it around his shoulders, and went on with his walk. In spite of the gathering darkness his white head still showed where he was. Peter, who was leaning against the port rail, followed with his eyes the tall, dark figure of the Admiral.

'My Lord the Admiral'... that was what the page with the hair like a black spaniel's had called Columbus. His master had not corrected him, although everyone on board knew that Columbus would not really be an admiral until he had discovered land. Land to the west, the road to the Indies. Cipango with its roofs of gold.

Had he been so gentle with his clumsy page partly because he liked the sound of those words: 'My Lord the Admiral'?

'Perhaps,' Peter thought, 'even a great man likes to know that someone believes in him, even if it is only a cabin boy.'

Peter was alone at the port rail staring down at the water. Now he raised his eyes and stared at the faint line of light in the west that marked the place where sea met sky.

Was it really there? he wondered with his first shudder of doubt. Were Marco Polo's cities there with the scarlet bridges and the walled gardens? Or was there only water? Water and a wind that blew only from the east, tossing three small boats over dark waves, thinking no more of them than a child thinks of chips he has thrown into a millpond?

He turned and looked back at Teneriffe. As he did so, he saw that Pedro had left the group of grinning sailors on the starboard side and was now standing at the port rail, not far from Peter. Like him Pedro was looking back at the shadowy peak of Teneriffe.

As they both looked, it happened.

The high mountain that had been only a shadow opened and spouted fire.

Behind him Peter heard sailors groan, mutter, curse. He looked at them and saw men who had been smiling throw themselves on their knees and begin to pray. The fire from the mountain threw a strange reddish light on their faces. Rolling eyeballs, open lips, salty, tarry hands were all stained by the red glare. Above them the new sails were pink.

Pedro de Salcedo grasped Peter's arm saying: 'What is it? What is it?' in a choked whisper.

Peter did not have to answer.

Columbus had walked quietly into the group of frightened sailors. The red light turned his white hair to something like the color it must have been in his youth. He looked young and strong and calm.

'It is only the volcano,' he said. 'I have seen it many times. Some of you must have seen Vesuvius in Italy. A volcano is only dangerous for those who are underneath it. For us at sea it is only a light to speed us on our voyage.'

He stood there quietly with the last of the red glow on his face.

Then he added in a voice that was louder than the noises of the ship: 'For to dark places we carry light.'

He climbed back to the poop.

One of the pictures that Peter always remembered was the Admiral—that was how he thought of him now—standing with his back to the smouldering volcano, looking westward. Behind him rust smoke stained the sky. Shining lava was running down the mountain like rivers of hot lead, but the Admiral stared into the empty sea to the west.

Hardly realizing that he spoke aloud, Peter said: 'He is a great man.'

The boy at his side said eagerly, turning his soft eyes on Peter: 'Oh he is, he is! He took me for his servant because they would have sent me to Africa. You saw that shipload of Jews we passed as we left shore—you heard them sobbing and wailing, I suppose? Well, my father's mother was Jewish. My parents are dead. They were good Catholics. And so am I, but they would have sent me, just the same.'

He murmured a prayer for his dead parents and said: 'Our priest tried to help me, but it did no good. The mayor said I was a Jew and all the Jews must go. They took the little inn my father kept. I had nothing. But the Admiral—when he was poor and sold printed books in the streets and drew charts for his living—my father gave him food for himself and his son even if he had not sold any books and could not pay.

'My father believed in him. "What's a loaf of bread and a little sausage?" he used to say. "Why, Señor Colon, when you come home from the Indies, you will bring me a sausage spiced with rubies!" The Admiral remembered that and took me for his servant.'

'I'm not,' Pedro added, 'a very good one. I spilled the soap-suds when the barber was shaving him yesterday. And you saw me with the cloak. I was all right on land, but here I am dizzy all the time. When I put my foot down, the deck is so often somewhere else. I ate something that disagreed with me the first day. I thought I was going to die. And I did not care if I did.'

Peter looked away so that Pedro would not see him smile.

'I think we have the same name,' he began. He had meant to go on 'Yours is Pedro, mine is Peter,' but he remembered in time that Peter was his name no longer.

Pedro was already saying: 'No, mine is Pedro de Salcedo. Yours is Martin, is it not—Martin Alzate? I asked the barber today. He knows you well, he says. I am glad he is going to be on the *Santa Maria* now, because part of my work was that I was to learn to shave the Admiral and I think it would be better if I did not. Juan de Niebo agrees. He cut the Admiral's chin a little yesterday, because the ship pitched. He said I would probably have killed him and then we would not have found the Indies. I am glad the volcano opened, because now I know you. I hoped you would speak to me when I went past the hourglass sometime, but you never did.'

'I thought you were too proud to speak to *me*,' Peter said, laughing, and added: 'I wish you would call me Peter. It is English for Pedro. My mother is English. They—they used to call me that at home.'

A wave of homesickness swept over him as he spoke. Would he ever see Melcote again? The fading light from the volcano suddenly changed in his mind to the glow of a dying fire in the Great Hall. He could see his mother's pale face and white hands warmed to a soft pink. The light sparkled on Meg's bright hair. Esteban stalked through it, his crimson velvet glowing like hot coals. Only Gwen was outside the circle of warmth. She stood at a window. Moonlight streamed over her pale blue dress. She seemed made of moonbeams and frost.

He had forgotten how beautiful Gwen was. Yet even after he had remembered, it was of his mother he thought. She had looked ill when he went away. How must she look now, thinking her son was drowned?

In the group around the fire he had not seen Don Diego's handsome face, but he would be there of course, all smiles and sympathy for Lady Aubrey and for Gwen.

Peter thought, grating his teeth together: 'I ought not to be here. I ought somehow to have got to England.'

He began to go back over what he had done. It was all very well to say he ought to have gone back to England, but how could he, without a ship, without money, with Gonzalo Palma at his heels, ready to have him thrown into prison for a thief, or killed and pitched into the river?

'No,' Peter decided for the hundredth time, 'I did what I could. It is too late for regrets. The voyage to the Indies is short by the westward passage. The Admiral says so. In six months, or a little more, I shall be back in England. And then, Don Diego Medina-Barrios—I suppose you call yourself James, Lord Aubrey now, you thief—you may smile all you like...'

'What did you say?' he asked Pedro, whose tongue, once loosened, had gone on steadily.

'I said the fire had all faded,' Pedro answered. 'I must go now. My Lord the Admiral will want me. I must get his warm water and put perfume in it and lay out the scented soaps and the damask towels that our gracious Queen gave him.'

Pedro trotted off about his important tasks.

It was time for Peter to stand his watch at the hour glass. Pedro, climbing up to the Admiral's cabin with his pitcher of hot water, heard a voice that rose above the splash of waves and the creak of cordage,

Holy the hour Our Lord was born:
Holy Our Lady, Holy Saint John:
Down flows the sand; while you are sleeping,
The guard his watch is quietly keeping.
The wind is fair, the sails are filling,
Peaceful our voyage—if God be willing.

'That is my friend's voice,' Pedro thought happily.

CHAPTER 8

BIRDS FLY WEST

"BLUE-WATER SAILOR"—I heard an old man who used to work for my—an old sailor say that once. I know what it means now,' Peter said to Pedro.

It was noon of the tenth day of September. The *Santa Maria* was travelling westward under a light breeze that made the waves sparkle.

'It's never like this near shore,' Peter went on. 'It looks so clear, so cool—it's like sailing in the sky.'

'I'd like to swim in it,' Pedro said.

'I would not'—Peter gave a little shiver.

It was a long time since he had thought of his last swimming lesson. On the *Santa Maria* it was easy to forget that he had ever known anything but this world of sea and sky. At first each day had seemed like a week. Now they slipped away quickly. There was little to mark one from the next. Yet in spite of the calm sea, the gentle breeze that carried them always toward the west, in spite of the softness of the air and the clear brilliance of familiar stars, the crew were afraid.

More than once the Admiral had to rebuke the sailors for steering badly. They let the ship fall away to the northeast so often that it could not be an accident. Everyone knew that the farther north they steered, the easier it would be to turn back towards Spain. This thought was in all minds, but no one spoke of it. Even as the sailors lay in their stifling bunks in the dark forecastle there was no talk of turning back. This very silence had something strange about it.

It was a waiting silence, Peter thought, though he could not have said clearly what he meant by the word 'waiting.'

Their silence grew heavier the day that the mast of a great ship tossed out of the blue waves and drifted past them. No one of the crew wondered—aloud—what had happened to the men who had once climbed that mast, but it was not hard to read what went on behind the sullen faces on the *Santa Maria*'s deck.

'On the fifteenth of September,' Columbus wrote, 'we saw fall from the sky a marvellous branch of fire. It seemed to enter the sea about five leagues off.'

The men did not pray and groan over this sight as they had over the fire from the volcano. It would have made Peter less uneasy if they had. He spent as little time as he could in his bunk. Everything about the forecastle—its stuffiness, its darkness, the hard shelves with the mattresses of rotten straw and the greasy sheepskins over them, the snores of the men when they slept, their gloomy silence when they were awake—all made any corner of the deck seem pleasant. Peter was often wet by fog and salt spray, often chilled by the night wind, but at least he could breathe clean air and watch the stars.

Pedro slept on a mattress beside the Admiral's door, but in the morning the bed in the cabin would be empty. Often it had never been slept in. Columbus had stepped over the sleeping boy and had gone on deck to be sure that the ship's course was west—always west.

During the day the Admiral spent more time in his cabin. He slept sometimes, but mostly he wrote in his journal or read in his book of prayers or studied charts. He seemed to need little sleep, but as the days went on there were dark circles under his blue eyes, the arch of his nose seemed to thrust forward sharply, his cheeks were hollow under his high cheekbones. He ate little for so big a man, and hardly seemed to know what he ate or drank. Some biscuit and some water with a little wine in it was often his food for the day.

In spite of his carelessness about food and sleep, he was particular in other ways. Even the officials of the Court who had come on the voyage had given up being shaved and were growing beards of different shapes and colors. At least they were already different colors. They were not yet long enough so that it was possible to tell whether the owners preferred to look like goats or bears.

'At present,' Peter thought, 'they look like the big field at Melcote when the corn is cut!'

The Admiral, however, always had a cleanly shaven chin. Juan de Niebo became an expert with the razor as the voyage went on. The Admiral's shirts were beautifully clean and scented with spiced roseleaves that the Queen had sent. The rosary of fragrant amber hung around his neck. He was never too tired for his prayers, or to read in his book with its jewel-like pictures and letters of scarlet and gold the Latin words of devotion. And he was never too tired to write in his journal.

On the sixteenth of September he cut a new quill and wrote:

'We kept our westward course day and night and made more than thirty-eight leagues. There were clouds and a little rainfall. We meet now with warm breezes, so that it is a delight when morning comes. It is like April in Andalusia. All we need is some nightingales! We saw today many tufts of grass, very green. They must have been torn from some land: but it must be an island, for the mainland is farther on.'

On the next day, he says, they went fifty leagues.

'We saw much grass, drifting always from the west. We must be near some land. At night the pilots found that the compass needle did not point exactly to the north. The sailors were alarmed, although they did not say so. In the morning the needles pointed due north again. I told the sailors that it was the North Star making a small circle around the Pole that made the needles vary. We saw much grass. It seemed to be grass from rivers. One of the sailors fished a live crab out of the grass and I kept it. This is certainly a sign of land.

'The water is less salt than that around the Canary Islands. The breezes are softer. We saw many tunny fish, and the men on Vicente Yanez Pinzon's ship, the *Niña*, caught one. Early this morning we saw a white bird, called a boatswain bird, asleep on the water. All these are signs of land. They come from the west, where I trust that Our God in whose hand are all victories will soon show us land. We went on our way greatly rejoicing.'

On September eighteenth Martin Alonso Pinzon in the *Pinta*, which was the fastest of the three caravels, did not wait for the *Niña* and the *Santa Maria*, but called to the Admiral that he had seen a great crowd of birds go towards the west and that he hoped to sight land that night. For this reason he went ahead. A great bank of dark clouds that appeared in the north was also considered a sign of land.

Land... Signs of land... Plenty of signs—but no land.

They saw a bird like a tern, which is a river bird. There was so much grass that the sea looked like a meadow. A whale came up and spouted a thin jet of steamy water close to the ship.

'Whales never go far from land,' a sailor said.

A pigeon and a pelican flew past.

'They are river birds,' said Pero Izquierdo. 'They must be near their nests.'

Sandpipers skimmed over the sea.

'There must be a beach near,' Juan de Moguer said hopefully.

Yet on the twenty-fifth of September the sea was still as empty as ever. It was very calm. The Admiral and Martin Alonso Pinzon talked across the green water about a chart that the Admiral had lent to Captain Pinzon a few days before. Martin Alonso thought they must be near the islands shown on the chart. The Admiral thought so too, but added that currents might have carried them too far north. He asked Martin Alonso to send back the chart. Martin Alonso put it in a box and sent it back on a rope.

The sea was so calm that afternoon that sailors from all three ships went swimming. For a while they splashed and ducked each other and dove as happily as a school of porpoises that went tumbling through the water a little way off. Then Peter, who was leaning over the rail watching them, saw that a change came over them. Suddenly the laughter and shouts stopped. As if each man felt a cold hand clutching at his feet, they swam for their boats, scrambled into them, and rowed hastily back to their ships.

What were they afraid of?

No one admitted he was afraid. Yet they looked as if they had seen a sea monster. There was something about their chattering teeth, their sunburned faces with drops of water caught in the fast-growing beards, something about their wet white bodies and shrivelled blue fingers that meant fear as well as cold.

Fear, Peter thought, of the vastness and emptiness of that ocean, fear of being left behind with only their small boat, fear of signs of land that were not signs of land. He, for one, did not blame them.

The men were quarrelsome after their swim. A fight broke out over the wooden bowls from which they ate their food. One man's bowl was missing. He accused another of taking it. The owner had carved a dolphin in his bowl. Now he pulled out the very knife he had used. He made a sound in his throat like a dog getting ready to snap.

Luckily at this moment Martin Alonso called out in great excitement that he saw land.

'I claim the reward the Queen has promised,' he called to the Admiral.

The crew fell on their knees singing '*Gloria in excelsis deo—* Glory to God in the Highest.' Then they swarmed up the masts shouting that there was land about twenty five miles off.

A breeze sprang up. They sailed all that night and half the next day for the place where the land seemed to be. Then the sky blew clear.

The land was only clouds.

Now the men were more sullen than ever. When two or three were together on the deck or in the forecastle they muttered to each other. Even the boldest and gayest were afraid now.

'This wind,' Alfonso Claviga said, 'always blows from the east. How shall we ever get home? We cannot run against it all the way to Spain.'

'Sea devils made that land to cheat us,' Juan de Moguer said. 'They show it—then take it away. It is a trick to lead us on forever.'

Pero Izquierdo was of the opinion that it was a floating island and that the wind would always blow it ahead of them.

'Like a donkey with a bunch of grass tied in front of his nose, we fools sail after it,' he said gloomily, and added that he was sick of the calm sea and the warm breeze, sick of birds that had no nests and fish with wings.

There had been flying fish landing on the deck that day.

'It is unreasonable,' Izquierdo said. 'Fish ought not to fly. Suppose in this ocean the whales begin to fly? Will that be pleasant?'

Approving groans answered him...

The Admiral walked the deck without noticing the dark looks that followed him. He kept his eyes on the great flocks of birds. On the seventh of October Vicente Pinzon's ship, the *Niña*, went ahead. Before long she hoisted a flag at her masthead and fired a lombard to show that she saw land, but again it was only clouds.

More and more birds were seen. They always flew southwest. The Admiral knew that the Portuguese had discovered the Azores by following the flight of birds. He decided to turn his course southwest. The Pinzons were in favor of this course, but on the *Santa Maria* there was grumbling. The men wanted to turn back to Spain.

The Admiral told Martin Alonso that his men were losing courage, but Pinzon only roared: 'Well, string up half a dozen of them, then! And if you need any help, I'll come over!'

There was something about that hearty roar that gave everyone courage. The men were more afraid of Martin Alonso than of the sea.

Pero Izquierdo began to look cheerful again. He asked Pedro de Salcedo to find him a left-handed hammer. Being left-handed, he said, he could not work with the ordinary kind. The cabin boy's search for such a tool amused the sailors for most of the morning of the eighth of October.

Peter thought it was a mean trick to keep Pedro trotting about on his short legs looking for a hammer that existed only in imagination. After a while he gave Pedro some advice.

The result of it was that Pedro said solemnly to Izquierdo: 'I have found the hammer, but the Admiral needed it to drive some left-handed nails, so it is in his cabin. If you ask him for it, I am sure he will be glad to lend it to you.'

The men laughed, but not at Pedro.

'Here's a boy that was not hatched yesterday,' Alfonso Claviga said, and Izquierdo grinned, saying: 'Never mind. I'll use my own head for driving nails.'

Everyone was cheerful that day and the next.

Columbus wrote in his journal: 'We had a sea like a river in Seville. Thanks be to God, the breezes were softer than April there. It is a pleasure to be in them, they smell so sweet. All last night we heard birds passing.'

That was a strange night with the air so full of beating wings. No one slept. In the morning the crew were more sullen than ever.

'They could now bear no more,' the Admiral wrote. 'They grumbled bitterly about the long voyage. I cheered them as best I could, telling them of the gains they would make. Then, when they still remained sullen, I told them it did no good to complain, for—I said—"I am going to the Indies and I will pursue my course until, with God's help, I find them."'

The grumblings and mutterings went on, but not where the Admiral could hear them. If there had been a leader among the men, they might have mutinied, but there was no leader. Besides, the presence of Martin Alonso in the *Pinta* was no encouragement to mutiny. Martin Alonso was only half-joking when he suggested hanging grumblers. He would certainly not hesitate to deal harshly with mutiny on the *Santa Maria*. His own crew of friends and relatives and Vicente Yanez Pinzon's crew in the *Niña* were loyal and fearless.

Sailors on the *Santa Maria* who thought about mutiny also thought how—after Martin Alonso's lombards had shot holes in the *Santa Maria*'s side—they would look hanging from the yardarm of the *Pinta*. That conspicuous position did not seem attractive.

There was something about the Admiral, too, that kept them quiet in his hearing. Many believed that he had magic powers. Once when they had grumbled because the wind was always blowing from the east, he had looked—only *looked*, mind you—quietly towards the west, and a great wall of water had suddenly risen ahead of them with the west wind back of it and had dashed itself against the bow of the ship. That showed the Admiral could raise a wind to blow them home, if he liked. The man who had complained was quite sure of that; he was soaked through by the spray.

Some said the Admiral had whistled very gently, but there was dispute about that...

Others claimed that the signs of land that had deceived them so long—the floating grass, the river birds so far from shore, the land that came and vanished, the scented breezes—were all magic. The Admiral made them and waved them away. There was nothing around them but sky and water. The rest was all illusion.

'It is clean magic, then,' Alfonso Claviga said. 'It is well known that the Admiral is firm in his devotion to Our Lord and the holy saints.'

No one could deny this. Some fell back on the idea that sea devils were tempting them. The birds they were following might look real enough—in fact, some small ones had even sat in the rigging and twittered away as simply as sparrows in Seville—but they were only ghosts of birds. Those were the wings of dead birds that beat the air all night... ghosts, flying to a place of ghosts. Their own spirits would wander there too, before long.

With such cheerful talk the *Santa Maria* pitched through the roughest sea they had met during the whole voyage. The waves were too much for Pedro—or else again he had eaten something that disagreed with him. Whatever the reason, he was too sick to drag himself to the galley for the Admiral's dinner.

Peter, finding Pedro lying in a corner looking pale green, offered to take his friend's place.

The Admiral was writing in the great cabin when Peter came in with the dinner. Pero Gutierrez, a gentleman of the King's bedchamber, and Rodrigo Sanchez de Segovia, whom the King and Queen had sent as Chief Inspector of the fleet, were both there. These two fine gentlemen had spent most of the voyage in the cabin drinking and gambling. On their few visits to the main deck they had looked at the sailors as if sailors were a different kind of animal, perhaps a slightly superior sort of monkey. If a sailor had lost his teeth or a finger, or had a twisted shoulder or a blind eye, Sanchez and Gutierrez made witty and amusing remarks about him.

Peter had forgotten he would have to wait on them as well as on the Admiral, but having undertaken the task he did it as well as he could. In spite of the motion of the ship he spilled nothing. Columbus as usual ate little, but the others stuffed

their fat faces with the delicacies kept especially for the cabin—
the big Spanish olives, the raisins, the sardines in olive oil, the
marmalade made of Seville oranges.

They talked to each other about their own affairs and made
no attempt to include the Admiral in their talk. Like the sailors,
Columbus was regarded apparently as an inferior specimen of
animal. However, after Gutierrez had finished gobbling the last
olive, he began asking questions of the Admiral, who—having
finished a dry biscuit and a glass of water and wine—had gone
back to his writing.

'More signs of land today, I suppose,' Gutierrez said with
his oily smile.

Columbus paid no attention to the sneering tone, but
answered quietly: 'Yes, the men saw a green branch. It was
covered with dog roses. A sailor on the *Niña* fished it out.'

Gutierrez smeared sardine oil from his beard to the back
of his fat fist and said: 'Wonderful!'

Sanchez with a yawn asked, 'Any more marvels?'

'I myself saw a piece of cane, like sugar-cane, but much
larger than any I have ever seen. I think the men on the *Pinta*
got hold of it.'

'Solid gold, I suppose!' Gutierrez said.

His smile reminded Peter of his Uncle Diego. How, he
wondered, could the Admiral listen so quietly to these men's
jeers?

Columbus made no reply to Gutierrez. His deeply sunken
eyes seemed fixed on something a long way off, something
that the dark walls of the cabin could not shut away from
his gaze.

Peter cleared away the odds and ends of the meal. He had
hoped for a stray olive or a sardine, but there were only olive

stones left and the sardines had vanished down to the last silvery tail.

The ship was pitching violently as he came back with water for the diners' hands. Gutierrez and Sanchez, he thought as he climbed up to the aftercastle, ought to take baths all over. Especially Gutierrez, who had a habit of seizing three sardines by their tails, tipping back his head, and dropping them all into his big mouth. Sometimes the oil dripped from his beard and ran down over his embroidered shirt.

'What a treat he must be in the King's bedchamber!' Peter thought.

Sanchez was daintier in his habits, but his hand was unsteady from drinking too much, and he had spilt wine on his sleeve as well as on the table.

They both, Peter was delighted to see, looked distinctly pale as he poured the scented water over their greasy hands. At a particularly bad lurch of the ship they both left the cabin and went to their own. The Admiral was still sitting with the napkin with which he had dried his hands crumpled in his fingers. With the departure of the others, he came back to the world around him, asked kindly about Pedro, thanked Peter for his services.

'I am going on deck now,' he said, getting up.

His white hair almost brushed the roof of the cabin. He had on an old suit of brown homespun, faded by the sun and stained by salt spray, but with his neatly shaven chin and clean linen he looked far better dressed than Gutierrez in his oil-smeared velvet or Sanchez in his wine-spotted satin.

'I shall need no supper,' he said, and then added—with a smile that lightened his usually grave face—'And I think my guests will need none.'

'But—' Peter began.

'Ah—now I remember—the young man who says *"But!"* Well, what is it now?'

He was half-smiling down at Peter from his great height. Peter felt very small and unimportant, but he kept on.

'It is only, my Lord the Admiral, that I have a message for you—from England.'

'A message from England! Did a bird bring it?'

'No, my lord. I forgot it that first day, and since then I have had no chance to speak to you.'

'It is good news, then. Bad news would have travelled faster.'

'It is from your brother, my lord. I saw him in London and bought a chart from him. He told me that if I saw you in Spain to say that he had not had any promise of help from King Henry, so he would try France and then, if he had no luck there, go exploring wherever he could find a ship to take him. I think that was what he said. He sent you his love, my lord, and his prayers for your good fortune.'

The Admiral was smiling widely now.

'Bartholomew! By all that's wonderful! This does me more good than birds or floating branches—a Birds Fly West better sign than any yet! Did you ever have a brother?'

'No, my lord. I am an only child.'

'I am sorry. There is nothing like a brother. He halves your burdens; doubles your strength. How did Bartholomew look? Well?'

'Well, my lord, yes, but a little like a caged eagle. He sat in a dark shop and drew charts. I think he was very tired of it.'

'No doubt, no doubt. I know about that. Well, that is over for us both, Bartholomew. It cannot be long now...'

He seemed again to have forgotten where he was.

'It cannot be long now,' he repeated.

There was weariness in his voice, but firmness too.

'Thank you for your message,' he added. 'Your name—I have it on my roll, but my memory for names grows poor—you wrote it well. Martin—something, is it not?'

'Yes. It is written Martin Alzate.

'It will be remembered,' Columbus said. 'Fame brushes us with her wings, Martin Alzate.'

He left the cabin with a kindly nod.

'If there is fame,' Peter thought, 'I am glad it is for Martin.'

CHAPTER 9

MEN FROM HEAVEN

ALL that night the Admiral stayed on deck straining his tired eyes into the darkness. Towards ten o'clock when he was on the poop he saw a light. He called Gutierrez and Sanchez, and told them that there seemed to be a light in the west and that they must watch for it.

It was like a small wax candle which was being raised and lowered, the Admiral said.

Gutierrez, who came on deck rubbing his eyes, said that he saw it too, but Sanchez only shrugged his shoulders wearily. A sailor, Rodrigo de Triana, said he had already seen the light before the Admiral spoke of it.

The other sailors muttered that it was only another false sign to lead them on to destruction. The pilot said that it was probably the light on the *Pinta*, which was on ahead somewhere. The wind had dropped at sunset, but the sea was still rough. The light could be on the *Pinta's* aftercastle, tossing up and down. Sometimes it went high enough so that they saw it above the waves that rolled between. Someone else murmured that it was only the moon breaking through the clouds and flashing on the tumbling water.

No one said any of these things in the Admiral's hearing. The crew sang their evening hymn, the Salve Regina, as usual. After it the Admiral urged them to keep a good watch from the forecastle. He said that, besides the reward that the Queen had promised, he would give a silk doublet to the man who first sighted land.

He ordered everyone to stay on deck. There was grumbling at this. Peter heard the mutterings of the crew uneasily. There was something especially threatening about them tonight.

'We'll make him turn back tomorrow,' he heard one sailor growl. 'We're on the edge of the world, I tell you. Feel how hot it is growing! There's fire beyond us—it's the edge of the pit we're heading for.'

It was Peter's turn to stand at the hourglass. His voice seemed to be blown away into emptiness by the warm breeze as he started his song.

A good hour's gone. A better one's coming.
Down goes the sand...

He saw the Admiral's shadow fall across the glass. The moon had come up out of the waves behind them. It had changed from hot copper to cool silver, and now it was painting the deck with shadows of ropes and sails and masts.

Peter heard the Admiral whisper as he passed: 'I smell it. I smell land. Spices... perfumes... Cathay...'

He must have spoken out loud without knowing it. Gutierrez had heard him too. As the Admiral turned away, Peter saw Gutierrez nudge Sanchez and tap his forehead. A meaning grin

'I smell it. I smell land'

creased his fat cheeks. Sanchez only shrugged and yawned. The scowl he wore did not lighten.

But out of the darkness came a flash and a shot. There was a strange moment of silence, a moment during which each man stood straining his ears dizzily to hear above the sizzling water and the creaking timbers another sound.

Then it came, from their own masthead above them, a hoarse, choked shout: '*Land! Land, ho! Land!*'

Peter never forgot that sound nor those that followed it. The running feet. The noise of men on the ropes. The laughter. The yells. The ship swept on. They could all see it now. A low island edged with white sand. Palm trees dark against a pale sky. No bank of clouds ready to melt away, but land. Land to walk on, to lie on. Land with things growing on it. Land with a strange perfume of spicy sweetness rising from it.

The ships all shortened sail and lay to until dawn. The morning hymn had never been sung with such joy as it was that Friday morning of the twelfth of October, 1492. It echoed from all three ships over the silver water:

> *Blest be the holy light*
> *That comes at God's command.*
> *We bow before His might,*
> *Our lives are in His hand.*

Peter could hear Martin Alonso's voice. It came roaring across the water like a great horn blown in the fog. He could see Juan de Bermejo opening his mouth and pretending to sing. It was Bermejo who had first seen land from the *Pinta*. He was a fat little man. How grand he would feel in his silk doublet! The pension from the Queen would be ten thousand *maravedis*. A *maravedi* is a small coin, but ten thousand of them would be about ten English pounds. For Juan every year that would be riches. No wonder Juan grinned and tried to sing, even though he made no more noise than a cricket!

Peter's own voice was too shaky to sing. He could hear the Admiral's ringing out above him. It was not so loud as Martin Alonso's hearty roar, yet it had some thing that the other lacked. Its mellow sweetness made Peter think again of a bell.

'I feel it in my finger-tips,' Peter thought as the Admiral sang the second verse:

> *Blest be the morning bright.*
> *He sends this day for all.*
> *And on us till the night,*
> *Let His own blessing fall.*

Peter looked up into the Admiral's face. Columbus had lost his look of strain and sleeplessness. His eyes were as blue as the shining water around him. The rising sun struck on his silver hair, and for a moment it was red gold. He had changed his shabby homespun, and stood now on the poop wearing the scarlet and gold of the Admiral of the Ocean Sea. He was a splendid figure—taller than the men around him, stronger, with his great courage and his invincible faith written clearly on his face.

Peter never forgot how Columbus looked in those first moments when at last he saw his dream come true. The Admiral always looked strong and confident. Now his face shone with something else. He looked happy, so happy that for a moment it gave Peter a strange feeling, a shudder it was almost. He shook it off quickly and forgot it—for a while.

Later he was to remember that he had thought: 'He will never look so happy again.'

That thought was soon forgotten in the excitement of approaching the island. There were crowds of naked people among the green trees and bushes near the shore. More and more came to stare at the Spanish ships and at the armed boats in which Columbus and the Pinzons were being rowed towards the land. The Admiral carried the royal standard. Each of the Pinzons had the flags that were flown on all the ships, the one with the green cross, the letters F and I and over each the sovereign's crown. Gutierrez and Sanchez and Escobedo, the notary, were in the Admiral's boat to witness that Columbus took possession of the island for King Ferdinand and Queen Isabella.

All was done in order and according to the law of those times. Any country that was not Christian became the property of the first Christian King whose captains took possession of it. Peter knew that, and yet the thought went through his mind: 'But the island belongs to these people. They were here first. They have done us no harm. Suppose they came to England and took Melcote.'

He must not think about Melcote. It only made him sad, and this was no day for sadness. The Admiral was on his knees on the beach. The great folds of the bright banner flapped over his white head. His scarlet-and-gold clothes looked strange against the white sand and the brilliant green leaves with the naked brown men peering out of them.

Columbus began to speak. On the ships everyone was silent. By straining their ears they could just hear the words of the prayer for taking a new country.

'O Lord, everlasting and mighty, who made the heavens, saying "Let there be light"; who made the land and the sea and all that in them is, blessed and glorious be Thy name; let Thy

Kingdom come, O Lord, through Thine unworthy servant, and let Thy power and majesty be known and praised evermore in this new world.'

Peter wished he could go ashore. So, of course, did everyone else. Their feet ached to feel the white sand between their toes. The shade of the green forest looked all the more tempting as the sun began to blaze down on the decks. However, the Admiral refused all requests for permission to land. His orders that no one should go ashore were given in a tone that Peter had never heard him use before, a tone of impatient authority. It seemed as if with his Admiral's scarlet dress he had lost his patience and reasonableness.

'How will the proud Spaniards like this new pride?' Peter wondered.

If Columbus had trodden on notions of Spanish courtesy, he was ignorant of having done so. He wrote happily and for a long time in his journal that night.

'In order that these Indians might feel great friendship for us,' he wrote—after he had told about the discovery—'and because I see that they are a people who will be turned to our holy faith by love rather than force, I gave some of them red caps and glass beads and other trifles. At this they were greatly pleased and became so friendly that it was wonderful to see. Afterward they came swimming to the ship's boats where we were and brought us parrots and balls of spun cotton. We gave them more glass beads and hawks' bells in exchange. In fact they took all and gave all with great good will, but it seems they had not much to give.

'They are tall, very well built, with fine faces. Their hair is black and straight. They wear it down over their eyebrows. A few strands behind are long. Some of these people are painted black, but their skin is brown. Others are painted white or red or any color they can find. Some paint their faces. Some their whole bodies. Some only their eyes or noses.

'They do not carry arms or understand them. I showed them swords and they grasped the blades and cut themselves. They have no iron. Their spears are reeds, sharpened or tipped with a fish tooth. I saw some had scars of old wounds. I asked them by signs how this happened and they showed—by signs—how people came from other islands and fought with them. I believe they came from the mainland to take these people for slaves.

'They are of quick intelligence. They soon say the name of anything that is told them. I believe they can easily be made Christians. I plan when I go back to Spain to bring six to Your Highnesses so that they may learn to talk and be made Christians.

'I saw no animals of any kind in this island except parrots.'

On Saturday, the thirteenth of October, Columbus wrote: 'As soon as day broke there came to the shore many young men. Their hair is not curly but loose like a horse's tail. They have broad foreheads. Their eyes are handsome and not small. Their legs arc very straight: none are bow-legged. They have good figures, not fat. They came to the ships in a tree-trunk hollowed out and carved into a large boat. About forty-five men came in one. Others are smaller. In some only a single man came. They row them with paddles like bakers' shovels and they send them along at a great speed.

'If a boat upsets, they all begin to swim and bail it out with gourds which they carry for this purpose. Some of them wear a small piece of gold hanging from a hole in their noses. They told me by signs that gold comes from a land to the southwest, where I will go and seek it. These people are gentle, and so eager to have something of ours that they give things such as fruit, or spun cotton even, for pieces of broken pitchers.

'I shall forbid this. Any cotton taken in fair trade I will bring to Your Highnesses. It grows on this island, but I cannot say how much is grown. I shall not waste time here but will try to reach the island of Cipango.'

By Cipango Columbus meant Japan.

Because he believed the world much smaller than it really is, he thought he had reached the Indies, as all the countries of the Far East were called. He always thought so to the end of his life.

Yet there were no houses roofed with gold. And where were the elephants? Where were the great cities with scarlet bridges?

He told the interpreter, Luis de Torres, to ask the people about Cipango and Xanadu and the great Khan. This Luis de Torres was a hook-nosed little man with thin hands that he jerked while he spoke. He knew many languages and tried them all on the Indians, but without success. At last by signs he learned some words of their tongue and taught them some words of Spanish.

Torres had a lively imagination. His talks with the Indians gave him many ideas. They were chiefly ideas that the Admiral wanted to believe: the great Khan was not far off; there was plenty of gold, only on another island; yes, Cipango was its name.

The natives were eager to please these bearded strangers who came riding on birds with enormous wings. Sailing ships had never been seen in that sea. The Indians were frightened of the great birds that came out of the endless sea to the east. The pale-faced, bearded men must come from heaven, they thought. The Indians paddled in their canoes from one island to another spreading the news.

As the Spaniards came to each new green island they were

greeted by cries of 'Come and see the men from heaven! Bring them food and drink!'

It was pleasant sailing over that clear water and landing on islands where the trees were as full of leaves as they would be in Castile in May; pleasant to breathe the soft air, to eat the fruit brought by the friendly Indians, to catch fish like rainbows, and see the parrots flashing through the trees. Columbus called the first island San Salvador, the next *Santa Maria*, another Fernandina for the King.

The people of all these islands lived cleanly in neat houses. Their beds were nets of cotton. They called them hammocks. There were no animals except some small dogs that did not bark.

The Admiral wrote about all these things in his journal. There were showers, he said, every day. The land was the most fertile and temperate anywhere in the world. He was sure there must be spices, he wrote, but he did not know the leaves and this caused him sorrow. The flower-scented breezes in the mornings were the most delightful in the world, the people the friendliest, the song of the birds the sweetest. The flocks of parrots were so large that they darkened the sun.

Everything in fact was the best of its kind—the mountains the highest, the water the clearest, the trees the greenest. Only, where was the thing for which men took the perilous road to the Indies? *Where was the gold?*

There were bits of it, to be sure, dangling from men's noses, and they would trade them for a hawk's bell. There was an island called Cuba farther on where there was plenty of gold, Luis de Torres learned—or thought he learned. The Admiral thought Cuba must be Cipango at first. Later he thought it must be the main land of Cathay.

Cuba was a beautiful place full of palms. Fishermen thatched their houses with them. The Admiral jumped into a boat and went ashore. The owners of the houses near-by ran away. He found a dog that did not bark but only made a choking growl; some nets, some fish hooks; but no gold, no pearls, no jewels. They must be farther on.

So he sailed on, naming rivers and harbors and capes. Wherever he landed he set up a cross and took possession of the land for the King and Queen.

They were fortunate in their weather. There were few storms. Yet in spite of the beauty of the new country the men began to grumble again. Except for getting wood and water they were not allowed to land. When they did land they were not allowed to trade with the natives. Columbus frowned on the trading of ends of leather straps and broken porridge bowls for spun cotton that would fetch a good price in Spain. It was cheating the Indians and also the King and Queen. Ferdinand and Isabella had supplied money for the ships and for trade goods. Profits from trade belonged to them. Columbus knew that trade cannot be based on cheating.

Peter heard plenty of talk from the sailors about their ideas of trade.

'He promised us gold, didn't he? Heaps of gold! But if I try to trade my own cap that my mother knitted for a cotton hammock to take home to her—I'd planned to hang it between the two pines near the door and she could lie in it on hot evenings while I talked—well, I'm cheating the King and Queen! Does the King need my cap? Does the Queen want my hammock? The Indian can have his wife make another hammock and he wants my cap. What's wrong with that?'

'I think the Admiral has tried to make a rule that's fair to all,' Peter said.

'Fair!' The sailor gave a short laugh and moved away. 'Ask Juan de Bermejo what he thinks about fairness. Ask Rodrigo de Triana who is going to get the Queen's pension,' he said over his shoulder.

Peter did not answer. He had no answer. He had been present at the argument between Martin Alonso and the Admiral over who was to have the reward from the Queen for first finding land. He could not see that there was anything fair about it.

It was certainly Juan de Bermejo of the *Pinta* who had first seen land. Everyone on all three ships knew that the *Pinta* was well ahead of the other ships, that the call had come from her masthead.

Yet in spite of Captain Pinzon's roars and curses the Admiral insisted calmly that when he saw the light some hours earlier, he had really found the first land. Captain Pinzon finally agreed that the Queen herself would decide. He agreed unwillingly and with many rude words. They did not ruffle the Admiral's calm. He spoke gently and went on eating a pineapple.

His calmness only made Martin Alonso angrier and redder in the face. He gulped down his wine, slammed the cup on the table, shoved away the food that Pedro brought untouched. When Peter brought him water for his hands, he shook his head, keeping his red fists clasped behind him, and scowling at the Admiral.

At last he stamped off, thumped into his boat, and went back to his ship, looking as if he had swallowed a thunderstorm.

Sanchez and Gutierrez laughed after he had gone. These gentlemen were all smiles and politeness to the Admiral now. They called him Don Cristobal and uncovered their heads while he sat with his plumed velvet cap covering his white hair. They remembered all about the Admiral's seeing the light.

They laughed when Rodrigo de Triana claimed he had seen it before the Admiral had.

'Why had he not called out, then?' Sanchez asked.

The Admiral sent for Rodrigo de Triana after Captain Pinzon had gone. The sailor was a wild-looking young fellow with a way of twisting his fingers in his long hair. He stammered. It was hard to understand him.

In answer to the questions about why he had not called out when he saw the light, he stammered something about 'So many false alarms.'

'You did not believe it was land, then?' Escobedo the notary asked, scribbling with his pen.

The sailor stammered again, contradicted himself, admitted at last that he was willing that the Queen should decide.

'B—but,' he said at last, turning his wild, light eyes on Columbus, 'if she d-does g-g-give it to you I'll—*I'll become a M-Mohammedan!*'

Columbus only looked at him gravely and moved his head and hand slightly toward the door. Rodrigo stumbled out of it with a sound that was almost a sob, but it was drowned by the laughter of Gutierrez.

'B-become a M-Mohammedan,' he mimicked. 'That's really very amusing. The Queen will be overcome!'

Columbus did not smile. He thanked the notary and the others for their company and dismissed them. They followed Peter, who had left just before carrying away dishes.

'I feel as if I had left a royal audience,' Gutierrez said with a sneer. 'What do you really think about that light, Sanchez?'

'I am not paid to think,' Sanchez answered, 'but it is my opinion that you cannot see a light on a flat island forty miles away, and San Salvador is as flat as those cassava cakes the Indians bring.'

He spoke without caring whether Peter heard him or not. Peter was a boy who on a voyage watched hourglasses and scrubbed decks, and sometimes waited on table and washed dishes. Therefore to a fine gentleman like Sanchez, Peter had no ears.

Sanchez went on about cassava cakes.

'They taste like sand. Pretty, white sand, to be sure, but sand just the same, with just a hint of ground up fishbones to stick them together. I wish I were back in Segovia. There was a little inn there where they fried chickens with olive oil and cooked sausages and chestnuts with them...'

'Be quiet, you are breaking my heart, you glutton,' Gutierrez groaned. 'About that light, Sanchez. What you say sounds sensible. We must have been at least forty miles off when I saw it, so it could not have been on the island. I think it was on the *Pinta* after all.'

'But you know which side of a biscuit has honey on it,' Sanchez drawled, 'and you had better remember when you get back to Spain that the whole island was lighted with candles to welcome us.'

Peter went to the galley with his dishes and heard no more of their talk. He did not need to hear any of it to know that Sanchez and Gutierrez had a strong sense of what was best for themselves. The Admiral would be a powerful man at Court now, they thought, and they would take some pains to stand well with him.

They and their selfishness did not trouble Peter, but Martin Alonso's angry face did and Rodrigo de Triana's wild look, and

Juan de Bermejo's way of pinching his lips together whenever the Admiral's name was mentioned.

Peter was not surprised when, on the twenty-first of November, Martin Alonso Pinzon sailed off in the *Pinta* without telling the Admiral he was going.

'He went,' the Admiral wrote, 'contrary to my wish and through greed, thinking that an Indian he knew would show him much gold. He has done and said many other things to me.'

The *Santa Maria* sailed on south with a light wind. It was a long time before they saw the *Pinta* and her angry captain again.

CHAPTER 10

CHRISTMAS EVE

BY THE end of December they had left Cuba and reached the beautiful island that the Admiral named Española. Peter was in a boat rowing towards the shore when an Indian canoe suddenly appeared from around a wooded point. It slid through the water like a snake going down a rut in a road. The arms of the paddlers rose and fell together. Water dripped off their paddles like chains of pearls.

Near the boat the paddlers stopped the canoe's swift motion and held it still with slight pressure of their paddles. The sea was choppy that morning, but the canoe never seemed to tip. The Indians managed it as if it were part of their own bodies. They were all painted with red and black so that their skins hardly showed at all. Their faces were covered with streaks and dashes.

A tall man, whose nose was painted scarlet, whose eyebrows had black tents above them, and whose mouth was surrounded by a white border that ran into the middle of his cheeks, began to speak.

Peter had learned all the Indian words that he could from an Indian of San Salvador who was on the *Santa Maria*. The speech of the different islands was much the same, so that he knew what the man was saying.

'Guacanagari, a great cacique, the Lord of the Island, lives here,' the Indian said. 'He wants the ships to come near. He will give the Admiral all that he has!

There was a boy about Peter's age sitting near the man who was speaking. His body was not painted but pricked in an elaborate pattern of dots and lines, with colors rubbed into the pricks. Peter had read about that kind of decoration in Marco Polo's book— tattooing it was called. On his back the boy had the picture of a lizard and on his chest a parrot. His face was unpainted. He had large, gentle eyes and a smile that showed very white teeth. When the man stopped talking, the boy reached down into the canoe, picked up something, and, leaning across the strip of water between the canoe and the boat, gave it to Peter.

It was a sort of belt of finely woven cotton cords. Instead of a purse there hung from it a mask, carved out of wood. The eyes, the nose, and the tongue were of beaten gold.

The word 'gold!' went from one mouth to the next. Greedy eyes looked at the bright spots. Greedy hands stretched out to touch them.

No one spoke it, but the thought in the boat was, 'These poor fools of Indians—they don't know what gold is! If they have this, they have more. For a few glass beads—the end of a broken strap, I can be rich, rich...'

The boat was heavy with this thought as it rowed back to the ship.

The Admiral was pleased with the mask.

'I will take it to the Queen,' he said.

He sailed towards the village where the Cacique Guacanagari lived and anchored near it. Canoes began to dart out from the land. Before they got within a crossbow shot from the ship, the Indians would stand up in the canoes and hold up things they had brought, crying: 'Take! Take! Men from heaven, take what we bring!'

More than a thousand Indians came to the ships. Half of them came swimming because they had no canoes, although the *Santa Maria* and the *Niña* were anchored two miles from shore. Some of the canoes had whole families in them—men, women, and children. In one of them was the boy who had given Peter the mask. His name was Cacibi. He and Peter talked to each other. Cacibi had already learned a few words of Spanish. With Peter's words of the Indians' tongue and with the aid of signs they got on very well.

Columbus sent a party ashore that afternoon. Peter was one of the party. He saw Cacibi again in the village. It was a clean place of palm-thatched houses neatly arranged around a square. There must have been two thousand people there, counting the children.

The Cacique Guacanagari himself spoke to the Spaniards and gave them food. He sent some parrots and some cotton cloth and some pieces of gold to the Admiral. The common people gave the Spaniards cotton cloth and some fat geese and fruit. When the sailors went back to the ships, the Indians went to the shore with them, carrying the presents. They even carried the Spaniards across a marshy place and laughed and chattered happily in their soft voices while they did it. They swam beside the boat, laughing, diving under it, pushing at the stern to make it go faster. The whole bay seemed full of brown arms and splashing water.

It was Christmas Eve as the Spaniards rowed back to their ships with their boatloads of presents.

They sailed that evening. There was only the lightest possible breeze. An hour before midnight the Admiral, who had not slept for two days and a night, lay down to rest. So did the pilot of the ship. So did the sailors. So—at last—did the sailor who was steering. There was a rule against letting the ship's boys steer, but the sailor, after a good deal of yawning, called one of them and gave him the helm.

Peter was at the hourglass. He wished he could have steered the ship, but the sailor had called to Tomaso, a boy who had done his best to make life unpleasant for Peter. It was Tomaso who had put fish scales in Peter's dinner; Tomaso who had greased the mast and bet Peter he couldn't climb it (he couldn't!); Tomaso who had tied a rope across the passage outside the Admiral's cabin so that Peter would trip (he had tripped and dropped cassava cakes on the floor and a pewter plate on his toe). Tomaso, in fact, had a sense of humor.

'Put him in a red-and-yellow suit, sew some bells on him, and he'd make a fine jester,' Peter thought crossly. 'Esteban would like him. I ought to take him home to Melcote. "See what I have brought you," I'd say, "Don Esteban. A gentleman with your wit will enjoy this fine fellow, I am sure."'

Peter yawned. He was as sleepy as anyone else on the *Santa Maria*. He kept himself awake by thinking of Christmas at Melcote. It was cold there. A great log would be burning in the fireplace. The light would glow on the painted crimson velvet of his father's robe in the portrait with the peep-holes back of its eyes. Peter pretended he was looking through the holes. There was Henry Tallard catching Meg under the bunch of mistletoe and kissing her. She was pulling his beard and he called her a wildcat... Dame Butts was spicing some wine in a big pewter can beside the fire... The smell of it drifted through the room and mixed with the smell of wood smoke and of roasting fowls... Gwen had on her new dress of Venetian velvet... His mother sat close to the fire putting the last stitches into the tapestry that showed the battle of Bosworth Field. Outside in the snow the men from the village were singing carols...

Peter yawned again. The sand had nearly run out. It made him sleepy to watch it as it trickled down in a faintly glistening stream. The night was so quiet he could almost hear the grains of sand fall. The air hardly stirred. The sea was as still as milk in a small bowl. The *Santa Maria* slid over it so slowly that she scarcely seemed to move.

Peter nodded over the falling sand. By a great effort he pulled himself back from sleep. He must sing his call in a moment and his head was heavy, too heavy to hold up. It was like being dizzy. There was a noise in his head like water beginning to boil in a kettle. Peter shook his head, but the boiling noise only grew louder. The last grains were falling. He had his hand out to turn the glass, the words of the call were on his lips when the thing happened.

At first it was only as if a hand that no one could see had reached out and touched the *Santa Maria* gently. Then a shudder ran through the ship. Peter heard Tomaso scream. There were no words. None were needed.

The *Santa Maria* was aground.

The noise in Peter's head had been waves whispering over a sandbank.

Before anyone else woke, the Admiral was there. Then the pilot and the master of the ship, whose watch it was, came stumbling on deck half asleep with the sailors of his watch behind him. The Admiral ordered them to launch a boat at the stern. He meant them to try to shove the ship off the sandbank before she sank deeper. Instead of obeying, they rowed to the *Niña* some distance behind. Captain Vicente Yanez Pinzon refused to take them aboard. He called them some names, of which 'coward' was the politest, and ordered them back to the *Santa Maria*. He also sent one of his own boats to help.

It was too late. The tide was running out fast now. The ship was broadside to the sea. The Admiral ordered the mast to be cut and thrown overboard to lighten the ship, but the *Santa Maria* only sank more deeply into the treacherous sand.

At last even the Admiral gave up the attempt to save the ship. He sent the crew to safety on the *Niña* and sent Gutierrez ashore to ask Guacanagari for aid.

When the Cacique heard the news, he wept. He sent all his people in their largest canoes to take everything off the ship. All that Christmas day the canoes went back and forth between ship and shore. The care with which the Indians worked was a marvel.

'Nowhere in Castile,' Columbus wrote, 'could I have been able to keep all safe without even the loss of a strap. Guacanagari ordered everything to be put into some houses which he had emptied on purpose. He sent his own brothers to watch over the houses night and day. He and all his people wept at our misfortune. They are a race full of affection and without greed. I believe there is no better race anywhere. They have the sweetest, softest voices in the world and are always smiling.'

While the Admiral was talking to the Cacique, a canoe came from another part of the island. The men in it showed pieces of gold and cried out: '*Chuque! Chuque!*'

This was their word for the hawks' bells which the Spaniards had given to some of the Indians in trade. Nothing pleased the Indians so much then as those small, tinkling bells. A good deal of gold was brought to the Spaniards that day. The Cacique told the Admiral that there was plenty more gold in a place called Cibao. As usual Columbus thought that must mean Cipango. He had not yet stopped expecting to see roofs tiled with gold instead of thatched with palm leaves.

He dined that day with the Cacique on shrimps and yams and cassava bread. The Cacique wore a shirt and gloves that Columbus had given him. He was particularly delighted with the gloves.

Columbus treated the Cacique with great courtesy. The sight of Guacanagari wearing the fine white linen shirt and gloves of scarlet velvet although his feet and legs were bare did not amuse the Admiral. Barefooted or not, Guacanagari was King over these smiling, kindly people, and Columbus treated him like a King. To entertain his host, after the feast was over, Columbus ordered one of his men to shoot at a mark with his cross bow and another to fire a lombard.

These things were wonderful to the Indians. They fell on the ground at the sound of the firing. Shortly after this the Cacique brought the Admiral another mask with gold on the eyes and ears and other gold ornaments. Guacanagari himself hung the mask around the Admiral's neck and put a gold crown on his white hair.

By the end of the day Columbus had begun to think the loss of the *Santa Maria* was really a piece of good fortune. He would settle a colony here, he decided. Gold was plentiful; the people so gentle that they would never attack the Spaniards. The only danger was from a savage tribe from another island called Caribs. Luis de Torres said that the Cacique had told him the Caribs sometimes came to Española and made slaves of the people.

Columbus decided to build a fort, using the timbers of the wrecked *Santa Maria*. It was not possible for the little *Niña* to carry all the men of both ships back to Spain, and as Martin Alonso had vanished with the *Pinta*, Columbus could not count on help from him. The Admiral planned to leave about forty men with bread and wine for a year, seeds to sow, arms, and armor. Skilled workmen were among those chosen to stay.

There was no trouble in getting men to remain. They had seen the gold.

They would probably, Columbus thought, collect a barrel of gold before he came back. Five Caciques had visited him with gold crowns on their heads. One of them traded his crown for the Admiral's cloak of scarlet cloth.

Peter had fortunately not been chosen to stay at the fort. He was eager for the *Niña* to sail back so that he could reach England. His plan was clear in his mind now. With his wages he would take ship for England from some Spanish port—Cadiz, perhaps. He would sail to London. He could see himself walking past the Abbey to Master Studley's house and hear himself telling the lawyer about all that had happened. Soon he would be telling his mother that he was not dead after all. They must have told her of his death long before this. There must have been some uneasy moments for Don Diego and Gonzalo when they realized, by hearing about the scar on his wrist, that it was not Peter who had been drowned, but by this time they would feel sure he had gone forever. Sailing with Columbus was considered as good as being thrown into the sea!

He worked hard all that week helping to build the fort. Columbus had named it La Navidad because the *Santa Maria* had been wrecked on Christ's birthday, the day of the Nativity. The building went on quickly with the help of the Indians. They did not act as if they were used to hard work. They smiled and laughed and chattered while they moved logs. It took a dozen of them to put a log in place that two Spaniards could handle easily. They stopped work and went swimming whenever they felt like it. There were always some of them sitting under palm trees with some brown leaves rolled up into sticks about four inches long in their mouths. They lighted the sticks and drew smoke out of them into their mouths and blew it out again.

Some of the Spaniards tried this smoking and were very sick. Peter took one puff that set him coughing until the tears ran out of his eyes. He never did find out why the Indians liked the smoke.

Even though the Indians made a game of building the fort, it grew rapidly. There were always some to pick up a timber that others laid down. In a week it was finished. It had a high tower, a cellar for storing food and gold, loopholes for guns and lombards, bunks for the men, a room where the officers could dine. Gutierrez and Sanchez were to stay. Diego de Arana was the Commander, the other two were his lieutenants. The goods for trade were in their care. The *Santa Maria*'s largest boat was anchored in a little inlet near the fort. It could be used to sail along the coast and discover the mine from which the gold came.

Gutierrez and Sanchez were another reason why Peter was glad he was sailing on the *Niña*. He had heard them laughing and sneering at the Admiral—not in his presence, of course, but when the crew were listening. This was their way of getting even with Columbus for his haughty manner towards them.

Haughtiness was something in which they were expert

themselves. They treated the Indians to plenty of it. They made fun of Guacanagari in his Spanish clothes. It was very funny to them to see the Cacique wearing a crown, paint, feathers, and a pair of gloves. They would solemnly praise his splendid appearance and, as soon as his back was turned, go into fits of laughter.

Guacanagari was not a stupid man. It would not be long, Peter thought, before he understood the Spaniards better than they did him.

The *Niña* was to have sailed on the third of January, but the sea was so rough that her boats could not go ashore to get the men who were still working at the fort. There were several among them, including Peter, who were going to sail on the *Niña*. An Indian in a canoe brought a message from the Admiral to say that he would not send the boats till evening. The wind would probably drop then, and he would send for the men and also for a load of fruit and cassava bread that Guacanagari had promised him. He planned to sail at dawn.

Peter wandered about restlessly. There was nothing to do at the fort. He wished Pedro were there, but Pedro was on the *Niña*. The other men who were going fretted over the delay. Those who were staying were anxious to have the others go.

'It is often so when a departure is postponed,' Luis de Torres said to Peter. 'Those who stay behind wish to begin their new life. Those who go wish to see the last of that life for a while. Both are impatient. Nothing is more wearisome than farewells. Never say good-bye—go: that's the best plan.'

'I could get a canoe to take us out,' Peter said. 'Indians don't mind getting wet, and I have no silks and velvets to trouble about.'

'You had better obey the Admiral,' Luis de Torres said.

Peter knew that was true. He strolled away from the fort. It was hot that afternoon. One of the sudden showers that fell so often on the island had drenched everything an hour before, and now there was a damp, steamy heat that Peter found stifling. He felt annoyed with the fort and everything about it.

'I'll find an Indian who has a parrot and trade for one to take home. Meg would like a parrot. And one for Gwen, too, of course,' Peter thought, and he kicked impatiently at a rotting log. There was one thing about Española, besides its green and fertile beauty: he would never have to marry Gwen there. 'She may have married someone else,' he thought. 'Perhaps she has seen an earl by now. And she thinks I am dead. Well, anyway I will get her a parrot.'

None of the Indians near the fort had any parrots, but they told him there were plenty in a village farther along the coast. Peter had seen the little collection of huts from the ship. It could not be far, not more than a mile or two. He would have plenty of time, he thought, to go there and get back before the *Niña's* boats came ashore.

There were no parrots in the village. They had given them all to the Spaniards. Peter asked if they could catch some for him, but either they did not understand or they did not want to go hunting. They all had hawks' bells. The whole village tinkled with them. They told him about another village farther inland where there were parrots—many parrots. It was not far, they said, and they showed him the trail that led to it.

Some of the young boys went with him along the trail. They laughed and jumped and the hawks' bells jingled. They wore them around their necks on cotton cords. Most of them wore very little else.

It was pleasant along the trail with the sound of palm fronds clicking in the wind and the bells ringing. The path went near the shore at first. At a sandy cove where the waves foamed in white on a white beach the Indians decided to go swimming. Peter watched them, and wondered at the skill with which they hurled themselves through the breakers and came out into the tumbled blue-green water beyond.

'They've forgotten me,' he thought after a while, 'and forgotten they are not dolphins.'

He decided to follow the trail himself. It led inland from the cove. The ground was packed down hard by the many bare feet that must have passed over it. Peter hurried along it. The village, he soon realized, must be farther than the Indians had said, but before long he had a piece of good luck. The parrots began to come home. A great flock settled down squawking and chattering in some trees and bushes only a little way ahead of him. The trees looked as if they had suddenly blossomed with bright flowers. Even the ground was gay with scarlet and green and yellow.

'I'll catch one—no two—myself,' Peter thought. 'It ought to be easy to get one of those on the ground. I'll sneak up and throw my cap over his head.'

He moved forward quietly, cap in hand. He was careful not to make any noise. The parrots themselves were making a great deal. Many of them sidled slowly over the ground hunting for seeds.

'I believe I can get two at once; Peter thought. 'They're so slow. I'll drop my cap on one and grab another by the neck.'

There were two not far from him now. He edged forward, keeping a big palm between them and him. He made no noise—he was sure of it—yet the two parrots flew ahead a little way and the rest of the flock moved on, too, after some chattering, to another clump of trees.

This happened three times, each time just as Peter was getting ready to drop his cap. Evidently catching parrots was not so easy, but he was only more determined to get one. By the fifth time the bright wings had flapped just out of his reach, one seemed plenty. One for Meg. He would give Gwen the gold ornament for which he had traded his cloak. She would like gold better than she would a parrot.

It was hotter than ever in the forest. There was little wind here. Mosquitoes buzzed around him. He slapped at one, and the big parrot he was chasing flew into a bush a dozen feet ahead and sat there chuckling to itself.

'I believe it's laughing at me,' Peter thought crossly.

Just then the parrot flew down from the bush. This time it flew near Peter and landed close to the tree behind which he was hiding. It turned away from him and began to pull at something on the ground.

'Now!' Peter thought, and jumped forward, throwing his cap over the green head.

The air was full of squawking and of flapping wings. Feathers beat in his face. Claws dug into his chest. Something gouged his forehead. The pain was so sharp that he let the furious bird go, and stood dizzily wiping away the blood that ran down into his eyes.

A dark, screaming shadow went over him, the shadow of a thousand birds. In a moment it was only a faint sound in the distance.

Peter tore a strip from his shirt and swabbed the blood that still ran down from the place where the parrot had bitten him. He still felt dizzy as he tore another strip and tied it around his head, but in a few minutes the dizziness passed away, though the wound was still sore. It was too late to keep on to the village now. He must find the trail and hurry back to La Navidad.

'The trail... Find the trail,' he said aloud, and his voice sounded strange in that hot silence. Now that the parrots had gone he could hear only the buzz of insects—and the blood singing in his ears.

'I must keep my head,' he muttered, and it seemed as if a dozen parrots chuckled in answer: 'Keep your head. Yes. You must keep your head!'

He shook off his feeling of fear and haste.

'Slowly. There's no hurry,' he thought. 'And I won't talk to myself aloud... Now I know I was behind that tree. Yes, there's my cap.'

He picked it up and put it on over the bandage. The blood on his hands was drying, he noticed. He went on in silence, carefully figuring out how he had come. The impulse to hurry, to move ahead quickly no matter in what direction, rose in him, but he beat it down. He must find the trail and he could do it. Then he would be all right. He must only be patient and keep calm.

He did find it, but the search had taken time. How much time he had no idea, but he knew it was nearly sunset. The sun had gone below the tops of the palms. The air was so still that he could see each palm-leaf finger cut in black against the bright western sky.

He started running along the trail. He reached the cove where the Indians had gone swimming, but it was empty now. The sea was only whispering on the sand. There was more— much more—sand showing. It must be hours since he was here.

He could not see the *Niña* from the cove. The arm of land

that protected the harbor where she lay hid her from him. He ran on, stumbling over roots and stones until he reached the western side of the point.

The sun was sliding into the sea. The *Niña* was there, he saw and shut his eyes against the glare. Small green and blue and yellow suns slipped across his eyelids. He opened his eyes, shading them now with his hand.

Yes, the *Niña* was there, but what was that?

He began running again almost before the words—they seemed to be shrieked at him in a parrot squawk—made their way into his brain: 'The boats—they're gone. And they've left *me*.'

He still kept running.

'I'll catch her... get a canoe... she won't sail yet... No wind...'

In spite of the pain in his head and the stitch in his side he kept on, but his feet were like lead. He had never been an especially good runner, and the months on shipboard had made him soft. His breath came in gasps, but he kept on, stumbling now.

Suddenly it was dark. Twilight is short on Española, and a shower was coming. The stars pricked out, then vanished. Drenching, blinding rain made the path slippery under Peter's feet.

It was no wonder that at a turn of path he took the wrong fork, no wonder that he tripped when a trailing vine twisted around his tired ankles, no wonder that he fell, striking his head against a sharp rock.

He was still lying where he had fallen when the *Niña* sailed that night. Captain Vicente Pinzon, hearing that the deck boy had not come aboard with the others, said that he was glad. Deck boys were always a nuisance. With his crowded ship anyone's room was better than his company.

Pedro appealed to the Admiral. Columbus asked why the boats had not waited for the missing boy. Someone said that Peter had been heard saying that he was going to get an Indian to take him to the ship. Everyone thought he had gone out to the ship ahead of the boats.

The Admiral told Pedro that his friend would probably get a canoe and come aboard before they sailed, unless he had stayed behind to be with the gold hunters.

Pedro watched all night, but no canoe came.

That is why the name of Martin Alzate was added to the list of those who stayed at La Navidad, although—strangely—Peter never saw the fort again.

PRESENT FOR GONZALO

CHRISTMAS at Melcote was not much like Peter's picture of it. There were the big logs burning in the fireplace and the voices singing outside, even the drifting flakes of snow that he had imagined, but the Great Hall was not as he had seen it.

Sir Henry Tallard was not there. He had been killed by a fall from his horse while riding after a stag. The son of a distant cousin had inherited Tallard.

Lady Aubrey was not there. It was hard for her to understand that the house that was her husband's and her son's was hers no longer, but she accepted the fact without caring greatly. After she heard that Peter was drowned, nothing else seemed to matter. She lived now in a small gray stone house in the old gray city of Lincoln, a long way from Melcote. Meg was with her, and Dame Butts.

Dame Butts and Meg had both told Don Diego—the new Baron Aubrey—what they thought of him, but their words had done no good. Baron Aubrey had smiled and bowed in the most courteous way, but he had seen no reason why his brother's will should be set aside. He reminded them gently that he had been made his brother's heir in case Louis Aubrey died leaving no children. This had—sadly, of course—happened. Naturally Lady Aubrey would always be welcome at Melcote, but as her husband had left her a large sum in gold—which, by the way, had almost emptied the treasure chest of the estate—and the manor near Lincoln and a comfortable house in the city—well, it was clear what his brother's wishes were...

The new Baron Aubrey paused here and smiled sweetly. He did not say that Meg and Dame Butts would be welcome at Melcote.

Most of the faces at Melcote that Christmas Eve would have been strange to Peter. Baron Aubrey's friends were not the hearty, red-faced Melcote neighbors. Most of the splendidly dressed men in the Great Hall were from London, although there were some Spaniards among them. There were fine ladies from London, too. Gwen was not there. She had stayed on at Tallard with her cousin's wife. Gwen had a large fortune of her own, and the new owner of Tallard, Sir Roger, had a son Charles whom he planned to marry to Gwen, with the prudent idea of keeping the money in the family.

Esteban had ridden over to Tallard Castle to ask Gwen to come to Melcote for Christmas, but Sir Roger had met Esteban at the gate and told him that Mistress Gwendolen was still in deep grief over her father's death and could see no visitors. Esteban had ridden off sulkily and had still looked glum and glowering when he got back to Melcote.

His father asked him what was the matter, and on being told said—always with that charming smile of his: 'You are a fool, Esteban. You should have stayed there.'

'Knocked down the walls of the Castle with my knuckles, I suppose!' Esteban said peevishly.

'Used your brains. Your horse could have gone lame. They could not have turned you out on Christmas Eve with a storm coming on. However, there is time. I hardly think she will accept that stooping, squinting Charles Tallard—the matter can wait till you return from Spain.'

'I am not going to Spain.'

His father said sweetly that he had saved the news as a surprise, a sort of Christmas gift. It was time someone attended to the Medina-Barrios property. Esteban was to have that pleasure. And if Esteban intended to wear the face of a sulky bear, he had better take it to his own room.

Esteban had replied by leaving the Hall, stamping and kicking the door open and upsetting a small fat boy and a pitcher of wine, so his face did not cheer the Christmas feast. In fact, except for Don Diego's there were only two faces in the Hall that Peter would have known. One was that of the Jester, who was amusing the guests with his dancing and singing. When Tom danced, he fell down. When he sang, the notes were sometimes like a skylark's and sometimes—more often-like a crow's. The ladies from London held their sides laughing at him. When he lay down before the fire, put his legs back over his head, and went to sleep, they laughed still harder. And when Tom opened one green eye and winked at two who stood near, they pulled him to his feet and sent him spinning around with a great tinkling of bells.

Tom was splendidly dressed in a new suit half of scarlet and half of gold, with gilded silver bells at his elbows and knees and shoulders and on his fool's cap.

'Which do you like better, Tom,' someone asked him, 'your new suit or your new master?

'Oh, the new suit,' Tom said in his high voice. 'Masters come and go. Swords strike them, or arrows, or stones, you know. They get drowned—a wet death, drowning, and a clammy one—most unpleasant. This very year I've had three masters. But a new suit that's harder to get. And easier to keep.'

He gave a cracked wild laugh and another tinkling spin, and the crowd laughed again.

The only face in the Hall that remained gloomy was the other that Peter would have known. Gonzalo Palma still looked like a frog, a fat frog, and an angry one.

He said in a low voice to Don Diego: 'That fellow's tongue would be better with a couple of knots tied in it.'

His master smiled and bowed, but his voice was sharp as he said: 'No one listens to the fool in red and gold and he means nothing, but all the fools do not wear bells. If you start and turn green every time Peter Aubrey's name is spoken, you had better find work out of England, Gonzalo.'

He finished with another of his courteous smiles and a graceful motion of his long hands.

'You'd turn me out—in spite of what I know?' Gonzalo muttered.

The new Baron drawled: 'I know that you killed my nephew. Tell that and you will find how the inside of a prison looks before morning.'

'It was at your order.'

'Not at all. My nephew fell overboard and was drowned, a sad accident. Everyone knows he could not swim. As to this tale of your having, at my orders, sent him over the side by slinging a stone, there is no evidence of any such thing. The only possible witness went across the sea with that madman Columbus and is by now telling his story to the mermaids, no doubt. Be sensible, Gonzalo—keep a pleasant face—'.

Don Diego started to move on, but Gonzalo caught him by the sleeve, saying with a grin: 'I have something to tell you, my lord. Something you will be glad to know. Step into the next room. No, don't try to shake me off—your guests will notice.'

Don Diego smiled and bowed and moved on with Gonzalo behind him. His guests all admired his splendid appearance. He was, they thought, all a nobleman should be.

Behind the closed door Don Diego dropped his smile.

'What is it now? You want more money, I suppose.'

'Money is always acceptable, my lord. I am sure you will give me some when I tell you the good news. Your nephew is not dead after all.'

Don Diego choked out: 'You lie in your teeth, Gonzalo.'

'Oh, no, my lord. I do not. I only saved something to tell you in case you showed signs of growing tired of a faithful servant. The boy who left the *Speedfast* had *a scar on his wrist like the track of a dog's foot.* He had black eyes too, whereas young Alzate's were light blue—very noticeable in his dark face. It was your nephew, my lord, who left the ship!

Don Diego had sunk down into a chair, panting for breath. After a moment he regained enough composure to say: 'Well, in any event, he has gone with Columbus. He will never return.'

'Do not be too sure of that. There are many people in Palos who say that with the Pinzons to help him, Columbus will come back safe—and before long. If you wish to bet on it, there are plenty who will stake gold that he will return before Easter. And what then?' Don Diego said quietly: 'Why, then, Gonzalo, you killed young Alzate and my nephew saw you do it. Let us not be such fools as to put both our necks in one rope by quarrelling. You will go to Spain with Esteban next week and see to affairs at Barrios. If Columbus returns, you will know it

'You lie in your teeth, Gonzalo'

in Spain sooner than I shall here. And you will take measures to make us both safe. I leave them to you. In the meantime I have gold for you—a Christmas gift—and when the task is safely accomplished, you shall have something more substantial. One of our Melcote farms would please you, perhaps. You have often admired our fertile soil here. We will speak of that later. In the meantime, I neglect my guests.'

He went back into the Hall smiling. Gonzalo was smiling too.

The face that looked into the Hall for a moment without a smile was that of the old priest, Father Patrick. He had come from praying in the chapel and was on his way to his room to rest for a while before it was time for the midnight Mass. His plump face had grown thin lately. He felt very old and ill and tired. The smell of the rich foods still on the tables—the boar's head cut and hacked out of shape, the half eaten haunches of venison, the roasted peacock with its bright tail feathers trailing over the edge of the table, the richly spiced wines—did not make him hungry. In spite of having fasted all day, he had never felt less like eating as he stood in the gallery and looked down at the brightly dressed crowd.

He murmured, looking at the men in their doublets sewn with jewels, at the women in their puffed and slashed silks and velvets: 'Peacocks—screaming peacocks!'

For a moment he hated the thought that these men and women would be kneeling in the chapel at midnight to hear him say Mass.

'But I must not feel so. If it touches one heart, brings even one nearer to you, oh Lord, that is enough,' he thought sadly. 'And my prayer will be for his soul, for Peter's, for my boy, drifting in that cold sea.'

He turned away to his bare, cold room. The snowflakes went

softly down past the leaded window panes. He could see the boys from the farm laughing and throwing snowballs. The waits were singing a song about the running of the deer.

It was a merry Christmas at Melcote.

CHAPTER 12

GREEN VALLEY

THE little party of Indians moved slowly through the forest. They were in no hurry. Their village was far away in the hills. It would take days to reach it. One day more or less would make no difference. There was plenty of time to carry the wounded White Boy carefully.

Even a White Boy from Heaven could be ill, it seemed, if he cracked his head on a rock. They were surprised to learn that the Men from Turey (heaven) had heads no thicker than their own. The men who had come in the Canoes with Wings had frightened the Indians by their strength. Besides, the bearded strangers with the pale skins had magic weapons that cut you if you touched them.

With a few strokes they could chop down a tree big enough for a canoe for a whole village. It was a marvel how the trees had fallen while the Men from Heaven were building the high fence around their house. Getting a tree down was a work of many days for the Indians. Hollowing it out for a canoe might take months. They had no tools but sharpened stones and sticks, shells and fishbones, and fire. Their work was more marvellous than that of the Spaniards, if they had realized it. It took endless patience and the strength of many people helping each other.

When a canoe was finished it belonged to everyone. When the men went fishing the fish they caught was for everyone. It never occurred to them that those who had many fish spears ought to have enough fish to make them sick and that others might have nothing to eat at all. They chose their chiefs because they were wise, and a wise chief would of course not allow greed and stupidity.

On this particular morning they stopped to eat near a pool in a cool stream. They swam in the pool. The older boys taught the small ones to swim. Even those who had to be carried by their mothers most of the way were like slippery brown fish in the water.

They slung a hammock for the White Boy from Heaven between two trees. One of the women brought him water to drink from the clear stream above the pool. She bathed his hot face—it was red now rather than white—and put a fresh cap of herbs and leaves on the deep gash above his temple, and on the place where the parrot had bitten him.

He seemed half asleep, but he drank thirstily from the polished gourd, smiled, and thanked her. He spoke in English, but the woman understood the words without knowing their meaning. He dozed for a while. The woman sat beside him and fanned the mosquitoes away with a dried palm leaf. After a while Cacibi came and took the palm leaf and went on with the fanning.

It was Cacibi who had found Peter lying in the rocky gully into which he had fallen. The Indian boy's sharp ears had heard Peter's moans. Cacibi had been running ahead of the rest of the people of his village. He was a good runner, but not especially strong. He was panting and tired by the time he had carried Peter up the steep slope to the path. After he had brought water and washed Peter's wounds, Cacibi was ready to rest.

He lay down beside Peter and they both slept. Cacibi slept when he was tired and ate when he was hungry. Sometimes he had to work, but never for very long. Most of the time he simply enjoyed life.

Cacibi woke up at dawn. He looked at the White Boy from Heaven and wondered what to do with him. The White Boy did not open his eyes or answer when Cacibi spoke to him. He was too heavy for Cacibi to carry back to the fort, even if Cacibi had felt like doing so. Cacibi had taken a dislike to Gutierrez. Gutierrez had promised the Indian three hawks' bells for some gold, but when Cacibi brought all he had, the Spaniard had scowled and said it was not enough. He had given only one bell—Cacibi's pleasant picture of himself with three bells around his neck was spoiled. Why should he get hot and tired to please the thundercloud-faced white man who sat in the shade while everyone else hauled logs?

Cacibi knew that the man at the fort thought that the White Boy had gone out to the ship in a canoe. When the boats came in from the ship the night before, the men had been calling and hunting for someone. The Man with Two Tongues—Cacibi's name for Luis de Torres—had made Cacibi understand that it was Peter they wanted. Then Torres told him that it was no matter, that the White Boy had gone to the ship in a canoe.

One of the men who was waiting to go in the boat said so. Cacibi wondered if he knew. He did not think the White Boy had gone in a canoe, but the men were making angry noises.

The sun was getting near the sea. They did not want to lose their way among the rocks and sandbanks in the dark.

The *Niña* had sailed before Cacibi found Peter. She had fired a farewell shot from one of her lombards and the men in the fort had fired back.

'It is too late,' Cacibi thought, 'to catch the Canoe with Wings even if this White Boy could hear what I say. No paddle can catch her now.'

Cacibi went to sleep again. When he woke up the people of his village were there. He asked them if they ought to carry the White Boy back to the fort. Guarion, Cacibi's father, settled the matter. Guarion was the Cacique of their village and the priest too. He said he would ask their Zeme what to do. The Zeme was a twisted root with a roughly carved face, eyes and ears of shells, and hair of parrots' feathers.

Guarion set up the Zeme in the shadow of a rock near a waterfall, and after the proper respect had been paid, he asked the Zeme what to do with the sick boy.

Cacibi could not hear what the Zeme said, but that was partly because of the noise of the waterfall, though mostly because Cacibi was not a priest yet. Guarion understood the Zeme perfectly. The Zeme told him not to carry the White Boy from Heaven back to the white men's new house. The house was not built in a good place. The spirits there were bad. The White Boy would die, and then the men from Heaven would be angry and make smoke and thunder with their logs and sticks.

The Zeme said that Guarion and his people must take the White Boy from Heaven to their village. He would get well there and bring them good fortune. The women could carry him, the Zeme said. They could stretch a hammock on sticks and make a litter. Their steps would be gentler and smoother

He asked the Zeme what to do

than the men's. It was very important for the sick boy to ride smoothly. The women must remember that they were carrying one who would bring them good luck.

Guarion was naturally tired after talking so much with the Zeme. He took a swim, ate some cassava bread and two bananas nicely spotted with brown and with no green at the tips. He sat down to rest in the shade of a tree big enough to make a canoe for the whole village. His wife brought him a hot coal, and he lighted one of the brown sticks of dry leaves and smoked it.

He said it would keep the mosquitoes away from the White Boy.

Peter knew nothing of that journey. The fever never left him for long. Most of the time he lay in a stupor. When he spoke it was in a tongue that even Cacibi, who prided himself on knowing the white men's talk, could not understand. Even after they reached Guarion's village, Peter still lay in a waking dream in which he was a small boy at Melcote. His mother had made him a ball of scarlet-and-white leather stuffed with Melcote wool. He was throwing it for Meg to catch. Or he was taking Minotaur down to the stream for his evening drink. Or he hid in the passage back of the Great Hall and heard Gwen and Esteban looking for him. Sometimes he was at Tallard Castle or outside a church in Seville waiting for the Queen to ride by. Sometimes he was on the *Speedfast*.

Those were the times he would call 'Martin! Martin! Where are you?' and Cacibi's mother would bring him water to drink and sing to him. He would be quiet then, for a while, but later he would be somewhere else—on the *Santa Maria* or in a bookshop. He was anywhere indeed except in an Indian village on Española.

Yet when his senses at last came back, the place was familiar. In spite of fever and pain he had come to know it: the cup-shaped green valley with the jagged mountains around it, the pines that were bigger than four pines at home, the strange birds, the butterflies, the clean little houses with the hammocks hanging in them. The houses were scarcely more than roofs for shade and to keep out rain. There was always clean air blowing through them.

Peter liked them. He liked drinking from a polished and painted gourd. He liked the food—cassava cakes as thin as paper, the tapioca that looked like pearls and that had different kinds of fruit with it, and fish broiled over coals and hot enough to take the skin off his tongue.

The Indian women brought him all he could eat, and smiled with pleasure when he asked for more. They laughed at his attempts to speak their language and taught him better in their soft voices. He taught them English and Spanish words in exchange. A queer mixture of all three tongues served most purposes, but there were things he could not learn. At first he was too weak to care. As his strength came back he became anxious to know where he was and how to get back to the fort.

Neither the women nor Guarion nor Cacibi ever gave him any satisfactory information. The white men's house was many days' journey away, Cacibi said, but on being asked to count on his fingers how many, he simply opened and shut his hands several times. This was his way of saying that it was too many to count. There was no way of telling from the valley where La Navidad lay. That was a question which Cacibi answered only by twisting his handsome face.

Cacibi had been busy tattooing his legs lately. He was much more interested in his art than in questions about the Spaniards.

Probably, he said, they were getting much gold. And eating. They ate like sharks...

How long it had been since the *Niña* sailed was another thing Peter could not find out. There was no marked difference in the seasons to give him any clue. Perhaps the valley was a little greener, the sun a little warmer, the flowers a little more plentiful than when he had first come to Española. Perhaps it was spring, but as trees seemed always to have fruit and flowers and buds on them all at once, it was hard to tell. It might be March, but for all he knew it might as well be June.

As his strength came back he grew restless. Suppose the Admiral came back and went away again? Columbus had promised to return at once from Spain and bring more supplies to the men at La Navidad and more men to found a real colony on Española. He might even now be sailing towards the island.

The very thing Peter feared had happened: the Admiral made his second visit to Española and went away again while Peter was still in Guarion's village.

How lucky he was to be safe in that green hollow in the hills, Peter never learned till long afterward.

Chapter 13

ESTEBAN SEES A PROCESSION

It WAS on Friday, the fourth of January, 1493, that the *Niña* sailed from La Navidad, leaving Peter behind. On Sunday the Admiral saw for the first time in nearly two months Martin Alonso Pinzon's ship, the *Pinta*. The meeting between Columbus and Martin Alonso was not a pleasant one. Martin Alonso was not used to taking orders. He resented them especially from a man he always regarded as a foreigner and a landlubber. He never forgot that first sight of Columbus, dusty and shabby at La Rabida.

Martin Alonso would never admit that Columbus knew anything about the sea. Columbus was a good navigator when he had a good pilot, was Captain Pinzon's opinion. Without the Pinzons Columbus would never have made his discovery, he always said. It was galling to his pride that Columbus was now Admiral of the Ocean Sea while the Pinzons were only captains of two leaking, rotting tubs.

Things were made no pleasanter by Martin Alonso's comments on the loss of the *Santa Maria*. Columbus made the mistake of explaining that it had happened while he was asleep: that it was everyone's fault but his. Martin Alonso's answer was a laugh that echoed from the shores of Española across the sparkling water.

The *Niña* and the *Pinta*, badly caulked, badly provided with food, set out for Spain carrying men who had in their hearts more hatred than joy in their great discovery. Most of both crews were hostile to Columbus. Pedro de Salcedo loved him. Columbus was still a hero to his cabin boy, but except for Pedro's look of dog-like faithfulness, the eyes that followed the Admiral were unfriendly. The Indians whom he was taking to the Sovereigns were miserable. Some of them died on the way, apparently from homesickness and from fear rather than from any definite disease.

It was an unlucky voyage. The *Pinta* sailed badly. Columbus says in his journal that Martin Alonso should have had her mainmast replaced instead of spending his time hunting for gold. Whatever the reason was, the *Niña*, originally the slower of the two ships, now had to wait for the *Pinta*. There were storms that threatened to sink both ships: gales that blew them off their course; lightning that flashed above them and set strange balls of fire alight on the mastheads and spars; waves that broke over them.

Of the fourteenth of February, the Admiral wrote: 'This night the wind rose and the waves were terrible, one meeting another, so that they crossed and held back the ship, which could not go forward out of them, and they broke over her. We carried the studding sail very low, trying to escape from the waves, and went on for about three hours. Then the sea and wind rose so high that we had to run before the wind wherever it took us. The caravel *Pinta* began to run before the wind too, and disappeared. We sent up flares and for a while she answered, but at last we saw no more of her. At dawn the wind and waves were more terrible than ever.'

'It seemed to me,' he wrote after the storm, 'that God was punishing me for my little faith. My desire to bring the news of my discovery and to show the Sovereigns that I had been a truth-teller was so great that I had been afraid all these months that even a mosquito might prevent my safe return. I knew that I ought to have trusted more in God's mercy and I saw that I ought not to fear this storm, but in my weakness I could not calm my mind.

'I thought, too, about my sons and about what would happen to them in a strange land, if I did not return. If Their Highnesses only knew of my discovery, they would take care of my sons, I thought. For this reason, and that Their Highnesses might learn of the finding of the Indies even if I were lost, I took a parchment and wrote on it all I could of what we had found. I enclosed the parchment in a waxed cloth, and put it in a barrel, and threw it into the sea.'

That barrel never came ashore, but the ships came safely to port at last, in spite of more storms and in spite of trouble with the Portuguese.

Friday was always a lucky day for Columbus. He sailed from Palos on a Friday. On a Friday he first saw San Salvador, and it was on Friday, the fifteenth of March, that he crossed the Bar of Saltes with a rising tide and found himself again in the port from which he had sailed six months before.

He set out almost at once for Barcelona where King Ferdinand and Queen Isabella were. There was nothing to keep him in Palos. There was no pleasure in meeting the tears and sighs of the women whose sons and husbands had been left at La

Navidad. Nothing would convince them that their men would soon be back loaded with gold. From the men of that seafaring town there were scornful looks when they heard about the loss of the *Santa Maria* on a bright night, in a calm sea.

Strangely enough, the *Pinta* arrived at Palos the same day as the *Niña*. No dark looks greeted the Pinzons. Everyone was glad to see Martin Alonso. His story of the voyage was the one they believed in Palos. There was anger over it; anger and grief over Martin Alonso's illness. People said it was of a broken heart that he died, because the King and Queen did not honor him for his share in discovery.

But if in Palos they were glad to see 'the foreigner' shake the dust off his feet, in other towns people were more enthusiastic. Women came to their doors as he passed. Men left their oxen in the fields and hurried to the roadside. Small boys and girls ran after the strange procession and stared at the painted Indians, at the sailors with the parrots on their shoulders, at the Admiral of the Ocean Sea in his scarlet and gold.

The Indians stared back. They had lost their gay smiles. This was a terrible country to them, this place where one day dust puffed around their feet and the sun scorched them; where the next day they might be shivering as they plodded through mud. They felt uneasy at night in the stuffy inns where they slept—if they slept at all—on mattresses of dirty straw. How could people sleep without clean air and a swinging ham-mock? They were hungry, so they ate the strange food, but it made them sick.

Worst of all were the animals. In every village there were barking dogs. To the Indians, who had never seen a four-footed creature except their own small dogs that did not bark, and rats and lizards, the Spanish dogs were as frightening as wolves or lions would have been. Still, even the dogs were less terrifying than horses and mules. These great beasts with the rolling eyes and the flying feet whose kick was death were a constant source of fear.

The Indians were surer than ever that Columbus came from Heaven when they saw him mounted on a mule for his journey and saw that he was not afraid of the foaming mouth or the thudding hoofs. The noise that the creature made—a noise like the scream of twenty parrots—did not frighten the Man from Heaven either. They had known he was brave on the ship when they saw how calm he looked when the waves were like mountains, but that was nothing, in the Indians' opinion, to riding a mule. Because he did not have to ride the mule. He might have walked!

The Indians were not at all embarrassed by walking through Spain dressed in a little paint and some parrots' feathers. They would have liked some gloves—there was something attractive about gloves. It was always an amusing surprise that a glove and your hand had the same number of fingers. Still, they were content to wait for the gloves. The Admiral had promised them each a pair.

Aside from the lack of gloves, they were well pleased with their appearance. The Admiral had made them wear more feathers than usual and more gold ornaments. One of them wore the crown that the Cacique had given to the Admiral in Española. The wearer was not a Cacique, but he enjoyed wearing the crown, and the mask with its gold eyes and nose that the Admiral put around his neck.

The Indians all painted themselves freshly just before they reached Barcelona. They were anxious to look well to please the great White Cacique and his wife. They wished they had their gloves, but they did the best they could with red and white and black paint, doing each other's backs in handsome patterns.

They liked the King and Queen very much, and thoroughly approved of the fact that the Sovereigns received them in the open air. The thrones were set up outside the palace where everyone in Barcelona could see the discoverer of the Indies, and the Indians he had brought back to Spain.

To the surprise of the Indians the King was a little man, shorter than themselves, or than the Admiral or than the Queen. To them the Admiral with his white head and tall figure looked grander than anyone. There was no voice like his, so rich, so strong, so gentle, though the Queen's soft voice was pleasant to hear, too.

The Square was packed with people. Two of them watched the procession as it came in with especial eagerness. They had pushed and shoved their way through the crowd. An elbow in ribs here and there, a toe trodden on carelessly, a shoulder wedged into any empty space, had done the trick. In spite of dark looks and some few curses that followed them, they had reached the front row just as the drums and trumpets were heard far down the street.

'We must watch carefully,' said the handsome young man to the fat man with the frog face. 'He may be changed, you know, this mysterious cabin boy.'

Gonzalo Palma muttered: 'You talk too much, Don Esteban.'

Esteban Medina-Barrios did not enjoy being corrected by his father's steward, but he only shrugged his shoulders and was silent. Gonzalo smiled his oily smile and rolled his prominent green eyes over the scene.

The King and Queen had come out of the palace and were sitting under the cloth of gold canopy that had been set up to shield them from the April sunshine. Crimson velvet embroidered with the arms of Spain hung behind them. A splendid carpet from the Orient covered the platform on which their thrones stood. Their son, Prince John, sat beside the King. Beside the Queen there was an empty chair.

The noise of the drums grew louder.

'They're coming! They're coming!' someone called. People began to edge out into the Square.

'Get back there,' growled a soldier, striding along the line of chattering women, squealing children, and shouting men.

'Back! Out of the way!' said the soldier behind him. 'Make way for the Admiral of the Ocean Sea.'

'Make way, clear the way for the Viceroy of the Indies!' shouted another. 'That's right, Señora, move back just a little. You'll see him well enough.'

'I want to see the Indians! I want to see the Admiral!' squeaked a small boy back in the crowd.

'Come on up, then,' the soldier said, and hoisted the boy to his shoulder, where he sat drumming on the soldier's helmet and looking very important.

'Now I can see them,' he squealed. 'I can see better than anyone. Here they come!'

Soon everyone could see them.

Two sun-browned sailors came first, carrying the Royal Standard. Armed seamen came behind them. Bearded men they were, with red caps on their heads and rough clothes stained with salt spray.

Behind them came more sailors carrying strange things from the Indies: branches of trees, enormous reeds, gourds big enough for a cat to sleep in, great mounds of fluffy white cotton, and spun cotton made into nets and hammocks. There were lizards and strange birds, stuffed, most of them, but there were living parrots, too, of different kinds. The parrots were a rainbow of color, a rainbow that squawked back at the yelling crowd.

There were Indian weapons—their bows and arrows, their lances tipped with sharks' teeth. Then came the Indians themselves. Their painted coppery skins, their gold bracelets and anklets, the bright feathers in their black hair, the quiet dignity with which they moved, silenced the crowd for a moment.

Then, as they passed, a murmur followed them: 'Gold! Gold! Did you see the gold? Those islands must be full of it.'

The murmur soon changed to shouts of: 'The Admiral! Long live the Admiral!'

'Live the Admiral!' panted the small boy, throwing his arms around the soldier's neck.

'Stop choking me, or I'll put you down,' the soldier grunted.

The boy stopped choking him.

'Live the Admiral!' he called, and then asked: 'What *is* an Admiral?'

'Sit still, small one. I'd rather have a chestnut burr in my boot than you yanking my hair. That's the Admiral there—the big man with the pink face and the white hair.'

'I like him—he smiled at me. What is an Admiral?'

'A man that sails the sea to a new country where the gold grows on trees and you have only to pick it up.'

The people near the soldier were laughing and listening to the boy's talk.

Esteban, seeing that no one was near him for a moment, said softly to Gonzalo: 'Did you see him?'

Gonzalo shook his big head.

'Might be with the mules,' he muttered.

Then came the Indians

Fourteen mules with closed baskets on their packs plodded through the dust, but the figure for which Gonzalo was looking was not there.

'We must get speech with the sailors,' he said. 'We may have missed him, or he may have stayed at Palos. He may even have sailed for England.'

'Suppose he has? I thought we came over here to collect rents.'

'So we did, but your father asked me especially if by any chance that madman Col—that is, the Admiral—returned, to find this young Alzate and—

'And what?' Esteban asked, yawning.

'And give him a message.'

'Well, he's not one of these bushy-bearded sailors, you say. Is he one of the Indians? I hope it's that one with the gold crown. I'd like to take him back to Melcote.'

Gonzalo Palma made an impatient noise in his throat.

'I told you before—' he began.

'Yes, I know. To keep quiet. But a crowd is the best place for privacy, I always say. How many in this one speak English, do you think? Find your sailor or someone else who knows this boy, and let's get out. I am sick of breathing garlic. It's hot in the sun.'

'We'll soon be back where it's cool,' Gonzalo said, edging through the crowd towards the place where the sailors were standing.

'Cool—yes, and dull. Turnips and cabbages and red-faced yokels and oxen. Sometimes I can't tell the men from the oxen, or from the cabbages. I'd like to go where these Indians and their gold came from. Look at the stuff they are taking out of those baskets. That fruit looks good. And there's more gold— lumps of it. Those islands must be worth seeing.'

'You'd like it no better than any other place. You carry your discontent with you,' Gonzalo muttered.

'Oh, don't preach!' Esteban made his impatient movement of the hand, palm down, thumb up. 'It's evidently worth going there. Look, the Queen is making that upstart from Genoa sit down beside her. That's what you get by finding new lands and gold. See, the King is taking grains of gold in his own hands and pouring them from one to the other.'

Esteban's fretful voice was drowned by the shouts and cheers of the crowd as the sailors unpacked the baskets carried by the mules, and new treasures were placed on the steps where the Sovereigns could see them.

After a while the Admiral began to speak and silence fell on that great crowd. He said that the fruits and plants and the gold were only samples of the richness and fertility of the new lands.

'What we—so few in numbers, strangers, ignorant of the language—have found on our first voyage is only a foretaste of the treasures that can be found with more ships and more men,' he said to the crowd. Then he turned to the Sovereigns and added: 'These seven Indians who now stand trembling before Your Highnesses are only forerunners of whole nations that Spain will rule and of the thousands of souls who will follow Our Lord Jesus Christ.'

At these words the Sovereigns knelt down and raised their hands to heaven. The great people of the Court, the roughly clad sailors, and the people in the Square did the same. The Indians at last knelt, too, and bowed their feathered heads. From all that great crowd rose the words of the Te Deum:

> *We praise thee, O Lord.*
> *We acknowledge thee to be our God...*

The solemn words of the chant were ended. The last echo of the Amen rang from the gaily decorated houses. The King and Queen rose and went into the palace. The Admiral's towering white head moved slowly behind them.

The crowd began to scatter. Men were hungry for dinner. Women wondered whether the stew would be burned. The sailors began to pack the goods from the Indies back into the baskets.

One of them turned and answered the frog-faced man who asked him a question.

'Alzate? Martin Alzate? Yes, I know him well. Deck boy on the *Santa Maria*. He stayed at La Navidad. Was to have come with us but he missed the boat. Has his pockets full of gold by now, I expect. Some people have all the luck.'

He turned away whistling and began tossing coconuts to another sailor, who dropped them into a basket.

'Well, we shan't see him for a while,' Gonzalo said in English with a gusty sigh of relief.

'You may not,' Esteban said coolly. 'I shall.'

'What do you mean?'

'I have been talking to one of the pilots. There is another fleet going soon to the Indies. I am going with it.'

'You are joking.'

'You think so? You will not when I come back loaded with gold. Come, too, Gonzalo! You can find this young Alzate—as you call him—whose name you never speak without turning green. Find him before he comes back to Spain or perhaps to England. Finish your *business* with him—whatever it is. It need not take long. Six weeks, the pilot says, now they know the course. A month there, perhaps; long enough to complete your—er—business, and pick up some gold. Another six weeks to get home. Say four months in all!'

'Your father—'

'My father—as you very well know—will be greatly pleased.'

Gonzalo and Esteban had been strolling away from the sailors as they spoke. They were standing now in the centre of the fast emptying Square with no one hear them. People had either gone home or were crowding around the Indians, who stood still without seeming to see the staring pale faces.

'You and my father, Gonzalo, always treat me as if I were feeble-minded. I found out long ago that you killed this Martin Alzate, mistaking him for Peter Aubrey. You are so afraid of what will happen—no, don't try to pull away, it does not look friendly—that you would run a knife in me if I should step up to the Admiral and tell him so.'

'You—you wouldn't do that,' Gonzalo stammered.

'You are quite right. I would not, since I do not wish to lose my inheritance. I merely wanted to see your face, Gonzalo, when you knew I knew. You ought not to have mentioned that scar on the wrist when you wrote to my father. I can read—you know. A little, but enough.'

'You young—'

'Now, now—no names! We are friends and must be courteous. You see I am cleverer than my much respected father. I saw at once that there was no use fighting you. Our interests are the same. We all want to be quite sure that this "Martin Alzate" is going to stay where he is. So we are going to the Indies!'

CHAPTER 14

SILENCE ON *ESPAÑOLA*

THE fleet that left Cadiz harbor in September, 1493, was very different from the first one. Instead of three badly caulked caravels, there were seventeen ships well supplied with everything to found a colony. There were grains for food and seed, vines and fruit trees, horses, pigs, mules, dogs. Besides arms of various sorts there were tools for building and farming and mining. Corners not otherwise filled were packed with bells and beads and bright cloth for trade with the Indians.

No pardons had to be given to wrongdoers this time. It was hard to choose among all who wanted to go. There were fifteen hundred who went, and from the proudest gentleman adventurer to the humblest cabin boy, all had the same idea. Gold. They were coming back with their pockets lined with it.

It was on the fifth of November that they saw the first land, an island that the Admiral named Dominica. It took two weeks longer—cruising among new islands, landing on them and taking possession of them—before they reached Española and once more anchored outside the shore near La Navidad.

The men at the fort would be watching for them, they thought. Trees and bushes had grown up around the fort, so that they could not see it from the ships, but surely the men in the fort would see the fleet.

Darkness came before anyone in the fort saw the ships. There were no lights on shore that night. There were lights on the ships. They must have looked like fireflies as the ships swung at anchor and dipped with the waves, but no one on shore saw them. The island lay as dark and quiet as if no one had ever set foot there. Even Guacanagari and his Indians had vanished. There were no brown arms splashing through the water, no canoes full of yams and cassava bread. The breeze from the shore brought a faint sweetness. Except for that, Española might have been a cloud shadow that would vanish at dawn.

It was still there at dawn. The Spaniards spent that day charting the channel through the hidden shoals on which the *Santa Maria* had been wrecked. Towards evening they sailed a little nearer in shore, but night again found them waiting, watching, listening for some sign from the fort. The island was only a little nearer, a little darker, and—somehow—a little more threatening.

Everything was very still that night. The Admiral ordered a lombard fired. A sound came from the shore, but it was only the echo. After it died away, the silence seemed heavier than ever. The men on the ships spoke softly to each other. They seemed afraid to break that strange silence. The tide came whispering in over the sandbanks. It was like faintly heard voices that sometimes chuckled, sometimes sobbed.

'It's only the tide,' the men whispered to each other.

'Yes, only the tide.'

'They're asleep in the fort.'

'Yes. that's it—asleep.'

'Hunting for gold all day, probably.'

'Yes, off in the hills, hunting for gold. Tired tonight with carrying it.'

'In the Kingdom of that Caonabo we heard of, that's where they've been. The houses are built of gold there.'

'Perhaps they have stayed there to sleep.'

'Yes, that's it. They're with Caonabo.'

A voice louder than these whispers said suddenly: 'I heard something. A boat's coming out from shore. I hear the oars chunking.'

There was movement on all the ships. Others had heard the boat. Men ran to the rails holding lanterns and torches high above their heads to guide the rowers.

The sound was not made by oars. Paddles made it. An Indian canoe slid quickly out of the darkness and stopped near the flagship.

'The Admiral! The Admiral!' one of the Indians called.

The Spaniards said the Admiral was there, and asked the Indians to come aboard.

'The Admiral—show us the Admiral,' the Indians called, making no motion to bring the canoe nearer the ship.

Columbus came on deck. Someone held a torch above his head so that the Indians could see him. They knew that tall figure, that shining hair, that grave but friendly look, even in the orange glare of the torch. When they heard his voice speaking in their own tongue, they had no more doubts, but came aboard.

They smiled at first in their old way. Then the face of their leader grew sad. Their chief, Guacanagari, was ill, they said. Caonabo had come with many bad men. They had burned their village. Guacanagari was hurt in the fight, otherwise he would have come himself to see his friend the Admiral.

One of the Indians who had been to Spain interpreted what the other Indian said. They both spoke slowly and clearly. They stood with Columbus in the circle of light made by the torch. Outside it gathered the crew of the ship, staring at the Indians. The torch light turned their skins a strange coppery orange.

'The white men—ask them about the white men in the fort,' Columbus said to the interpreter.

'It was very sad about the white men,' the Indian said. Tears slid over his painted cheeks. The Spaniards could see them shine in the flickering light. 'Very sad. They had quarrelled with each other and some had been killed. And there had been a sickness. Some had gone to distant parts of the island and probably they were very well. But Caonabo, who was a bad man and very fierce, had killed some. Yet no doubt some were still alive. It was a great sadness to Guacanagari, and he had sent these two masks to the Admiral.'

The messenger held out the masks and the light caught the gold eyes. He said that his master hoped the Admiral would visit him soon.

He would go to see Guacanagari the next day, Columbus said.

While he was speaking, the interpreter had been talking to another of the Indians. When the canoe had melted into the darkness, the interpreter told Columbus what he had learned.

The Spaniards were all dead.

Columbus could not believe it. The first speaker had said clearly that some were still alive, perhaps in another part of the island.

'He did not wish to tell you all the evil news at once, my lord. They are all dead.'

Still Columbus could not believe it. Death to all the garrison, and from the Indians, the kindest, gentlest people in the world? Death to men armed with swords and lombards from naked people with sharpened reeds for weapons? Surely there must be some still alive. Surely the morning would bring better news...

But there was no laughing, shouting crowd on shore next morning, no splashing swimmers, no canoes full of painted figures, no presents of bananas and balls of cotton. No calls to 'Come and see the Men from Heaven.'

It took courage to land on that silent shore where their comrades had died, but the crews landed that morning. They marched close together with swords and spears ready. The green, sweet-smelling place was hostile now.

No one came near them. The shadows in the forest were only shadows. Or if they were really watching Indians, they moved no more than shadows. The Spaniards reached the place where the fort was safely. It was only a pile of ashes and charred timbers now. There were around it broken chests... torn clothes... rotting flour... bones.

Guacanagari's village was a heap of ruins, too. Some of the Spaniards thought that Guacanagari had been one of the attackers. Others, Columbus among them, pointed out that the Cacique would hardly burn his own village. The story of the destruction of La Navidad and of its garrison was never fully known, but talk with various Indians convinced Columbus that he understood it well enough.

Gutierrez and Sanchez had lost no time after Columbus left in making plans to get gold for themselves rather than for the Sovereigns. They had revolted against Arana, the man Columbus had left in command of the fort, and had gone off into the country of Caonabo, taking a party of men with them, to look for gold.

Caonabo was a fierce warrior belonging to a tribe of Caribs. Six years before he had come with his band of Caribs from another island and settled on Española. He had taken some of the best land and trained the people who lived there in warlike ways. He had captured Gutierrez and his little party without trouble and had put them to death. Then, finding that these Men from Heaven could be killed, he had planned his attack on the fort.

Things had in the meantime been going badly at La Navidad. There was a quarrel in which some of the men had killed each other. Many of the men had fallen ill with a fever—malaria, they called it—and some had died. Those who had recovered were still weak. They were so sure that the Indians were harmless that they kept no watch. When Caonabo and his Caribs attacked the fort, the Spaniards were all asleep.

In the fight that followed, some died in the burning ruins, some escaped and threw themselves into the sea, where they swam until they were too tired to swim any longer.

After the victory the Caribs burned Guacanagari's village because they were angry with the Cacique for letting the Spaniards settle on Española. Columbus would never believe that Guacanagari had helped Caonabo in his attack on the fort, but there was something strange about Guacanagari when they found him.

He was in another village, a collection of fifty huts. The Spaniards marched there armed with muskets and swords and spears. Many of them wore armor of polished steel inlaid with gold. Others were richly dressed in silks and velvets. Brilliant banners fluttered under the swaying palm fronds. Drums and trumpets announced their coming.

Guacanagari was lying inside his hut in his hammock. His leg was bound with a thick bandage of white cotton. The Spaniards could see that, although it was dark in the hut. Columbus suggested that Doctor Chanca, who was with him, should look at the wound, and that the Cacique had better come out into the sunshine where the doctor could see better.

Guacanagari came, but with evident unwillingness. He walked with a great deal of pain and groaned as he moved, but when Doctor Chanca unfastened the bandage he could find no sign of there ever having been a wound under it.

The injury had been made with a stone, the Cacique said. He wept over the fate of the Spaniards, and he gave Columbus a gold crown and three small gourds full of gold dust.

Many of the Spaniards thought that Guacanagari ought to be punished for what had happened at La Navidad. It would be well to put fear of the white men into the Indians' hearts, they said.

Columbus refused to attack the Cacique. He believed in his innocence and in his friendship. He said that the Spaniards must take advantage of whatever friendliness they found. Perhaps Guacanagari understood that many of the Spaniards were hostile to him, even if he did not know what they were saying. The looks on the faces of the gentlemen—adventurers—Esteban's, for instance—were probably clear enough.

When they next came to his village, it was deserted.

He and his men and their families had vanished in the night.

CHAPTER 15

BATTLE OF GOURDS AND REEDS

IT WAS a long time before the news of death and terror on Española came to Peter's ears. Everything was peaceful in the Green Valley. The Indians planted their crops and harvested them as usual. The women did most of the work in the field. They spun the cotton, too, and made it into nets and hammocks. The men smoked and fished and hunted for utias, a kind of rabbit, and for lizards. Peter learned to eat both. Broiled lizard was as good as partridge, he said.

The boys caught parrots, which is not, as Peter had found out, so easy as it seems, and spent hours teaching them to talk. Sometimes the boys ran races. Some times they fenced with sharpened sticks. Scratches and cuts from this sport were common. Scars from them were considered an honorable distinction.

Both men and women danced and sang. *Areytas* was the name given to a kind of ballad and a dance that went with it. Composing the music, the dance, and the song was a skill that was much admired and applauded.

It was a pleasant life and it slipped by quickly. Peter never learned exactly how long he had been ill. It might have been weeks. It might have been months. The Indians never counted higher than their ten fingers. All he ever got for an answer was that fluttering motion of the fingers that meant the days were too many to count.

He began to keep count of the days himself and of the full moons. A stick of soft wood was his calendar. For a while he kept it carefully—a notch for every day, a cross for a week, a circle for a full moon. After a while he let the days go by: one was so much like another. He kept marking the full moons, however, and almost without his realizing it, there came to be twelve of them.

As he did not know in which month he had started to keep his record, he could not tell exactly what month it was, but he had a system of his own that pleased both him and the Indians. He cut signs opposite the different moons. The first was the Moon of the Parrot. The next was the Moon of the Fish. Lizards, butterflies, and flowers all found their place on the wooden calendar.

The carving pleased the Indian boys and girls. They would crowd around Peter, breathing loud in his ears, joggling his elbows, laughing with delight when they recognized what it was he had carved.

There was something very wonderful about Peter.

He had a knife!

It was in a leather sheath and was hung around his neck by a leather strap. When he found Peter, Cacibi had taken the knife out of the sheath and had cut his fingers on it. That had given him great respect for the knife. He was quite sure it had cut him because it was angry with him for touching it.

Cacibi had told Guarion and the other men of the tribe that the knife was 'Turey'—from heaven. No one touched it after that.

The moment when Peter first unsheathed it and tried the edge of the blade against his thumb was a great one. The White Boy from Heaven was surely brave. The cleaning of two small spots of rust from the blade, the polishing with fine sand and palm oil, the whetting of it on its own sheath, were all ceremonies of great interest.

Before long the name White Boy from Heaven was shortened simply to Turey. Indeed the name White Boy was no longer suitable. Peter had stopped wearing his Spanish clothes in the Moon of the Fish. He had given them to Guarion as thanks for his kindness. Guarion sometimes wore them on occasions of ceremony and looked exceedingly ill at ease. He found his own skin far more comfortable than clothes.

So did Peter. He was so tanned now by sun and wind that— with his long black hair stuck full of parrots' feathers and the patterns of red and black that Cacibi had painted for him—he looked very much like any other young Indian. Only an observant eye would notice that his eyes were brown rather than black and that his hair was softer than a horse's tail.

He moved like an Indian now. His feet were as hard as theirs. He could walk through the forest without making much noise. He had learned to swim at last and could plunge into a mountain pool without shivering. He spoke the language of the tribe, sang their songs, ate as they did. At times he thought as they did.

Yet one thought of his own never left his mind for long. It would come when the Indian men were sitting smoking. The Indians always smoked when they were making up their minds about something. They said it helped them to think. Perhaps they were thinking. Peter had an idea that generally they were just smoking.

What Peter thought about was how he could get back to England.

It had become clear to him before he had cut many moons that he was a prisoner in the Green Valley. The prison was a pleasant one. Later he was to wish that he had never changed it. There were many miles of it through which he could range. There was only one way out of it—a narrow pass at the eastern end through which the sun shone at dawn. Everywhere else high, jagged hills shut the valley away.

Peter could follow any trail up into the hills alone. It was only when he went towards the east end of the valley that someone always went with him. It might be Cacibi and half a dozen other boys going to hunt lizards. It might be two or three of Guarion's bodyguard or even the Cacique himself. There was always someone to keep him from slipping out of the valley.

He gave it up after a while. He had had no real plan about what he would do if he got out of the valley. He had no idea of the distance to La Navidad or even in what direction it lay. Once—months ago now—he had climbed one of the high peaks, thinking he might see the fort, or the harbor near it.

If the fort was in sight, he could not see it. Among the indentations of the shore none seemed more familiar than another. The sea was empty. Not even a canoe stirred on it. Yet if he had made his climb a week later he might have seen the sails of the Spanish fleet.

To leave the valley without food, without any knowledge of the trail to La Navidad, would be a fool's errand, he knew. He might, of course, meet some of the Spaniards or some Indians who would show him the way. He might much more easily wander around in the forest until he died of hunger and thirst: this time with no Cacibi to find him.

He decided to wait. The Indians might leave the valley to go on a fishing trip and take him with them. Or the Spaniards might come. There was gold in the sands of the stream that ran through the valley, and where gold was, white men might come.

Peter had a small gourd full of gold now. He had found that he could get a few grains at a time by scooping up sand and water in a gourd and swirling it around until he could separate the bright specks from the sand. The Indians had shown him how to do it, but they regarded his working so hard at it as foolish. Composing *areytas* or smoking while someone else danced and sang was a much better occupation.

No one stopped him, however, and no one thought of stealing the gold. The gourd stood on the ground under Peter's hammock. Cacibi found several grains larger than peas one day and added them to the heap. When Peter asked where he had found them, Cacibi obligingly pointed out the place.

'In the sand—between those two white rocks,' he said.

'Perhaps you are going to look for more there for yourself,' Peter said, but Cacibi only laughed.

'Bending over hunting for gold makes my back ache, Turey,' he said.

He climbed a tree and went to sleep in it while Peter made *his* back ache. His arms ached, too. So did his eyes from staring at the swirling sand and water. However, he had found a piece of gold as big as the end of his thumb and several smaller grains by the time Cacibi woke up and swung himself out of the tree.

He laughed at Peter's stiff way of walking as they went back to the village.

'Hunting for gold makes my back ache'

'You make yourself an old man, Turey, for the yellow stuff. What will you do with it? Will you make a crown? Or a bracelet?'

'I will leave it as it is,' Peter said.

Cacibi shook his head in a puzzled way. What possible good was gold if you did not wear it?

He began to dance and shake a gourd that had some dry seeds in it that rattled. The gourd was round with a straight piece that did well for a handle. Cacibi had spent the day before carving patterns on the gourd and painting it.

'My gourd is better than yours,' he said, shaking it. 'You can hear mine. It talks. It talks about rain and waves on the sand. Yours is heavy with yellow stones. It can say nothing. What good is it, Turey? You can not eat it, or drink it, or make music with it.'

Peter only smiled. Gold would help him get back to England. He might have to wait a long time, but his chance would come.

How long it would be in coming he—luckily, perhaps—did not guess.

This is how Peter at last learned about what had happened at La Navidad.

There was another village farther up the Green Valley. One day Peter, still hunting for gold, travelled up the stream until he was in sight of the palm-thatched huts. He was becoming wise about choosing a good place to wash for gold, but on this particular day his luck was bad. After working all the morning he had only a few grains.

He was tired and sleepy. It was hot in the sun. He left the riverbank and lay down to rest in the shade of a small clump of trees. He slept for a while. Then voices woke him. Small boys from the village were running and shouting in the sunshine.

They were playing a game he had never seen before. There were two groups of boys. Six or seven had gourds on their heads and heavy sticks in their hands. The others—a dozen, perhaps—were carrying the sharpened reeds that the young men used in their games. Those with the gourds marched along in a line. The others dodged behind bushes and threw their reeds.

They did not hit the first group. It was all in fun, apparently. The Gourd Boys had trouble in keeping the gourds on their heads. Often they would have to stop and pick them up. They would point their sticks at the others and shout. Sometimes one of the Reed Boys would fall down and roll over. Generally, how ever, it was a Gourd Boy who fell. At last there was only one left. The tallest Reed Boy seized him and put him against a tree, pretending to tie something around his feet.

Then all the Reed Boys threw their reeds at him and at last he fell to the ground. His gourd rolled over to the leader of the Reed Boys. He put his foot on the head of the fallen Gourd Boy and spoke to his people. Peter could not hear what he said, but he could see that the boy's face was smeared with black paint.

After he had finished speaking, he kicked the gourd aside and walked off. Then all the boys who had fallen down jumped up. They all chased out into the open field and began to play the game all over again.

Peter began to wonder what it was about—why did some of the boys wear gourds on their heads? Indians never covered their heads with anything heavy. Their long hair was enough protection from the sun. Why did the boys armed with reeds fall when a stick was pointed at them? Or rather, why did they fall when the boy who pointed the stick shouted?

Something about the whole thing made him uneasy. Why

did the boys with the reeds wear bands of cotton tied below their knees and above their ankles? That was not a custom of this village. The blood beat a little harder than usual in the wound near his temple as he watched the game through again.

It all went as before up to the time the Gourd Boy was tied to the tree. This time the boy with the blackened eyes threw his reed too straight. It went through the flesh of the Gourd Boy's arm, pinning him to the tree.

He gave a sharp scream of pain.

For a moment no one did anything. Then everyone except the leader ran away.

Peter hurried towards the tree. Just as he got there, the boy with the blackened eyes pulled the reed out of the other's arm. Blood gushed out of the wound and over the brown skin. The injured boy turned a strange color-like a brown stick with ashes dusted over it—and fainted.

'Give me those bands,' Peter said, pointing.

The boy who had thrown the dart tore the cotton bands off his legs. Peter pressed one against the wound.

'What is your name?' Peter asked.

'Yaqui,' the boy said sullenly.

'Well, Yaqui, take that gourd. Go to the river. Bring water.'

Yaqui brought the water quickly.

'What is this boy's name?' Peter asked, washing the wound and binding it up. It was less bad than he had feared. The blood had already stopped flowing.

'Mariem is his name.'

'Why did you throw the reed at Mariem?'

'It was in the game.'

'What game is this?I think Mariem's father will be angry. You are not old enough to throw the reeds.'

Yaqui had begun to cry now. The tears made tracks through the soot on his face.

'We were only playing Caonabo and the White Men. I did not mean to hit him. The reed flew away from me itself. It is an evil reed. I will break it.'

Peter said, trying to keep the uneasiness out of his voice: 'Tell me more about this game, Yaqui.'

In spite of Yaqui's sobs, Peter learned about the game, and found out also the fate of the Spaniards. The boys with the gourds on their heads were white men. The gourds were their helmets. The sticks were muskets. Yaqui was Caonabo, the fierce Carib Chief. Yaqui and his followers wore cotton bands around their legs because the Caribs wore them. Caonabo had killed all the white men, Yaqui said, only now more had come, but Caonabo would kill them, too.

Peter had thrown the rest of the water over Mariem's face. Mariem sat up now and began talking. He seemed to bear Yaqui no ill will.

'I will have a scar now like my brother's,' Mariem said. 'I hope it will be a big scar.'

Yaqui stopped crying. He and Mariem chattered about Caonabo, who was, it seemed, their hero. Mariem, Peter decided from their talk, must have been playing the part of Gutierrez. There was something terrible in this thought, but Peter could not feel any great amount of grief over it. He remembered the Spaniard's haughtiness on board ship, his impatience when Pedro had spilled a few drops of wine, his mocking of the Admiral behind his back. He remembered that Gutierrez said that an Indian who had picked up a piece of broken glass at the fort ought to have the tops of his ears cut off and be flogged for stealing, to show him the Spaniards would stand no nonsense.

The tales of Spanish cruelty that Yaqui and Mariem were now pouring forth may not have all been true, but Peter was afraid they were not all lies, either.

Perhaps his stay in the Green Valley had made Peter think like an Indian. He could not help feeling that Caonabo had only been defending his country against strange people who came to take it away from him.

He heard the word 'Admiral.' The Admiral was a good man, Yaqui said. He had come again with many Canoes with Wings—Yaqui opened his hands and held them up twice to show how many—but now (Peter's heart sank at this) he had gone away again. The people he had left were very bad.

They took away the women's cassava bread. One white man ate as much in a day as one of their own people would between one moon and the next. His father said so. They seized men and made them carry heavy loads. They beat the men if they sat down to smoke. But it did not matter. Caonabo would kill them as he had the others. Caonabo was braver than any white man.

'You must come from a village a long way off,' Yaqui said, 'or you would know these things. Is your village on another island?'

'Yes,' Peter said gravely. 'From another island, a long way off.'

Melcote's rose-red towers hung before his eyes for a moment. A long way off—but perhaps he might reach them after all.

'Why did you not tell me the Admiral had come back and that the men at the fort were dead?' Peter asked Cacibi.

'We thought it would make you sad, Turey. And our Zeme told us not to tell you. Our Zeme says it is good luck for you to stay here. We did not wish you to be angry and go away.'

'I am sad,' Peter said, 'but I am not angry. Why should

you let strangers take your country from you? Oh, I wish that white men had never come to this place. It was so beautiful before we came.'

He was to keep on wishing so in the months that followed. News drifted into the Green Valley and Peter heard it from Cacibi. It was bad news, most of it. Bad for the Indians. Bad for Peter.

The Admiral came back from exploring other islands, but he lay ill of a fever in the new town he had built and called Isabella for the Queen. Then came a rumor that he was dead. Peter heard it, and gave up a plan he had made for going to Isabella. He felt that only the Admiral could help him, and if the Admiral was dead what was the use? Later came the news that Columbus had recovered from his sickness and that his brother Bartholomew had come.

This was pleasant for the Admiral, but for the Indians it made things worse than ever. Bartholomew Columbus was an efficient organizer. The more efficient he was, the harder the Indians had to work. The Spaniards and the Indians had one thing in common: they were both lazy. Gold mining was hard work, and the Spaniards naturally thought the Indians ought to do it. In their annoyance at finding that gold did not grow on trees, they thought up several ways of making the Indians work. Those who did not learn died quickly. Those who did, died too, but more slowly.

All the tribes had to pay tribute to the Spaniards: a small gourd full of gold every three months from each cacique; a hawk's bell full of gold dust for each grown man. The small, ringing bells that the Indians had liked so much now meant only back-breaking labor. Still, the people in the Green Valley were free. No one had found the way there. Their peaceful life went on.

Outside there were forts being built by the Spaniards. There were attacks on the forts by the Indians, and many Indians were killed. The Spaniards quarrelled and killed each other. There were conspiracies against the Admiral and his brother. The rumors that came to the Green Valley were confused and not always true, but they were no more confused than life on Española during those dark years of bloodshed and cruelty.

Would the White Men find the way to their valley? That was what the Indians talked about around the fire at night. Peter's hope that they would come had changed to fear that they would come. He could not have told just when the change took place. It had happened without his knowing it. Like Guarion and Cacibi and the others, he wished only to be left in peace. But nowhere on Española could there be peace for long.

DANCE, CAONABO!

Sunlight had left the Green Valley. At the east end of it the moon almost filled the cleft in the hills. It hung in the violet sky like a shield of polished copper. The valley began to fill with its pale light. Trees and rocks made long shadows. They looked bigger than they did in sunlight, and the voice of the river sounded louder than by day.

Peter was walking fast because he was hungry. He could smell roasting yams and utias and smoke from the fires. The village must be getting ready for a great feast. He could hear the thumping of drums and the sound of men singing. Dark figures went dancing across the path of the firelight. Some had their arms spread like wings. Some shook gourd rattles. Others pretended to throw their reed spears.

Very faintly came the sound of Cacibi's voice. Peter could not hear the words, but he knew the tune and what it meant. He had heard before the yells from the dancers at the end of each verse, and the savage thumping of the drums that grew louder until his eardrums felt as if they would burst.

There had been a full moon that night, too. No one had told him where the dancers went on moonlight nights. He only knew that they did not all come back, and that those who did had wounds not made with Indian darts.

Peter slipped quietly into the yelling circle around the singer. In the red glare of the fire Cacibi looked as if he had been carved out of bronze. His song had ended and he was standing with one hand pointing down the valley. One knee was a little bent. His head was thrust forward. His dark eyes were on the rising moon. Although he stood motionless, his whole figure seemed ready to shoot forward towards the cleft in the hills.

For a moment the drums and shouts seemed to fill the valley with sound. Then the Indians were silent so suddenly that the echo of their voices came back from the hills as if it belonged not to the group around the fire, but to some distant tribe. Then the echo ceased and a man walked slowly into the firelight.

He was taller than the men around him. The black paint around his eyes made them look like the empty holes in a skull. His head was shaven in curious patterns. White bands on his legs and arms bound them so tightly that the calves of his legs and his upper arms were swollen to an enormous size. Gold shone around his neck and on his wrists.

Someone in the crowd murmured: 'Caonabo! Caonabo!' Others took it up and it swelled suddenly to a great echoing shout. 'Dance, Caonabo! White men coming!' sang Cacibi and the gourds rattled like pelting ram.

Caonabo smiled. His lips and the skin around them were painted black. The smile was like the grin of a death's head. He did not dance. He stood like a carved Zeme and began to speak. The voice in which he spoke had in it thunder and the sound of water in flood dashing down a precipice and the harsh scream of a hundred parrots.

Peter felt his heart begin to quicken its beat. It seemed to have moved up under his collarbone. The men around him breathed as if they had been running.

'Choose now, brothers,' Caonabo was saying. 'The White Men are close to your valley. Soon your daughters will be slaves. Your own shoulders will bleed from carrying these men. I, Caonabo, tell you that I have seen the sons of a cacique carry a White Man on their shoulders till the poles of the litter rubbed them raw and bleeding. A cacique's daughter walked beside him and held a palm leaf over him to shield him from the sun. And who was this man? One of their chiefs? The Admiral or his brother? No! He was a man who swept the streets of their village! And the tips of his ears were cut off to show that in his own country he was a thief!

'Will you have your daughters slaves to grind cassava for such a man? Shall your sons carry water for his feet while he lashes their backs? Help me now, brothers, for if you do not, surely this stream of yours will be red with your blood.'

He stopped speaking. Someone from the crowd called out: 'How can we fight the Giant Lizard Men that come with the White Men? I myself killed two of the first White Men, but there were no Lizard Men then. You, brothers, have not seen them as I have. They have six legs. Their eyes roll terribly. Foam spurts from their mouths. They are as big as six men. Hair like our own grows on their heads—that is, on one of their heads, for they have two. They have a tail of hair with which they can break a man's arm or blind him. Their feet arc like stones. To be trampled by them is death. Let us stay in our valley and not be killed by these Lizard Men.'

There was an answering mutter of: 'Yes. Let us stay. We can guard our pass. No one will come here. If they do, we can roll stones on them.'

Caonabo's great voice silenced the murmurs.

'This talk of Lizard Men is foolishness. They are men like the other White Men, only they are carried by these beasts. The White Men call them "horses." They are big, it is true, but so is a shark, yet I have a shark's tooth on my spear. The White Men have tamed these horses to work for them. The men are your enemies, not the beasts. And do not think the men will leave you in peace. There is gold here.'

Guarion, the Cacique, said quietly: 'Tell us your plan, Caonabo. If it seems good, we will go with you once more.'

The fort that the White Men had just built, Caonabo said, was close at hand. It stood on a hill. The river looped around three sides of it. On the other side the White Men had dug a deep ditch.

'We cannot take this fort,' he said, 'because the White Men have the sticks-that-speak'—Caonabo meant guns—'and sticks-that-cut (swords) so that they can kill us if we come near.'

'Then how can we kill them?' Guarion asked.

'By hunger. Their food is brought to them by our people. We have only to make a ring of men around the fort far enough away so that the sticks-that-speak cannot wound us. Then we can keep all food from reaching the White Men. That will be easy,' Caonabo said with one of his death's-head grins, 'because we shall want the food ourselves. We shall be hungry, and I think we can make our people see that it is easier to give us the food than to carry it to the fort. When the White Men are hungry they will go away. They will be weak and we will kill some of them easily. Some will get away, if their horses can still carry them, but the horses will be hungry too. A horse eats even more than a White Man.'

There was shaking of heads among the Indians at this statement. A beast that ate more than a White Man—impossible!

'Let horses into your valley and you will see! You have heard the name of the captain of this fort. You know it is a name that means death. Alonso de Ojeda!' Caonabo shouted in his hundred-parrot screech. 'Let Alonso de Ojeda have your daughters! Let your wives spin cotton for him! Let your sons grub in the dirt for gold! Let...'

Peter stopped listening to Caonabo. The name Alonso de Ojeda—Caonabo had said it plainly—carried Peter back to Seville. How long ago was it? Peter did not know, but he was a small boy holding his father's hand and looking up at a great tower. There were ladies on a balcony near the tower. He could see their bright clothes and the softness of their veils. The Queen was among them. He remembered her bright chestnut hair and her gentle blue eyes and the sweetness of her smile.

The ladies gasped and gave soft little squeals of excitement and clasped each other's hands. Some covered their eyes with their veils, but they looked through them just the same, Peter thought.

There was a great beam sticking out from the tower. The builders had put it there while they were making some repairs. It was so high above the ground that a man on it looked no bigger than a rabbit. And there was a man on it. He had just stepped out of a window, had swung himself across a yawning gap, and was walking out along the beam.

'Alonso! Alonso de Ojeda!' the ladies squealed. 'Oh, I cannot bear to watch him... Ojeda, yes it is Ojeda. Who else would do anything so mad?... It's as if he were dancing... dancing on air! He'll fall. I know he'll fall... Oh! Oh! Did you see that?'

The man on the beam had reached the very end of it. He swung one foot into the air, pivoted on the other, and walked back. His cloak swayed as jauntily, the feather in his cap nodded as carelessly, as if he were strolling down the street with all the girls peering at him from behind the window gratings. He reached the window, placed one foot against it, took an orange out of his pocket, leaned back, and threw the orange over the top of the tower.

There was a great sigh of relief as he sprang back through the window again. Peter remembered nothing else about that day. He had never seen Ojeda again, but he had heard of him often. Even Esteban admired Ojeda.

He was a little man—Esteban had said patronizingly—but he was the handsomest man in Spain, and the bravest. He had fought the Moors since he was fourteen years old. No one could count how many fights Ojeda had been in, but he had never been wounded or even scratched. He was the best swordsman, the best horseman in Spain. Which means in the world, of course, Esteban had added.

And now Ojeda was in a fort in the heart of the wild mountains of Española. That very river from which Peter had washed his gourd full of gold went foaming down and twisted like a bright snake around that lonely fort. There might be men Peter knew in the fort.

Longing to see the white men and fear of what they would do both filled Peter's mind. It was true what Caonabo was saying. If the Spaniards came into the Green Valley, it would be the end of that peaceful life, the end of the people who had saved Peter's life and fed him and sheltered him all these months. Enough months now so that it was years.

What must he do? Try to help the Indians starve the Spaniards out? Do nothing, but stay in the valley like a coward waiting to see which side won? Try to get to the fort and warn Ojeda?

'There is a road from this fort—a road clearly marked to the city of Isabella,' Caonabo was saying. 'Along that road we will post our men with plenty of darts. And when anyone comes along it with food…'

Peter knew now what he must do. He would go with the Indians as far as the fort. After that he would follow this well-marked road to Isabella. The Admiral was there, Caonabo had just said so.

'I will find the Admiral,' Peter thought. 'I will plead with him for our valley. And not just our valley. For all the island. The Admiral is not cruel. He was always gentle and patient. These things that Caonabo is shouting about have been done while the Admiral was ill with fever. Now that he is well, he will stop them if someone tells him.'

Caonabo's great voice was weaving the wrongs the Indians had suffered into a battle chant. He was dancing. Every movement of his great body was fierce, threatening. The drums were throbbing again. The dancers whirled around the fire.

'It is my chance to go,' Peter thought; 'the chance I have waited for.'

Guarion stepped forward, held up his hand. The dancing and drumming ceased.

Guarion said: 'Caonabo, my brother, we will help you close the ring around this fort. My people shall stand beside yours.'

The Indians left the fire. Soon they were only shadows moving through the green and silver of the moonlit valley. There was mist at the end of it where the river foamed into the cleft in the hills. One by one the shadows disappeared into the mist.

One of the shadows was a tall, thin, hard-footed Indian with a knife around his neck. His black hair hung over his eyes. His face was smeared with charcoal. His sunburned body was spattered with red and black paint. There was a parrot tattooed on his chest and a fish on his back. His name—although he had almost forgotten it—was Peter, Lord Aubrey, second Baron Aubrey, of Melcote.

He had a square of cotton knotted into a bundle and slung over his shoulder on the end of a spear. There were a little cassava bread and three cooked yams in it. It was a heavy bundle because there was also a lizard skin pouch inside it. The pouch contained a curious collection of things. Most of the space was filled with gold dust, but there was also a leather sling of the sort used in the Island of Mallorca, and a miniature portrait of a fair-haired English woman framed in gold and pearls. It was wrapped in a stained piece of silk. Wrapped separately, too, was a nugget of gold the size of a parrot's beak.

It was the largest lump Peter had ever found. He was taking it to the Admiral. It was of the Admiral he was thinking as he followed the rough path to the fort, trying to move as quietly as the man ahead.

Peter was slower than the Indians. Dark figures trotted lightly past him and vanished into the black and silver light under the trees. They made no more noise than the dew dripping off the leaves.

'I will tell the Admiral... stop cruelty... plenty of gold for all... only kindness. We must be kind. I will give him... parrot's beak nugget... he will send me... Spain, next ship... gold enough... take me... England... mother, Meg... Melcote, roses, roses...'

The English words formed themselves with difficulty in his

mind; the thoughts were hardly more than shadows. Suddenly one came clearly.

He stumbled over a root thinking: 'Why, Minotaur, he's an old bull now. Years—I've been gone years. I don't know how long.'

'Quiet, brother,' a voice said in his ear. 'The White Man's fort is near. Step carefully,' and another figure slipped past him.

When the sun blazed into the hot blue sky, Guarion's men had taken their places in the ring that surrounded the fort. The ring of painted, brown-skinned men was a long way from the fort. Many tribes joined in making it. Many hours passed before Alonso de Ojeda's men saw even one of the ten thousand Indians who were blockading the fort. By that time Peter was well on his way towards Isabella.

He had said good-bye to Guarion and Cacibi. Guarion had told him he was free to go on his mission to the Admiral.

'I wish you would stay in the valley, Turey. Our Zeme says you will have bad luck if you go. It says the Admiral will not hear your words, but if you wish to go, I cannot stop you. You are a man now. I will not try to keep you longer if you have chosen the White Men.'

'I hope to bring good luck to our valley by going,' Peter said earnestly. 'In that way I can show you that I am grateful for all you have done for me—you and Cacibi—and repay your kindness. It is the only way.'

'Yes, our Zeme said you would go,' Guarion said, 'but we had good luck in the valley while you were there, Turey. The yams grew well. There were many fish in the streams. And we had peace. Do not speak of a debt. It is already paid. A good journey, Turey. There is your road.'

The road to Isabella was, as Caonabo had said, well marked.

The prints of horses' hoofs were on it. Yet for a while Peter hardly saw it. He kept seeing instead the faces of his friends with their look of patient sadness as they watched him go. When he turned back to wave, Cacibi was wiping his eyes with the back of his hand...

Peter turned his thoughts firmly towards Isabella. He planned carefully the Spanish words that he would use to the Admiral, forming them slowly in his mind.

'My Lord the Admiral, I who stand before you am not an Indian, and yet I come to speak for the Indians. I am...'

But the Admiral never heard those words.

LIZARD MAN

THE tree under which Peter stopped to eat his cassava bread the second day was a huge pine. A plank cut from it would make the door of a house. Peter's long arms could reach only a small part of the way around the great trunk. There was no other tree so large anywhere near. It stood at the top of a hill. Below it the road wound down between the bottom of one cliff and the top of another. The sea was some where far below. The noise like the tide rushing into the river near Melcote was the wind in the pine boughs.

'This will be a safe place,' Peter thought. 'I can find this tree again. That cliff below is like the prow of a caravel. I cannot miss it. It will be safe here for a few days.'

He dug a hole with his knife, lined the hole carefully with pebbles, put the lizard-skin pouch in it, and covered it with more pebbles, with dirt, with pine needles. The hole was close to a root of the tree. It protected the hole like an encircling arm. It was on the side away from the trail. Peter cut away a slab of bark and carved the figure of a lizard on the tree-trunk.

His bundle was lighter as he started down the trail, and so was his mind. The bundle had in it now only two yams and the parrot's-beak nugget for the Admiral. His mind was free of the thought that someone might rob him of his gold before he saw the Admiral. Isabella could not be far off now. Not more than another day's Journey.

Soon he would hear the Admiral say: 'So you are neither that Martin Alzate, deck boy of the *Santa Maria*, nor an Indian of Guarion's tribe.' Columbus would wave to a servant—would it be Pedro, with his soft brown spaniel's eyes bulging with excitement? Well, to someone, anyway—and say: 'Find Lord Aubrey some clothes. Then bring him back. I must hear his plan for peace with the Indians...'

Peter slept under a palm that night, using his bundle for a pillow—a lumpy one. It was still there when he woke the next morning.

So was something else: something that made a sound never until lately heard on Española, a sound that changed suddenly from a snuffling growl to a savage bark.

A great mastiff stood over him with its angry red rimmed eyes fixed on his face, its white teeth showing as the bark became a snarl.

Peter jumped to his feet.

The snarl turned into a roar and the great dog sprang at him, knocking him to the ground.

'Seize him, Duke! Good dog! Hold him!' came a voice from down the trail.

The commands were given in a languid voice.

The dog had seized Peter's ankle long before they were spoken.

The teeth did not break the skin. The dog had been well

A great mastiff stood over him

trained. As the dog's master often said, an Indian with a wounded foot was no use at all. If you wanted to get work out of an Indian, you had to feed him—fortunately they did not eat much—and keep him well. That was only good sense. Otherwise they died. The least thing would do it—a dog bite, a small stab from a dagger. Sometimes it seemed as if they died to spite you.

So the teeth on Peter's ankle were more threatening than painful. They were ready to tear, but so far they were only like iron spikes pressing the skin. No blood flowed yet.

There were seven men looking down on Peter now. Six of them, the ones on foot, were grinning and laughing. They were soldiers, bearded men, sweating from tramping through the forest dressed in steel and leather. The seventh man was on a horse—a lizard man, Cacibi would have said.

Peter's eyes took in the horse first—its heaving black sides, the foam dripping from the bridle, its switching tail and tossing mane. Then his eyes travelled over the rider's mail-clad figure.

The horseman had taken off his steel cap and was wiping his forehead with a handkerchief of soft blue silk.

After a moment, during which his long fingers moved the fringed silk slowly and while the mastiff's teeth pressed harder and the low growl in his throat grew fiercer, the horseman pushed the square of silk into his saddlebag and Peter found himself looking up into the face of his cousin Esteban.

That handsome face had altered very little. That slight one-sided twist of the thin lips was still Esteban's smile. The lazy droop of the eyelids over the cool gray eyes had not changed. Perhaps the color of his skin was faintly yellow instead of ivory, but the lines of his cheeks and chin and the thrust of his nose were still worthy of being cut in marble. He was perfumed too, as usual. The heavy scent of musk mixed with the smell of the sweating horse.

Peter had moved involuntarily at the sight of his cousin's face, but then, feeling the breath from the mastiff's muzzle hot on his skin, feeling the pain from the teeth still increasing, he lay still, staring upward.

The words, 'Esteban, it's I, it's Peter,' moved slowly through Peter's brain, but he did not say them. He could hear the scornful laugh with which they would be greeted and the command that would follow: 'Run your lance through this Indian brute, Juan.'

Caonabo had told some of the things that happened to captured Indians who were not immediately obedient.

Esteban moved his hand in the old way, slowly, carelessly, palm down, as if he were waving away some trifle—a glass of wine, a piece of dry bread.

'Let go, Duke,' he said to the dog. 'Tie him up and send him back to the others,' he said in the same tone to the men. 'He will do instead of that fool that threw himself over the cliff last night. He looks strong. Shove him over here a moment so I can feel his muscle.'

Two of the soldiers pushed Peter over to the horse. Esteban bent down and thrust sharp, hot fingers into the flesh of Peter's arm.

'Stronger than most of them,' he said. 'Listen, you. Do you understand Spanish? Have you gold? *Caona? Turey?*'

Peter only stood staring straight into the gray eyes.

'Another dumb brute,' Esteban said peevishly. 'Doesn't even understand his own language. Well, he'll learn! If he doesn't, Duke can teach him. Duke is a fine teacher.'

Esteban laughed his thin, sharp laugh and the men all laughed too, but Esteban bit his laugh off suddenly.

'What's that in his hand?' he drawled.

One of the soldiers snatched the bundle away from Peter. In a moment the parrot's-beak nugget was lying in Esteban's thin ivory-colored hand.

Peter spoke then: 'Guamiquina,' he said.

It was the name the Indians called the Admiral.

'So you can talk after all,' Esteban said. 'I suppose you mean the *caona* is for the Guamiquina. Well, I will see that he gets it—sooner or later.' He twisted his lips into a yawn and then said sharply: 'Tomaso, take that knife off his neck. He stole it probably. I suppose I ought to kill him, but I need him. If he can smell out nuggets like that, he's too good to kill. Here, Juan, you can speak this Indian chatter. Tell him if he steals again I'll have his ears cut off. This stealing has got to stop,' he added, wrapping the nugget in his blue handkerchief and stuffing it back into the saddlebag. 'Get him tied up. We waste time.'

There were more soldiers coming up the trail now. They were driving a group of Indians ahead of them. There were nine pairs and one stumbling along behind by himself. They were roped together. In a few minutes Peter found himself roped to the stumbling man who had been walking alone.

Two more mastiffs growled and snuffed at his heels. Close behind him a whip cracked. Peter felt a tug on his neck as the men ahead started forward. His neck was rubbed raw by the rope long before they reached Esteban's division—his *repartimiento*, as the Spaniards called it.

Much of Española was divided up now among the Spaniards. Some of them raised food or cotton on their divisions, some of them collected gold. Whatever the work was, it was done by the Indians. Collecting tribute from the Indians had not produced enough gold or enough food or cotton. It would be better to give each Spaniard a certain number of Indians and make him responsible for seeing that they worked. The Spanish overseers got a surprising amount of work out of the Indians considering how lazy the Indians were and how easily they sickened and died.

Esteban was a good master. He did not starve his slaves—much. They were beaten only just enough to make them love their work. His dogs were trained to bark before they bit. By taking care of his slaves and of the goats and chickens and pigs brought from Spain that belonged on his division, Esteban was becoming rich. He had very soon found out that it is just as good to sell a chicken for gold as it is to dig the gold out of the ground, and much less work.

He raised a great many pigs—or rather his slaves did for him—and the slaves often had a bit of pork, perhaps a bone with a good lot of meat on it, to add to their cassava and yams and bananas. The Indians loved pork. Esteban himself was fond of a young roast pig. It was not served often because he felt it was more profitable for the pigs to grow up to their full size. However, when one of the Indian girls found in the river sands a piece of gold big enough for a platter, Esteban ordered a small pig killed and roasted. They served it on the gold platter, and the Indian girl was given a good thick slice of the pork and some of the crackling brown skin.

Esteban, of course, got the platter.

Esteban's division was not far from Fort St. Thomas, where Ojeda was besieged by Caonabo and his ten thousand Indians. Esteban saw no reason for going to Ojeda's aid. Ojeda, he thought, could look after himself. It proved that Esteban was right. Ojeda was able with his fifty men to hold off Caonabo and his ten thousand. Ojeda had no idea of sitting in the fort and starving. He and his men would dash out at some unexpected time and place, ride their horses over the naked, frightened Indians, slash at them with swords, and be back in the fort before the Indians had thrown a spear. He was never wounded on any of these raids. The Indians believed he had some magic that turned spears aside. They soon grew tired of the blockade. The White Men seemed as strong as ever. Only Indians were killed. One by one they left Caonabo and went back into the hills. Before Esteban's latest crop of pigs were well fattened, the siege was over.

Caonabo made peace with Ojeda, but Ojeda knew that while a man of Caonabo's brains and courage was alive on Española there would always be trouble with the Indians. Ojeda wanted a lasting peace, a Spanish peace.

He heard something strange about Caonabo. In spite of the fact that anyone in Isabella would have killed Caonabo for a grain of gold dust the size of a pin-point—or for nothing—the Cacique, it was said, often went near the town. What drew him there was the sound of the great bell.

One of the first buildings in Isabella was the church. Like other buildings in this first city in the New World, it was of logs, but it had a bronze bell brought from Spain. The voice of the bell was wonderful to the Indians. They saw that whatever the Spaniards were doing they would stop when it spoke and go where it was.

Caonabo told another Cacique that if he had the bell he would be as powerful as a white man, because the bell was stronger than a whip or a sword or a cannon—all the white men obeyed it.

Ojeda heard what Caonabo said. His plan for peace on Española was soon made.

Its rashness pleased Ojeda. He took a few horsemen with him and went to visit his recent enemy. Caonabo welcomed him in a friendly way. There was feasting and dancing and the games that the Indians loved.

Then Ojeda made his speech.

'I come,' he said, 'from the Admiral. He invites you to visit him in Isabella. He lies ill with fever or he would visit you himself. He wishes your friendship, for you and he are both great caciques. If you come to Isabella he will treat you like a brother.'

Caonabo did not reply at once and Ojeda went on: 'When you come to Isabella and become the brother of the Guamiquina, he will give you the great bell that sings. You shall have it always near you. Its magic will give you power over all people: over your own people and over White Men, too.'

Caonabo did not need much persuasion after that.

'I will come to the Guamiquina,' he said.

When they started for Isabella, Ojeda found that it was not only Caonabo who was ready for the journey. The Cacique was escorted by all the men of his tribe.

Ojeda said that such a large escort was not needed, but Caonabo answered that all the men wished to pay respect to the Guamiquina. Besides, many of them would be needed to carry the bell home.

'And one of my rank does not travel with fewer people,' he said proudly.

Seeing the crowd of painted Indians, Ojeda feared that he had fallen into his own trap, but he said cheerfully that the Admiral would be delighted to welcome Caonabo and his companions.

Ojeda was a gay and charming companion on the first stages

of that long journey. Caonabo walked beside the Spaniard's horse. Jingling on the saddlebow was a pair of polished steel handcuffs with a chain that shone like silver.

'What are these?' Caonabo asked, putting his finger on the bright metal.

'They are what our Kings wear in Spain when they go to visit other Kings,' Ojeda said. 'They are made from Turey. Only kings can wear them.'

Like all the Indians Caonabo was eager to have things that belonged to the white men.

'I am a great cacique,' he said.

'That is true'—Ojeda took up the chain and jangled the handcuffs together—'and since you are going to visit the Guamiquina you shall be dressed like a king. You shall wear them. And you shall ride with me on my horse.'

Caonabo hesitated at the idea of riding on the horse, but Ojeda laughed that frank and charming laugh of his and told him there was no danger.

'We will bathe in the river here,' he said. 'When we come out you shall be dressed in these bracelets that only our Spanish kings wear. Your people will be proud when they see how splendid you look and that you are brave enough to ride on horseback.'

So after their swim Ojeda put the handcuffs on Caonabo's wrists and locked them. Ojeda mounted his horse. The other Spaniards lifted the Cacique to the crupper behind Ojeda and tied him there—to keep him from falling, Ojeda said.

The Indians shouted and laughed when they saw their Cacique with the shining bracelets from Turey on his wrists, riding on the big brown horse. Caonabo's head rose high above Ojeda's. There was a broad smile on Caonabo's painted face as

Ojeda turned the horse first one way and then another, making it rush towards the Indians, who scampered into the bushes, laughing and yelling. Ojeda was laughing, too, as he trotted off down the trail with the other horsemen close behind him.

'Do not speak,' Ojeda said to Caonabo.

Ojeda was not laughing any longer.

Caonabo felt the point of a sword against his ribs. The cold thing pressed against him by the man on the other side was the muzzle of a musket. There were always two men behind all that long ride, ready to shoot or stab him if he called out. Soon there was no one to hear if he called. His escort was left far behind.

So Caonabo came to Isabella and heard the great bell ringing.

Chapter 18

ESTEBAN IS AMUSED

THE wooden hut where Caonabo was chained was near the bell. He had his handcuffs too, and other chains on his feet. The bell rang often and he could see the people hurrying across the Square. Some of the people were Indians. Few people, either Spaniards or Indians, cared to meet his fierce, proud stare.

At one man, however, Caonabo always looked with friendliness. This man, oddly enough, was Ojeda. When the Cacique saw that small, trim figure crossing the Square, he would watch it eagerly and if Ojeda turned towards the prison, as he often did, Caonabo would smile.

If Caonabo were sitting down when Ojeda came in, he would always stand and greet his visitor with the same friendly courtesy that he had shown Ojeda when the Spaniard visited the Cacique in his own mountains. Once the Admiral came to see Caonabo. Columbus was curious to talk to the Indian who had made the Spaniards so much trouble. Caonabo did not get up when the Admiral appeared. He sat staring down at his chained feet and hands. He neither spoke nor looked up while Columbus was in his cell.

After the Admiral had gone, the jailer asked Caonabo why he always stood up to greet Ojeda, who was only one of many captains, and why he had remained seated before the Admiral, the Guamiquina, leader of all the captains.

Caonabo's answer was: 'Brave men know each other. I know Ojeda. I have fought against him. He came to the very centre of my country with a few men and captured me by a trick. It was a good trick. I am his prisoner. If the trick had not been good, Ojeda would now be in a cave in my valley. As for your Guamiquina, I do not know him, so I do not speak to him.'

Never for a moment did Caonabo conceal his hatred of the Spaniards. He would do nothing to try to gain their favor or to make his acts against them seem less hostile than they had been.

'Yes,' he answered when they questioned him, 'I surprised and killed the white men at La Navidad. I wished to do the same at Fort St. Thomas and Isabella. I called other caciques to fight against you. I would burn the place now, if I could.'

They put more chains on him after that. The polished steel bracelets from Turey had rusted and tarnished in the damp air of Isabella. It was an unhealthy place. Clouds of mosquitoes buzzed there in the evenings. Their stings carried the fever that made the Spaniards who lived there look yellow rather than white. They called the fever 'malaria' because they thought it came from being out in the bad air at night. The air was not bad, only the mosquitoes. Many Spaniards died of this fever. Others carried it in their bones all their lives and the mark of it in their faces.

'All the gold they have brought is in their faces,' people said cruelly in Spain when thin, shivering scare crows of men began to come back from Española. Voyages to the Indies were no longer popular. When the sons of Columbus appeared on the streets, people shouted: 'See, here are the sons of the Admiral of Mosquito Land; the man who sent our sons to death and starvation.'

Yells, jeers, and bunches of rotten grapes greeted young Diego and Ferdinand Columbus, although they were the sons of the man who had found the passage to the Indies, and though they were pages at the Royal Court.

There was hatred of Columbus on Española as well as in Spain. The Indians hated him because his coming had made them slaves. The young Spanish noblemen hated him because he was an upstart who never spoke their Castilian tongue correctly, and because he expected them to work at founding the new colony. Those who had no gold hated him for that reason. Those who had some hated him because they had to turn it into the Royal Treasury. They had a share of it, but so did Columbus.

Columbus was accused both of cruelty to the Indians and of being foolishly fond of them. He was accused of stinginess and of extravagance; of tyranny over the Spaniards and of being too weak to govern the island. Not everything that was said against him could have been true, but it is certain that things were in a bad state in Española.

Caonabo's capture did not frighten the other chiefs as the Spaniards had hoped it would. It only made them angry and there was fighting in the mountains. News came to Esteban's division that a great force of Indians was being collected to drive the Spaniards into the sea. Esteban decided to leave Española before that plan was carried out.

Esteban had grown very tired of collecting gold. It was a

wearisome business. The overseers spied on the Indians to see that they did not conceal any nuggets. That was fairly easy, although occasionally one did hide one in his mouth. Esteban had the more difficult task of overseeing the overseers. He had to be on the watch constantly against being cheated, and he had not yet thought of any absolutely certain way of cheating the Admiral and the King and Queen. It was annoying to toil all day getting gold—lying in a hammock all day drinking pineapple juice was Esteban's idea of a day of toil—and know that the King and Queen and the upstart Genoese got most of it.

Esteban decided that he had had enough of Española. He had come for adventure and had found himself raising pigs. To be sure, the pigs had been profitable, and there was the nugget the size of a platter, which had not yet been sent down to be weighed at Isabella, and some others not so large. If he could get them to England without anyone's knowing it, he would be well satisfied with his voyage. For some time he gave all his attention to his plans for making the gold industry of Española work fairly—for him.

On one point his journey had been entirely successful. There was no doubt at all that his cousin Peter Aubrey had died under the name of Martin Alzate. The whole garrison at La Navidad had been slaughtered by that brute Caonabo. Esteban felt perfectly at ease in his mind about his inheritance.

Esteban never noticed the face of the tall Indian called Turey especially. All Indians looked much alike to him. They were hideous brutes, these big Caribs like Turey, with black paint around their eyes. They were strong, though, and this Turey was not afraid of horses. He worked with the blacksmith and learned to shoe the horses fairly well. He was a useful slave. He was never ill and never needed much flogging. An occasional lashing of course was good for any of them…

Turey was one of the last people Esteban saw in the valley just before he left for Isabella. The Spaniard who had come to take over the division had arrived and Esteban was showing him over the place—the pig pens, the kennels for the mastiffs, the stables, the slave quarters, the sheds where cotton was stored, the iron chest in Esteban's own room for keeping gold dust.

'Take good care of the mastiffs,' Esteban said. 'They'll save you from losing slaves.'

'I supposed the slaves were always chained.

'Oh, of course we keep them chained for a while, but they do better without. Good overseers and plenty of dogs turned loose is my idea. You get more work out of them that way. And they know they can't get far. Besides, they've seen a few who have tried it brought back. They are tattooed with our mark, you see. Look at this fellow's left shoulder—the one who is bringing my horse.'

'Fine, strong-looking Indian.'

'Yes. He's a Carib. Turey, they call him. Ugly beast, but useful. Knows a little blacksmithing. Most Indians, you know, would rather fight a shark than shoe a horse. They think horses are devils!'

Both men laughed.

The new master of the division, Juan Piombo, stared at the man who brought the horses. The Indian stared back and Juan Piombo looked away. Juan Piombo had once been a scullion in an inn in Seville, but he had no special reason to remember it just now.

'Neat piece of work,' he said to Esteban, pointing to the tattooed mark on the Indian's shoulder. 'What is it?'

'It is the coat of arms of my family,' Esteban said in his tired voice. 'Of course there is no reason for you to put it on your new slaves. Your own may be used, if you like.'

'Oh—this will do very well,' Juan Piombo said hastily.

The Indian held the reins while Esteban mounted. There was a wide bracelet of woven grass on his right wrist. A band of black paint edged it on both sides and seemed to extend under it. His face was freshly painted with black and red. Besides the tattooing on his shoulder there was the fish on his back and the parrot on his chest—Cacibi's work. There were red dots and stripes and dashes on his legs, also newly painted.

'Get Señor Palma's horse now, Turey.'

Gonzalo Palma came out of the house carrying a heavy box and panting: 'The mules, where are the mules?'

There followed the usual cursing and shouting with which loading mules is carried on. Even after Gonzalo had scrambled onto the back of his horse, having lashed most of the mules and all the slaves within reach, the mules would not start.

The overseer who was in charge of the mules scowled and muttered something about Gonzalo. Then he turned and said to Peter: 'Here, Turey, get them started. You are the only one who can. Walk with us a little way.'

Juan Piombo said hastily: 'Don't let him leave the valley,' and then as Peter spoke to the overseer, added: 'What's that he says?,

'He says he has no wish to leave the valley, Señor.'

'Well, all right, but don't let him go too far. Valuable man. I can see that.'

So Peter escorted his cousin and Gonzalo Palma on the first stage of their journey, and heard Esteban say in English to Gonzalo: 'Even Melcote will seem gay after this place, Gonzalo. You know, I think my father had better retire to Spain and let us manage Melcote. I think it would be pleasanter without him. I have always found him a very tiresome man.'

'Your father will not like that, Don Esteban.'

'Perhaps not, but when I tell him what I know about his old friend—I mean his young friend—Martin Alzate, I think he will. I have had such a good idea. It came to me when I was looking at the pigs—restful animals, we must have some at Melcote. I think I shall tell him Martin Alzate is alive on Española. That will keep my dear parent out of England.'

At the look on Gonzalo's face Esteban began to laugh.

'Go back now, Turey,' the overseer said.

The last that Peter saw of Esteban he was still laughing.

Esteban and Gonzalo sailed on the *Niña*. Properly caulked now, she was still a strong ship, in spite of her small size and the buffetings of many storms. The Admiral sailed on her too. He was going back to Spain to persuade the Sovereigns to send more men and supplies to the Colony. The ship carried various things to show to the King and Queen—gold and plants and carved idols and weapons and fruits. There was a great chain of gold big enough to chain a man's wrist. The gold came from the mines of Cibao.

It was not the only chain on board. Others, heavier ones, were around the wrists and ankles of the former owner of those mines, Caonabo. His name meant Lord of the Golden House.

He was lord of nothing any longer except his own dignity and courage. Luckily for him, he died on the voyage. He never had to walk in a procession loaded with gold, stared at by curious eyes, or laughed at for his painted face. He was never a slave; only a prisoner. He was fortunate—he did not die of torture. His heart broke, the other Indians said. They threw his body into the clean blue-green Atlantic waves.

Perhaps, they thought, the water would carry him back to Española. It would be better to be tossed up on some beach there, where the palms sang and the air smelled sweet, than to be alive in the white man's country. Yes, Caonabo was lucky.

Other Indians died on the voyage. It was always so. Of the thousands of slaves sent to Spain few lived. It was as Esteban said. They seemed to die on purpose.

The bags of gold dust and the great gold 'platter' nugget that he had concealed among his clothes were much on Esteban's mind. His chests were locked, of course, but he was always afraid that someone would lift them and notice how heavy they were. It had been one thing to get the gold on board the *Niña*—he had stowed it on his person on several trips that he had made to the ship before she sailed—but to get it off would be a different matter. The men who watched the port of Cadiz for the Queen were not likely to let those heavy chests by without looking into them.

Still Esteban was not without a plan. It was a good plan, too, depending only on bribing one man.

It was growing dark when the *Niña* slipped into Cadiz Harbor. That was lucky, Esteban thought. He was always lucky. He sat quietly at the table listening to the Admiral talk: or rather giving a very fair imitation of a young man listening.

He was thinking: 'Why won't the old fool stop crumbling biscuit and drinking water? He takes longer to eat a meal fit for an Indian than the Duke of Medina Sidonia would a banquet with roast boar and wine and truffles. He's said that fifty times, I swear...'

He said aloud, bowing politely: 'Yes, my Lord the Admiral.

Yes, I have no doubt that on your next voyage you will find the great cities of Cathay...'

('And about time,' he added to himself. 'The King and Queen must be sick of promises by now.')

Columbus got up at last, said thanks in a Latin prayer for the food he had eaten, while Esteban swallowed a yawn and stood in a beautiful attitude of deference with his gray eyes lowered.

He raised them and looked scornfully after the Admiral as he limped slowly away to his own cabin. The Admiral's tall figure was dressed in a shabby brown robe. It was fastened around his waist with a cord.

It was ridiculous for an Admiral of Spain to dress like a Franciscan monk, Esteban thought. Columbus ought to be in scarlet and gold. Was the old man getting a little crazy? Perhaps he—was a miser. The ship was stuffed with gold. Esteban felt sure the Queen would not see it all. And if the Admiral lined his brown serge robe with gold, why shouldn't Esteban fill his pockets?

Having satisfied himself with this reasoning, Esteban went on deck. It was dark and the wind had fallen. The Admiral had ordered the ship anchored until morning. She rode at her anchor with a gentle swaying not unpleasant to feel after being tossed by the Atlantic waves. The light near the hourglass made a pale circle of light. Outside it the deck was dim and shadowy. It was a chilly night. The crew, many of them still aching and shivering from the fevers of Española, were lying in their bunks trying to keep warm under dirty, moth-eaten sheepskins. The Indian prisoners shivered, too. They had no skins but their own. Their chains clanked as they huddled together for warmth.

A few faint lights close to the water marked where the shore was.

Esteban said softly to the man who had appeared quietly at his elbow: 'Do you know where those lights are, Gonzalo? Are they the docks? Are you sure where we are?'

Gonzalo muttered impatiently: 'The slingers—Phoenicians, men of my race—came into this harbor three thousand years ago and more. Of course I am sure.'

'Well, I hope you have been here since then,' Esteban said out of the side of his mouth, the one he sometimes used for smiling. 'Are we to lean on this rail all night? Where is this fellow of ours?'

'Getting ready to lower the boat. Go now and talk to the deck boy. Talk loud enough so that he will not hear us getting the boat into the water. Luckily this old tub creaks so, even on this calm night, that another squeak or so will not matter.'

The deck boy looked only half awake. He had his cloak around his ears and he was shivering.

'A cold night, my lad,' Esteban said.

'Yes, Señor. It seems to go right through me. I am always cold now except when I am burning with fever, but when I get home my mother will have a fine mattress of clean straw for me to lie on, and perhaps a blanket of her own weaving to cover me.'

'And a fine bowl of hot soup for you, too, no doubt,' Esteban said.

'Yes, Señor.' The boy smacked his lips and grinned. 'She makes the best soup of anyone in the village. Then my teeth won't ch-chatter!'.

'Plenty of garlic in it?'

'Yes, indeed! Garlic and onions and a chunk of beef as big

as your fist. A marrowbone, too, sometimes, and good hot pepper.'

The boy's teeth chattered again and he began to dance up and down on the deck and slap his arms. He made far more noise than the creaking of the boat being lowered and touching the water with a faint splash.

Esteban went on talking until the scraping and creaking had stopped. He had been standing where he would shut off any view the deck boy might have had of shadowy figures moving outside the circle of light. At last Esteban threw his cloak over the boy's shoulders, saying: 'That will keep you warm till morning,' and strolled off to his cabin. It was a light-colored cloak. The boy felt almost warm in it. His teeth stopped chattering and he thought sleepily about sausages. He did not see the black-cloaked figure that slipped out of Esteban's cabin a few moments later.

Esteban and Gonzalo rowed off towards the fishing village. That is, Gonzalo rowed. He moved his oars so gently that the noise they made was hardly louder than the ripples against the *Niña's* side. Neither spoke until the lights on the *Niña* were no bigger than glowworms on a log.

'What shall we do with the chest, Gonzalo?' Esteban muttered as they began to get close in shore. 'We cannot load it on a mule, it is too big.'

'I have canvas bags here. We will fill them and throw the chest into the water with stones in it. We will set the boat adrift. If they find her, they may think we are drowned.'

'We ought to have filled the bags on board and left the chest there,' Esteban grumbled.

'You have forgotten, Señor, the story that I told our friend when I bribed him to help me with the boat. How you wanted to see your mother, who perhaps thought you were lost at sea, and wished to bring her happiness as soon as possible. It would not have seemed reasonable if you had left all your chests on board. I explained that we would take only this one and get the others later.'

'He must have thought it strange that we took such a heavy one.'

'He was paid not to think,' Gonzalo said.

Esteban said peevishly: 'Well, it makes the boat move like a snail. A turtle could catch us the way we are going.'

'More thieves are caught by their own haste than by that of their pursuers,' Gonzalo muttered. 'And speak more softly. Sound travels fast over water.'

'All right,' Esteban said in a lower tone. 'But I don't like that word "thieves," Gonzalo. We are taking our own, that is all.'

'Of course! Naturally,' Gonzalo chuckled under his breath, 'that is understood.'

With this happy understanding the friends came at last to shore.

'The rope. Cut the rope,' Esteban whispered. 'I have the key.'

Gonzalo cut the rope that the sailor they had bribed had tied around the chest, but the key was not needed.

The lock had been broken.

The chest had stones in it instead of gold.

Esteban had bribed the wrong man.

The only metal in the chest was three gold coins wrapped in paper. It was too dark to read what was written on the paper. In fact, Esteban did not see that anything was written on it at the time. He stuffed the paper into his pouch and began to run. He did not see the words on it until after a week of skulking and hiding he was on a ship bound for England.

The words did not make the pitching of the boat in the English channel any more agreeable. They were in a handwriting that Esteban knew, and signed with a peculiar arrangement of letters also familiar to him.

'The pilot,' Esteban read, grating his teeth angrily, 'returns your bribe, Señor Medina-Barrios. Because you have not actually stolen the gold and because a member of your family, though I think not nearly related to you, the Duke of Medina—Celi, was once kind to me, and helped me somewhat towards my discovery of the Indies, I shall make no public accusation against you, but I advise you to leave Spain at once. If you ever set foot there or on Española, I think you will regret it.

'The Queen, I feel sure, will be much interested in the large nugget of gold somewhat resembling a platter in shape. I believe it is the largest yet found on Española. I shall take great pleasure in telling her that it was discovered through your diligence.'

Then followed the signature that Esteban knew was the Admiral's.

So when Esteban Medina-Barrios, sometimes known as Stephen Aubrey, heir to the Barony of Aubrey of Melcote, at last landed in England he was no richer than when he had left it and in a very bad temper.

VALLEY OF PIGS

PETER did not know that the Admiral had sailed on the *Niña*. He had hoped that when Esteban and Gonzalo left the division, he might find some way to get to Isabella. When he heard that Columbus had again left for Spain, the chance of being caught as a runaway slave did not seem worth taking. More and more the life of the division became the only life he ever expected to have. Less and less as the weeks became months did he think of ever getting away from Española.

Columbus did not come to the island again until late in August of the year 1499. It was his third voyage. He had seen the mainland of South America on his way, but he did not know it. The sailors whom he sent ashore were the first Europeans to land on the American continent since the Norsemen visited North America hundreds of years before.

The Admiral found misery, disease, war, and cruelty on Española. He did what he could to bring it peace and order, but it was not enough. Things on Juan Piombo's division, once Esteban's, were no worse than any other place, in fact they were better on the whole since Piombo, ex-innkeeper, ex-soldier, and ex-thief, was at least a good-natured man. He was an enormously fat man. He enjoyed life on his division. He was carried everywhere by half a dozen panting, sweating Indians. He ate tremendously and slept a great deal.

He did not have Esteban's interest in pigs. It took too much time for the Indians to raise food for them, so the pigs were turned loose to get food for themselves. The result was that they had eaten every green thing in sight. Cactus was now the chief thing that grew in the valley. People called it the Valley of Pigs. The Indians were afraid of the pigs that ran wild in the woods, but Piombo enjoyed hunting them. He would sit comfortably under a tree and wait until the Indians drove a pig near enough to him so that he could run a lance through it.

The tall Indian Turey was especially good at chasing pigs. He was a sullen-looking fellow, Piombo had thought at first. Most Indians tried to please their masters by smiling. Even when they had just been flogged they would try to smile. Turey had a grave way of looking down at fat little Piombo that made the owner of the division uncomfortable.

Esteban had told Piombo that Turey was a Carib, one of the dead Caonabo's followers. Piombo knew that Caribs were fierce brutes. There was a story that they ate people. No one had ever seen a Carib eating anyone, but a man of Piombo's build could not help knowing that he would make a good supper for quite a party of Caribs.

He was always careful not to be alone with Turey, but he boasted about him to other Spaniards who came to the valley. He would entertain them with a pig hunt. Afterwards he would call Peter and show him off.

'Here,' he would say in Spanish, 'look at the muscles this

boy has. Look at his teeth—white as a mastiff's! See those legs—like bronze, like bronze, aren't they? Ugly face, all that paint on it—he's a Carib, you know. Eat you as soon as look at you, but I've got him tamed—got him tamed, you know. That's my mark tattooed on his shoulder. Coat of arms of the family, you know.'

Piombo did not say whose family, and no one was rude enough to ask him. He would clap his fat hand on Peter's tattooed shoulder with the Aubrey sheep and anchor on it and add: 'Here, Turey! Take a pig. Carry home. Make fire. You good boy. Get a good bone tonight.'

'Bright boy. Just talk good and loud and he understands every word you say,' Piombo would brag as Peter walked off carrying the dead pig over his shoulder as lightly as if it were a bag of cotton. 'He's learned blacksmithing too. He helped the smith at the forge until the smith died of fever. Now Turey does as well as ever the old smith did. He'll turn you out a boar spear or mend your armor as neat as can be.'

The dogs would run after him whining.

'He's the only Indian that can manage the dogs,' Piombo often said. 'Seems to have a way of talking to them they like, so they mind him.'

One day Tigress, one of the mastiffs, was missing. Piombo sent Peter out to look for her.

'Find Tigress. Maybe find puppies—little dogs. You know what I say, Turey? You find. Get good supper—yams, cassava, maybe chicken leg. You understand?'

Peter nodded and went off.

It was hot in the woods that day, and Peter trotted along with Fury, one of the mastiffs, at his heels.

'We are going to find Tigress,' Peter said to the dog, speak-

'We are going to find Tigress'

ing in Spanish, and Fury whimpered and put his cold nose against Peter's knee.

'Good boy,' Peter said.

He had a boar spear of his own making in his hand. He tickled Fury behind the ear with the spear point. They trotted along, Peter's hard feet thudding on the beaten dirt of the trail; Fury's toenails clicking on rocks or padding softly in sand.

The woods were full of small noises: insects buzzing, parrots calling to each other, a goat saying 'mig—gig gig,' a young pig calling 'oink—oink,' and one farther away snuffiing. Both went plunging off through the underbrush when they heard Fury growl.

'Quiet, Fury! Heel! We are not driving pigs today,' Peter said.

They made a wide circle along the wooded ridge that shut in the valley. Many times Peter whistled or called 'Tigress! Tigress!' and stopped to listen for an answering bark, but only the echo came back.

At last, when they had circled most of the valley, Fury stopped with the hair rising on his neck, and growling. Peter could not hear what the dog heard. Fury looked up at him, whimpered, and set off down a trail that led away from the valley. Peter followed, straining his ears for any sound different from the forest noises.

At last he heard it—a low whine and a fierce grunting snort. He tightened his grasp on his spear and ran forward. The path led to a cave. Tigress was standing at the mouth of it. In front of her, snorting, grunting, making fierce little rushes and then retreating, was a boar nearly twice the size of the dog.

His long tusks had already torn her shoulder and the blood was running down it. As Peter arrived, the boar ran in again. The sunlight shone on his red bristles. Tigress bared her teeth and sprang forward, but too late. The boar's rush knocked her over and left her lying moaning on the ground.

'At him, Fury!' Peter shouted.

The boar turned his head. Fury's jump was just in time. His teeth seized the boar's throat.

The great pig tried to shake him off. From one side to the other he plunged, grunting, snorting, squealing, but Fury held on. Blood from the boar's throat ran down into the dog's eyes and from one of his legs where the boar's sharp hoof had gashed it, but he held on, still making a low half-choked growl. Tigress got to her feet and tried to stagger towards the twisting, swaying bodies.

'Down, old girl, lie down!' Peter called sharply, and the wounded dog stopped where she was.

For a moment the boar stood still. It was what Peter had been waiting for. He drove his spear into the boar's throat, drove it so fiercely that the pig swayed in his tracks and fell.

Fury held on. Even when the boar at last lay still, Fury's teeth were still clenched in the bristly throat. Peter had hard work to pull the dog away.

'Good work, Fury. If you hadn't held him still, I'd have missed. And a good job for you, I didn't. I struck close enough to your muzzle as it was.'

Fury seemed to understand. He wagged his tail and fell to licking his injured paw. Tigress rubbed against Peter's leg and whimpered.

'Have you something to show me, old lady?' Peter said.

Tigress had.

There were four half-blind, whining puppies in the cave, funny little short-nosed, fawn-colored things. Tigress stood over them proudly, looking up at Peter as if to say, 'Did you ever see anything so wonderful?'

Peter went back for a basket he had been carrying. He had dropped it when he saw the boar. It was lined with cotton and cotton cloth. Now he put leaves and grass in it to make it soft for the puppies and used the cotton to bandage the dogs' wounds.

It took a long time to get back to the village. Piombo was lying in his hammock under the palm tree. He was not asleep, but in that pleasant state when you know you are not asleep and it is too much trouble to open your eyelids. Yells from the Indian huts made him open them, however. What he saw pleased him so much that he sat up and swung his feet over the side of the hammock.

Stalking through the hot sunlight came Peter with the great bristly boar with the spear in his throat over one shoulder. In the other hand he held the basket of puppies. The two mastiffs limped along behind him.

'And,' Piombo said in telling about it, 'does he say a word? No, he does not. Not this Carib of mine. Not Turey. He just dumps the pig down, points to Tigress, shows me the puppies, all without a smile or a sound. He'd tied up the places where the boar hurt the dogs too. That shows you how different he is from these other Indians. I'd as soon bandage a lion as they would a dog! I tell you I wouldn't take three hawks' bells of gold for that boy. Not three hawks' bells.'

'You'll lose him now that they have made these new laws that the Admiral is trying to force down our throats,' the visitor said gloomily.

Piombo cursed the new laws heartily. A man's property was not safe under them, he said. The Queen was no doubt a fine queen, but she was a long way off. How could she know how to manage a division? It was hard enough if you were on the spot. Though very likely these ideas were the Admiral's rather than hers. A pity he did not stay in Spain and not come shoving his long nose into Española where it was not wanted.

The new laws that Piombo disliked so much were intended by Queen Isabella to make the lives of the Indians happier. They were to work only eight months out of twelve on the divisions. During the other four months they could visit their families and plant their crops. There were to be no slaves, she said, except prisoners taken in war. The Indians were her people. They must work—all her subjects must work—but they must be treated kindly and taught to be good Christians.

The misery on Española was not the fault of the Queen.

As Piombo said: How could she know? Spain was a long way off.

Peter began to keep his calendar again after he heard about the new laws. He knew the year now—1500—and the month— June. It was almost eight years since he had first come to Española. He could hardly believe that it was so long. Yet he had heard Piombo and his visitor arguing about whether 1500 was the end of one century or the beginning of another. They had drunk a great deal of wine during the argument and bellowed at each other, and still each thought what he thought at first. One thing they had agreed about—Peter had heard them say it over and over again. This was June of the year 1500. On the first of July his labor service would be over for that year. It had begun last November. After July first he would be free to go where he liked on the island. Piombo had said so.

Those June days seemed endless. Piombo kept him busy at the forge, making spearheads, mending armor, shoeing horses all day and most of the night. Peter's hands and face were black with soot. Sweat poured down over his painted back, but his arms and legs never seemed to tire. He could have worked longer but there was no more iron. He had made the last of it into nails before midnight.

He woke at dawn and went to the river. He set up a shield of polished steel for a mirror and scoured himself clean with a mixture of lard and sand and ashes. There were hairs sprouting on his chin. He pulled them out one at a time with a small pair of tweezers that he had made himself. Indians had no beards. Even Piombo would notice if an Indian had a beard and wonder about it.

Peter was safer as an Indian than he would be trying to prove that he was a Spaniard. He came back to that thought many times. As an Indian blacksmith, pig sticker, trainer of dogs, he was useful. No owner of the division would let him be damaged. He might be beaten a little, now and then—certainly: all slaves were beaten, but nothing really dangerous would be done to a valuable man.

Once he tried to show he was a Spaniard, everyone would be against him. Piombo would not believe him—he would not want to lose his blacksmith forever. It was bad enough to have Turey go on a four months' vacation. Piombo would say the big Carib had gone crazy and instead of letting him go free would decide that Turey had better be chained at his work with chains of his own forging. Peter had seen what happened to slaves who tried to escape. He thought about it as little as he could.

If he said he was Martin Alzate and was believed, it might be that Gonzalo and Esteban were back on Española and would kill him. Esteban would not rock in his saddle with laughter if he knew Peter was really alive on Española. He and Gonzalo had discussed calmly what they would have done if by bad luck Peter had been found alive at La Navidad. Esteban had said they could easily have taken care of him with a poisoned Indian arrow in the back. Gonzalo had favored poison in his food as being simpler and surer. It would have saved a great deal of trouble, he said, if they had used poison in the first place.

This interesting conversation had taken place while Peter and eight other Indians were carrying Esteban and Gonzalo in a litter. They spoke in English, of course, so that no one would understand them. No one did—except Peter.

Peter's hope was still the only one he had ever had—the Admiral. Columbus was at Santo Domingo, the new city on the south coast of the island. Piombo had said so. So it was there Peter was going. He was going openly with the bronze disk around his neck that showed that his eight months' labor service was completed, that he owed the Queen neither work nor gold.

No one would dare to touch him. He had only the journey to Santo Domingo between him and freedom.

'The Admiral—the Admiral will believe me,' he said, shaking his wet black hair out of his eyes.

Even after all these years of waiting, hiding, hoping, and planning, and having hope disappointed, he still clung to that idea.

He rubbed red clay into his face and said aloud:

'I am not an Indian, my Lord the Admiral. I came here on your ship the *Santa Maria* in 1492, under the name of Martin Alzate.'

His tongue stumbled over the Spanish words. He must talk aloud to himself on the journey so that he would speak more smoothly.

'But even if my speech is strange, the Admiral will believe me. He will set me free.'

Back in his hut he dressed himself in his skirt of parrot feathers, hung the precious bronze disk that Piombo had given him the night before around his neck by the strap of pigskin, picked up his boar spear, slipped it through the thongs of a pigskin pouch, and strode out into the hot, hazy morning.

The overseers were driving the Indians towards the gold mines in the hills. Men and women burrowed in the ground for gold now, instead of washing it out of sand in the sunshine on the riverbank. Indians died more quickly in the mines than on the river, but it was a quicker way of getting the gold.

These Indians had come to the division only six months ago. They had only two months' more service ahead of them. They looked ill and listless. Their ribs showed through skin that had a strange pale color, like the skin of a roasted yam with the ashes still on it. Their eyes were hollow in their thin faces. Their noses were pinched and sharpened.

When they smiled or spoke, it was as if it were an effort to move their lips. Some of them smiled now at Peter and said: 'Good fortune, Turey. A safe journey!' in their soft, tired voices.

Before he could answer, the whip cracked and the line of dragging feet stumbled along a little faster. Peter stood watching them as they plodded along, shoulders bent under the weight of pickaxes and spades, knees bent by squatting under the earth, heads bent by grief,

'Some of them will be free in two months,' he thought, but he could not help knowing that many would be free before that. Death would free them.

'I will make the Admiral understand,' he said aloud. 'He was kind. He liked the Indians. It is true the Queen has tried to make things better. Eight months is better than twelve, but still the work is too hard. The Admiral—I must find him. Standing here talking to myself will not help.'

He whistled to his dog. It was one of the puppies Tigress had hidden in the cave. Piombo had given him to Peter. He had grown into a strong, black-muzzled dog now, big enough to match his big, soft paws. Tiger was his name.

He came racing out of the hut, nearly knocking his master over with joyful jumps and bounds. There were other Indians leaving the valley. The overseer checked off their names on a parchment roll, and explained to them what would happen if they did not come back in four moons. He held up four fingers and folded them down one after the other. The Indians smiled and imitated him.

'Here you, Turey. Hold up your fingers. Back here in how many moons? You can count four, can't you?'

Peter held up four fingers.

'Don't wait till the moon starts to get small again either. If you are not back here before it's full—'

The overseer paused and cracked his whip suggestively.

'Open up your bundles now, and be quick about it, And if I find as much as a grain of gold—'

He cracked his whip again. It was his favorite remark.

There was no gold in any of the bundles. There was pathetically little in any of them: a little cassava bread for the journey, odds and ends of leather and iron, the few silver and copper coins in which their wages had been paid. The Queen had said the Indians were to be paid. They were, and after eight months' work some of them had enough to buy a Spanish shirt or even a scarlet sash.

Some of them had a hawk's bell or two, or a small steel mirror—presents for families who might still be alive in another valley. One of them had most of a smoked ham. The overseer grumbled about an Indian's having so much ham. However, after hearing testimony that Piombo himself had thrown it to the Indian because it was mouldy, he allowed it to leave the valley. It was quite true it was mouldy.

The Indians—all but one—turned west as they left the valley and took the trail towards Isabella. The city was deserted now by the Spaniards. There was no more gold there any longer. The Indians were welcome to it and its fevers. The great bell rang in Santo Domingo now. It was a healthier place than Isabella, with a better harbor.

Peter was bound there, but first he turned eastward. He had an appointment with a pine tree.

It was still standing. The mark he had cut on the trunk was still there, though the bark had almost grown over it.

He knelt down and began to scoop up pine needles with his hands and toss them aside.

'How deep they are!' he thought. 'My stones—I ought to have reached them by now. Can someone have found them?'

He breathed hard. A hot prickling ran over his neck and hands. He stopped to wipe the sweat off his face. It was lucky that he did so, for Tiger, who had been burrowing in the pine needles, stopped too and stood looking along the trail and growling.

Then Peter heard the sound of metal, leather, and hoofs. The pine was at the top of a steep rise. The trail descended in both directions. The noise was coming from the east. Outside the circle of the pine's shadow was thick undergrowth. Peter and Tiger took cover in it and saw the mule train go by. It seemed to take an endless time for the mules to lumber up the hill and go down on the other side. To the west the trail was stony and twisted along between a cliff and a precipice. The mules did not like to be hurried. They placed each foot deliberately, stuck their long necks out to admire the view down the precipice into the valley below, snatched bites of young leaves from cracks in the rocks, and stood still to chew them.

The Indian drivers had lost their fear of the mules, but their shouts and drubbings only made the mules bray like a dozen cracked trumpets. At last they were gone. The last swaying pack of gold dust from the mines of Cibao disappeared around the shoulder of the cliff that was like the prow of a caravel. Down in the valley below Peter could still see an occasional glint of sunlight on a helmet of one of the Spanish soldiers, or the tip of a lance. He could still hear the sound. It made him think now of the noise of a waterfall going over a rock. When the sound faded out and was softer than the wind in the pine, he went back to his digging.

Needles, more needles. Dirt. More dirt than he remembered, but at last stones and under them the lizard-skin pouch.

The pine had kept his gold for him, and, in the gold dust, still wrapped in faded silk, his mother's picture. He knelt for a long time looking at it. Then he turned west.

CHAPTER 20

SHAVE AND HAIRCUT

It TOOK Peter a month to reach Santo Domingo. No one in that busy town with its straight streets and its new stone buildings paid much attention to the tall Indian with the mastiff at his heels. Footsore, hungry-looking Indians were no novelty in Santo Domingo, and besides on the first day of August, 1500, the townspeople had something else to interest them.

There was a ship coming into the harbor, a ship from Spain—and everyone in Santo Domingo who could walk was on the shore to see her come in.

'The Admiral, where is the Admiral?' the tall Indian asked a Spaniard who was leaning in a doorway of a house near the stone fort and watching the cross on the ship's sail grow larger.

The Spaniard scowled and rolled his yellow eyeballs.

'Wait till you're spoken to,' he said harshly. 'Do you think I'm here to answer questions for every slave with a bronze tag around his neck? Admiral! Admiral! That's all you diggers want. You ought not to be allowed to set foot in this town,

238

and wouldn't if we had a governor with any backbone. This pampering Indians—I'm sick of it.'

He had spoken in Spanish up to this point, not caring whether the Indian understood or not. There was another Spaniard holding himself up by a hand against the wall who took the trouble to nod approvingly.

The first man, seeing Peter's eyes looking down on him, said impatiently: 'Guamiquina gone woods. Back soon. Now get out.'

'I hate these big Caribs,' he added peevishly as Peter walked away. 'That one stared at me so it made my spine creep. Murderous-looking brute! If the Admiral knew his business, he'd send every one of them to Spain. But what does he do? Look at those corpses on the gallows—Spanish corpses! Good men, hanged by his orders. Suppose they did kill a few Indians! If you think someone is going to kill you, you'd better kill him first, hadn't you? It's not right to hang Spaniards and leave them to rot where Indians can see them. I tell you this island's governed all wrong.'

'So it is,' the other agreed. 'Now, if I were the governor—'

Peter heard more complaining voices as he stared out at the moving ship, but he hardly listened to them. The ship was a beautiful sight with her bright banners fluttering and her painted sails swelling.

He thought: 'Can I be really standing here after all these years watching a ship—a Spanish ship? Can it be true?'

For a moment the blue flashing water and the moving ship dazzled his eyes so that he could see nothing. He covered his eyes with his hand. Then the anchor chains rattled... She was anchored... A boat was leaving her side... more boats... Then there were men marching up from the dock—armed men with an important looking man at their head: a big man with fine clothes on and a loud voice: a fine red-faced man who had never had fever.

He and his men marched to the Admiral's house. They stood in front of it with the hot sun blazing on their shields and helmets. People crowded around them and filled the Square while the big man spoke.

Even from his place at the back of the crowd, Peter could hear what the man was bellowing. Peter could hear it, but he could not believe it: could not believe that this loud-mouthed Francisco de Bobadilla had come from King Ferdinand and Queen Isabella with power to take over the government of Española; could not believe him when he roared that Christopher and Bartholomew Columbus should be sent for and brought before him.

The government of Española to be taken away from the Admiral who had discovered the island, and all the other islands of the Indies, and the westward passage to them! How could they take the government away from him when the King and Queen had promised that he and his family forever should govern the lands he discovered? It couldn't be true...

And yet it was true.

Peter saw Bobadilla take possession of the Admiral's house— the fine stone house for which the Queen herself had sent hangings embroidered with birds and flowers, sheets of fine linen, and bedcovers with the Admiral's arms worked on them in gold and colors.

He saw the two brothers being hustled along by the Spanish soldiers: the Admiral limping painfully, but holding his white head erect, and keeping his tired blue eyes fixed on something far away; Bartholomew striding angrily, and glaring at the hooting crowd so fiercely that they fell silent as he passed.

Peter knew him at once. He had changed little since the day Peter had seen him drawing charts in the dingy London shop. Since then Bartholomew had sailed the cold seas around the Cape of Good Hope, had fought both Indians and Spaniards under the broiling sun of Española, had starved one day, and had been given the title of Don by the Queen the next—yet here he was, unchanged, a proud eagle of a man, hating enemies, making new ones for himself and his gentler brother. There were plenty of people in the Square of Santo Domingo who were glad to see the brothers humiliated.

'Thief! Madman!' they yelled. 'Prison's too good for you!'

The Admiral and his brother lay in cells in the fort for two months. During that time Bobadilla carried on their trial—as he called it. They were not allowed to hear it or to speak in their own defence. The get-rich quick, greedy colonists, whether they were haughty noblemen or the sweepings of the jails of Seville, were all against the Admiral. The men of his ships were loyal to him, but no one listened to them.

The brothers were closely guarded in their hot, dark cells. Peter tried many times to see the Admiral, but he was only laughed at by the guards. The last time he went one of the guards seized the bronze tablet that hung around Peter's neck and turned it over.

'See here, what's your name with the parrot on your chest?... Turey? Well, Turey, it's time you were getting back to your division. What work do you do? Dig? Plant cotton?'

'Smith,' Peter said. 'Work iron.'

'Well, get back to your forge. Your time's almost up. One moon more. Understand?'

Peter nodded and walked off. He knew only too well that he could not stay much longer on Santo Domingo. If he stayed on Española at all, he must go back to his division. The Admiral could not help him. Even if Columbus should remember the deck boy of the *Santa Maria*, it would do no good now.

There were some deserted Indian huts in the woods back of the town. In one of these Peter lived. Ten days after the guard told him to start back to his division, the parrots—who were the only people to take any interest—saw something strange take place in Peter's hut.

The big Indian put down a bundle wrapped in a piece of cotton cloth, dug up the dirt floor, and lifted out a box. Out of the box he took white men's clothes: a shirt, a pair of stained velvet breeches, stockings with a hole in them, a greasy silk doublet, a cap with a limp ostrich feather, a dirty scarlet cape. He undid his bundle. There were shoes in it of soft leather that had once been crimson, with holes in the toes. It was just as well that the toes were open to the air, because the original owner's feet were smaller than Peter's.

Peter washed the paint off his face, put on the clothes, and looked at himself in a polished shield he had. The effect with his long black hair hanging down under the cap was so strange that he grinned sourly at his reflection.

A parrot on the ground near him squawked.

'I don't blame you, brother,' Peter said. 'But I'll look better when I've chopped my hair off.'

It had taken a long time to collect the clothes. First of all he had had to change his gold for coins. There were men in Santo Domingo ready to do this if an Indian brought the gold secretly. It was a good business for the Spaniard because he could always give the Indian very little coined money. If the Indian objected, the goldsmith could always threaten to report him for smuggling gold. Peter knew he was being cheated, but he had taken what coins he could get for most of his gourd full of gold dust.

He had bought the clothes one piece at a time from Spaniards who were glad to take advantage of an Indian's foolish love for the white man's garments, no matter how dirty and tattered.

Now he was ready, and only just in time. The shoes had been the hardest to get, but though they had cost too much, he had got them at last. The so-called trial of the Admiral had ended that day. Bobadilla had decided that Columbus must be sent back to Spain—sent back in chains. The ship *Gorda* was in the harbor ready to sail. It should carry the discoverer of the Indies away from Española. Peter was determined that it should carry him too.

He hacked away at his long hair with his knife and went over his plan. If it failed, he would be a slave on Española forever. He knew that, but this was his chance and he was bound to take it. He had been patient and prudent long enough.

He took one more look in the surface of the shield. He was a strange-looking vagabond, but no worse than many men who came in from the divisions. His face without its covering of soot and paint was pale rather than brown. His beard had started to grow and there were hairs pricking through on his upper lip. It had been ten days since he had pulled any out. Except for his raggedly cut hair he looked no worse than many of the men who hung around the Square in Santo Domingo.

'Every loafer on the island has come to the town to see the Admiral sent away,' Peter thought bitterly. 'One more will hardly be noticed. As for my hair—there's the new barber who came with Bobadilla. He was down with fever last week, I heard someone say, but yesterday I saw him shaving someone.

He will see plenty of hair not much worse cut than mine on Española, and since he has just come from Spain there is no chance that he will know me.'

He took off his cloak, shook the hairs off it, flung it over his shoulder, and swaggered off towards the town. He talked aloud to himself in Spanish as he went. He had done that lately when he was alone and the words no longer came so awkwardly from his tongue.

'Remember now who you are,' he advised himself. 'You are not Peter Aubrey. You are not Martin Alzate. You are not Turey—that dumb Carib blacksmith. You are that overseer that died on Piombo's division last June—the Spaniard Tomaso de Segovia. Remember to scowl and swing your arm when you walk as if you had a whip in your hand. Never step aside for an Indian—let him jump if he doesn't want his toes stepped on. Don't be in a hurry to get out of a Spaniard's way. Roll a little when you walk—that's better. And the cap over one eye. Never mind if the feather tickles your ear!'

No one in the Square of Santo Domingo paid any attention to the swaggering pale young Spaniard in the stained and ragged clothes.

The people who filled the Square all had their eyes on the gate of the fort which had for those long weeks been the Admiral's prison.

The barber's shop was across the Square from the prison. The door of the shop stood open. It was dark after the glare outside. The barber was only a thin, shadowy figure to Peter's dazzled eyes.

It was not until Peter was actually sitting on the high stool with the napkin around his neck that he recognized that long face with the twisted nose and the wide mouth. The man was thinner than ever now. His hair had grown gray. Yet it was still Juan de Niebo. Peter could not have spoken even if he had tried. Luckily there was no need of talking. Juan supplied the talk.

'So this is how they cut hair on Española,' he began. 'Tsk! Tsk! It was always a wild place, but I never knew it was so bad as this! Where do you come from, Señor?'.

'From the Valley of the Pigs,' Peter said.

His voice stuck in his throat and the words sounded strange in his ears, but Juan de Niebo only laughed and went on clicking his scissors and said: 'No doubt. And the pigs chewed your hair off! Well, we will soon fix that. You'd like it, I suppose, in the latest Court style? Not *too* long around the ears, brushed back a bit from the forehead—you have a fine forehead, Señor, if you will forgive a personal remark; it is a pity to hide it.'

He ran his hand admiringly through the thick stubble and went on: 'A wonderful head of hair! All it needs is training. Now, there are some that prefer curly hair, but I always say, leave that to the ladies. There's some thing manly about straight hair. And yours, Señor, is as straight as an Indian's... Pardon, Señor, did I nip your ear? I have been ill since I came. I fear my hand is clumsy...'

'No, no, it is nothing,' Peter muttered.

'I have a special ointment, Señor, that will keep the hair smooth and soft. I make it myself. Only the best materials used. It softens the hair and keeps it from falling out. Not that you need to worry—yet—but where the hair has been neglected as yours has—Thank you, Señor. A small jar? The large size is more economical, but—Thank you, Señor. Would you care for rosewater? Orange-flower water? Fresh from Spain. The same kind the Queen sends to the Admiral.'

'He has not had much where he's been these last two months,' Peter said in a voice rough with anger.

'No,' Juan de Niebo agreed. 'It's not exactly perfumed, that cell of his, I imagine.'

He was silent long enough to click his scissors twice. When he spoke, it was to say that all Peter needed now was a shave. Unless, indeed, he intended to grow a beard. A small beard kept carefully trimmed would be becoming, although with a strong, well-sculptured chin like Peter's—positively the kind one saw on the old Greek statues people were digging up lately—he would recommend shaving.

'At present, Señor, if you will forgive my saying so, the hairs on your chin are as far apart as palms in the desert. A man should make up his mind about a beard—half-measures are impossible.'

'Oh, shave it—shave it,' Peter said, and had hardly spoken when he found himself lathered up to the ears.

The wielding of the shining razor did not interrupt Juan's flow of speech. He had a way of taking Peter by the nose when he wanted him to turn his head. This habit and the fluff of lather around his mouth would have kept Peter silent even if he had wanted to speak. He shut his eyes, only half listening to Juan's talk and to the scraping of the razor. What he heard mostly was the noise of the crowd in the Square. The crowd was not shouting now. The voices had lowered until the sound was like the purring of a great cat before it lashes out with its claws.

'I never forget a face,' Juan de Niebo was saying. 'Not when I have shaved it. I would know yours any where—keep your head still, Señor—this little hollow under your lip, the crease in the left cheek, these high cheekbones like an Indian's—don't move, please. I never cut anyone who sits quiet... There, will you look in the mirror, Señor? See, not a nick anywhere. It's better, isn't it? Less like a garden after the pigs have eaten it. The towel—Thank *you*, Señor. Let me brush off these hairs.'

Peter stood up. The light from the door fell full on his face. Juan de Niebo leaned against the doorpost staring at Peter. He put his hand up to his eyes.

'Forgive me, Señor,' he said. 'For a moment you reminded me of someone. But he is dead. Martin Alzate his name was—I was fond of the boy. He had a scar on his wrist like the track of a dog's foot. It was a long time ago. I have been ill—my eyes play me tricks.'

Outside the crowd had grown restless again.

There were shouts of 'Bring out the Indian-lover. Hang him up beside the men he hanged! Come on, Admiral of Mosquito Land! Where is the gold you promised us? Cheat... dreamer... fool... Where are the men you starved at Isabella, madman, miser?'

Two or three voices took up this call. It was answered from across the Square by the word 'Ghosts! Ghosts!'

'Ghosts—ghosts walk in lsabella.'

'Ghosts of men who died of fever.'

'Ghosts of men who died of starvation.

'Ghosts of men who died of poisoned arrows.'

The voices began to spring up all over the Square.

'Let the Admiral's ghost walk with them,' yelled one, and an angry roar followed the words.

Juan de Niebo, still leaning against the doorpost, said: 'Why is it they hate the Admiral so, Señor? He was always so kind, so patient. The whole thing since I came is a bad dream. Is it the fever talking to me still? I was to have had employment with the Admiral. As soon as I set foot on shore, they threw him into prison. I have never been allowed to see him. Why have they done this thing to him? Why?'.

Peter answered slowly: 'I don't know.'

He stood still, half listening to the crowd, half thinking what he must do. Suddenly he decided.

'I don't know,' he repeated, 'Juan de Niebo.' Then, as Juan stared at him, he pushed back his sleeve and showed his wrist with five tooth-marks like the print of a dog's foot.

Juan stared at him muttering: 'Not... not...'

'Yes, Juan. The boy whose life you saved in Palos. There are ghosts on Española and I have lived like one all these years, but I am still alive. Though my name was never Martin Alzate.'

He told Juan briefly who he was and what had happened to him during those years.

'And now,' he said at last, 'my chance has come. I counted on the Admiral's help, but I must do without it.'

'It should not be hard,' Juan said. He had recovered from his first surprise and had been listening with his wide mouth in a happy grin. 'Walk up to the Captain, that wide-shouldered man in black—sign up as a seaman. He needs men, I know. I will speak for you.'

'And if someone recognizes me as an Indian who has been seen in the town lately, I'll be sent back to the division, or have a sword run through me, or be sold as a slave. And also perhaps get you into trouble. Your being a friend of the Admiral's is only a danger to you—listen to the crowd.'

'Are you afraid?' Juan de Niebo asked.

'Yes. And if you had lived my life for eight years, you would be.'

'I would indeed. And I like you for telling the truth.'

Juan drummed on the bottom of a basin of suds and then

said: 'The first thing is to put you into some clothes in which you look less like a parrot that's been in a fight. Have you money?'

'A little. Here's my purse.

'Then I know where I can get clothes. Lie down on my bed behind that curtain. If anyone comes, be asleep.'

Peter lay there for what seemed like hours. When Juan came back he was carrying a sack. In it were a plain coat and a cap of dark-blue cloth, breeches of leather, heavy stockings, and a clumsy pair of leather shoes.

'They belonged to a sailor who landed when I did. He sold them to the tailor and bought lighter clothes.

These are hot for this place, but on ship it will not matter. Your own shirt will do. The sleeves of the coat are short and it is tight across the shoulders, but we are not all giants. Now, what did you do on the division—what work?'

'I was a blacksmith, but I do not dare say so, because someone might remember Turey, the blacksmith from the Valley of Pigs. There are two men in the town who have seen me there. It might make them notice me. I planned to call myself by the name of one of the overseers who died lately. Tomaso de Segovia was his name. His time of service was over and I know he planned to go back to Spain. He was tall and dark, not too unlike me.'

'Very well, then. You are Tomaso de Segovia. You are not a sailor but you want passage to Spain, and you will graciously condescend to haul on a rope if necessary. Come. I know the Captain. Do not stop to think about it. Remember, we are doing him a favor. I happen to know half his crew is ill with this shivering ague. Come!'

It was easy, as easy as Juan had said.

The Captain of the *Gorda*, Alonso de Vallejo, was only too

glad to let the strong-looking, neatly dressed young man sign the roll that made him a member of the *Gorda's* crew.

'Be ready to go on board at once,' Vallejo said. 'We sail with the tide. Get your things aboard.'

'I have nothing, Señor Captain, except a dog.'

Alonso de Vallejo gave an impatient sigh.

'Gambling, I suppose. You are all alike on this island. Well, some haven't even a dog for a friend,' he said, looking towards the prison. 'You may take the dog. There's a kennel on board that we used coming over. Tie him up when you get aboard.'

'Yes, Señor Captain. Shall I go aboard now? I see a boat coming.'

'Yes, go and report to the master. But come back with the boat. I shall need you here before long.'

'Yes, Señor Captain.'

Peter called to Tiger, who had been lying panting in the sunshine outside Juan's shop. Peter and the dog hurried towards the shore and Juan walked with them.

'Not so fast, Tomaso de Segovia. There are no wild pigs chasing you, no frog-faced Mallorcans. Quietly, quietly. My legs are weak.'

'Forgive me, Juan. Every minute is an hour now. I wish you were coming.'

'So do I—almost; but now I am here, I will stay and make my fortune.'

'Gold?'

'No! Soapsuds—hair ointment. Yours looks better already.'

'Well, take some gold to start with,' Peter said. He took his old lizard-skin pouch from around his neck and emptied it into his hand. The leather sling and the picture of his mother slid out and fine grains of gold dust powdered them thickly. Peter poured the gold back into the pouch and held it out to Juan.

Juan said: 'I cannot take it.'

'They would only take it away from me at the dock. It's little enough to give a friend who has saved me—twice.'

Peter slipped the picture and the sling in to his pocket. 'I have a few coins left in my purse still,' he said. 'Come and see me, Juan, when you have made your fortune.'

'Thank you, my friend. Where shall I find you?'

'At Melcote. In Essex. In England. It *won't be long now*.'

CHAPTER 21

CHAINS

THE great bell was ringing. The crowd stopped its snarling and hooting. Men stood aside in silence, leaving a clear path for Francisco de Bobadilla as he and his soldiers tramped across from the Governor's house to the prison.

Vallejo still stood at the prison gate. There were a dozen sailors near him. One of them was Peter. He looked pale and the sweat ran down his face. His hot clothes stifled him and pricked him. His shoes pinched his toes, but he stood there quietly, trying to hold the arquebus they had given him as the others did.

'Alonso, de Vallejo!' Bobadilla said. 'Bring out the prisoners.'

There was a roar from the crowd.

'Silence!' Bobadilla shouted, and the roar died to a purring murmur that was a more dangerous sound.

Would the soldiers and Vallejo's dozen sailors be able to hold back the crowd if they once started to rush, Peter wondered.

The jailer unlocked the heavy door. Vallejo went in, followed by the sailors. It was dark in the cell. Peter saw the Admiral's white head move in the shadows, heard his voice, weak now, but with some of its old charm and sweetness say: 'Vallejo, where are you taking me?'

'To the ship, Excellency. To Spain.'

'You mean—I am not to be hanged, Vallejo? Is this true?'

'Yes, Excellency.'

'Thank you. I am ready now.'

The soldiers cleared a path through the yelling crowd. The sailors hurried Columbus and his brother along towards the dock. The Admiral looked ill and old and white. His feet stumbled, but he tried to hold himself upright. Bartholomew walked with some of his old vigor, but his hawk face had the prison pallor on it.

Bobadilla and the soldiers followed. The soldiers were carrying chains and handcuffs.

'See that he is strictly confined and kept in chains during the voyage,' Bobadilla said, as the soldiers threw the handcuffs on the deck with a ringing clank.

Bobadilla did not speak to the Admiral. He hardly looked at him. Perhaps he did not like to meet the Admiral's faded blue eyes. He did not stay to see the chains riveted on.

It might have been done more quickly if Bobadilla had been on the ship. His soldiers would have done it readily enough, but the sailors were different. Many of them had sailed under the Admiral. They knew him and understood him. When the master gave the order for the chains to be riveted, there was a general drawing back.

'I'm no blacksmith,' muttered one.

'I signed as deckhand,' another said. 'It's no part of my work to chain up the Admiral, who was always good to me.'

'He sent money to my wife when she was ill,' another voice said, and the man beside the speaker added: 'I have a lame arm.'

The master broke into these mutterings by saying harshly: 'There'll be no mutiny on this ship while I'm master of it. Draw lots for the job if you don't like it, but if those chains are not on when the glasses are turned, there'll be chains for the rest of you.'

He spun on his heel and stamped away and looked back at Santo Domingo, which was rapidly becoming only a gray spot on the green of Española. He had no more desire than the sailors to see the chains fastened on the Admiral's wrists and ankles.

It was the cook, Espinosa, a man who did not know Columbus, who struck the blows that fastened the chains.

'They are afraid I shall swim back to Española, I suppose,' the Admiral said with a smile. 'Thank you, Espinosa. The fetters are comfortable. I shall enjoy wearing them.'

Espinosa came away looking frightened.

'It is done,' he said. 'I wish it were not.'

When Española was only a faint blue mist on the horizon, Alonso de Vallejo came to the Admiral and offered courteously to have the fetters struck off for the rest of the voyage.

'Let it be as it was ordered,' the Admiral answered gently. 'These chains are my reward for my toil and labor. I will wear them, and I will keep them near me as long as I live to remind me that worldly glory and honor soon fade.'

Among the men who guarded the Admiral and brought him his food was Peter. He had hoped that Columbus would remember him, but there was no recognition in the Admiral's weary eyes. Once, when they were alone, Peter asked him if he remembered the deck boy on the *Santa Maria*, Martin Alzate.

Columbus only shook his head.

'My troubles have made me forgetful, I fear,' he said with a

'I am cruelly cast down'

smile. 'It is a kind of discourtesy that age brings with it. No, I do not remember your friend.'

He dropped the pen with which he had been trying to write and lifted his hand to his forehead. The chain clicked against the handcuff. Peter picked up the pen. He saw how the Admiral's wrists had swollen and how the iron had chafed them.

'Could I write for you, my lord?' he asked.

'You can write?'

Columbus looked up in surprise.

'I was not always a sailor—or a prison guard, my Lord the Admiral,' Peter said. 'I can write—slowly perhaps and clumsily, but—'

'But your hands are free. I thank you for your kindness. Throw away that sheet where I have blotted the words with my chains and begin again.'

Peter dipped his pen and began. It was a long letter, but the Admiral spoke slowly and Peter's fingers could keep up.

'Write "To the noble lady Juana de Torre,"' the Admiral said. 'She was governess to the young Prince, the son of our gracious Queen. My sons were his pages, but he died and our Lady the Queen took the boys into her own household. What has come to them now?... But no matter. Let me see what you have written. Why, it is a good hand! Print is no plainer... I sold printed books once... long ago.'

After a short silence he began again, speaking slowly, more as if he were talking to someone in the room than dictating.

'"Most kind and gentle lady: for the first time you hear me complain against the world. Always before I thought courage and good conduct would help me, but now I am cruelly cast down. Yet God has always sustained me with His divine strength and even now He says to me: 'Oh, man of little faith, arise! It is I. Be without fear.'

"'He has made me His messenger to new skies and lands. No one believed me but the Queen whose servant I am, and two priests. To Her Majesty God gave the spirit and courage necessary to the finding of the new world. All others were busy telling of the dangers of the journey and of the cost, but Her Majesty helped me in spite of them all.

"'There were seven years of planning. Eight more were spent in discoveries that will always live in men's minds. Yet now even the vilest man may insult me. If I had stolen the Indies and given them to the Moors, I could not be more hated by the Spaniards.'"

He was lying on his bed now. He wore the brown robe of a monk of the Third Order of Saint Francis with its rope girdle. His hands were folded on his breast. The little light that came into the cabin shone on the polished steel of the handcuffs. He shut his eyes for a time. When he opened them, he went on to tell what took place after Bobadilla came to Española. He spoke quietly, as if the things had happened to someone else a long time ago.

Still, at the last he sat up and spoke with energy. His blue eyes flashed. Color came into his pale cheeks.

"'Rightly I should be judged as a captain sent from Spain to conquer a warlike nation whose people live deep in the mountains; I should be judged as a man who, by the grace of God, has brought a whole new world under the rule of the King and Queen, our masters. I should be judged as a soldier who for years has borne arms, never once laying them down. I should be judged by knights of adventure, by men of arms, by men of the sea, not by those who sit at desks and scratch with pens.'"

Peter's pen had a hard time to scratch fast enough to keep up with this. He felt as he wrote a deep pity for this conqueror in chains, this knight unarmed, this eagle caged. Yet even in his pity for the Admiral he could not forget the Indians gay and friendly on the beach of San Salvador and now toiling in mines, lashed with whips, dying...

Then—'I will not judge him,' he thought. 'God will do that.'

Columbus spoke once more of Bobadilla's injustice to him. He ended with the words: 'May God use His power and knowledge as He has in the past and punish the unjust.'

He put out his hand for the paper, took the pen, and painfully wrote the signature he always used:

Seeing Peter looking at it he said: 'You would like to know what it means? It is simple enough. The first S stands for Salve. Then turn the paper quarter of the way around, to the right, and reading the next six letters running down and from left to right you have X S for Christus, M A for Maria, Y S for Josephus. Turn it back again. The first three letters are a Greek sign for the first part of my name; the "Ferens" is for the last part of my name and means "bearing." But you know Latin better than I do, very likely. I can see that you are a scholar. The whole thing says this: "Save me Christ, Mary, Joseph. I carry Christ."

'It is strange,' he went on, 'that my parents gave me the name of Christopher, the name of one who carried Christ across deep waters. For that has been my task—is still my task. So much to do—so little done. So few priests sent to bring the light... I built churches but they called me a robber. But—I shall not see it, perhaps you will not—but there will be sometime in this new world that I have found a Christian people caring for justice and honor, and right. God has time enough. We can leave it to him.'

The fire and light faded out of his face. He lay down again, saying quietly: 'Thank you for writing. I shall sleep now.'

The letter was not wasted. The King and Queen, on hearing that Columbus had arrived in chains, ordered him to be freed immediately and escorted to their Court at Granada. Peter was one of his escort when he arrived there in December and was received in the Moorish palace called the Alhambra.

Peter had heard his father tell about the pools everywhere that reflected the palace and how it seemed to be carved out of lace and sea foam. He had heard, too, of the fountains that rippled and splashed and tinkled in the Court of Lions, of great vases overflowing with water near the doorways, of orange trees with balls of gold among the shining leaves. It was all as beautiful as he had ever imagined, and yet to Peter the days passed slowly.

The sight of the Admiral, in his splendid dress now but still lame and ill, was more painful somehow than the chained figure in the *Gorda's* cabin. The Sovereigns received him kindly, but nothing was said about his returning to Española as Governor. The Queen had grown old and pale since the day Peter had seen her, the day Ojeda threw the orange over the tower.

She had many troubles besides those in the far-off island that she would never see.

She had kind words for the Admiral, kindness for his sons who were still in her service, but that was all. King Ferdinand had always thought Columbus a bragging adventurer quite unfit to govern a great country. He disliked Columbus, but he disliked even more the fact that Columbus, by that agreement made in 1492, was to have a share in all commerce with the Indies. The trade was beginning to make money.

If that Genoese upstart, Ferdinand thought, gets a tenth of the profits of every voyage, he will soon be richer and more powerful than I am. An unpleasant thought. If Columbus had really found the mainland of Cathay as he claimed, was he to have a tenth of the profits? It was ridiculous, agreement or no agreement.

Ferdinand did not say anything of the sort to Columbus. He simply smiled and drooped his eyelids over his bright eyes and said to his wife that they would have to wait and see. At waiting and seeing Ferdinand was as good as a cat at a mouse-hole.

The Admiral was sorry when the tall young man who had written his letter was paid off by Captain Vallejo and told he was free to go wherever he liked. He could not see why Peter wanted to go to England, a cold and foggy place, he had always heard, and full, Bartholomew had said, of people who thought they were better than anyone else...

'Stay with me. We will make another voyage to Española and the lands beyond. You remember how beautiful it is on Española—so green with flowers and fruit and buds all on the trees at once? You remember the smell of spice and sweetness that comes out from the land as the ship slides into the harbor? And how the parrots flash out of the trees like flying flowers?'

That was not the way Peter thought of Española. To him it meant hunger and cruelty and terror. He tried, gently, to tell the Admiral this, but it was no use. Columbus said the Indians ought not to have fought against the Spaniards. He had thought at first they were friendly, but after the killing of the Spaniards at La Navidad he saw that it was necessary to conquer the Indians to keep peace in the country.

There had been some suffering, he knew, but Spaniards had suffered as well as Indians. When he went back he would make things better. The Indians ought not to work so hard on the divisions. It was right to tell him these things and they should be seen to.

Peter saw with sadness that even lying in chains had not taught the Admiral what it is to be a slave. Perhaps you have to be one to know.

Many things were sold in the market place in Cadiz. On the day Peter walked through it they were selling slaves. They were from Africa mostly, woolly-headed Negroes with sullen faces and dark, shining skins. They looked strong. The owners would get plenty of work out of those powerful arms and legs; more work than a mule could do, very likely. The low moaning that Peter heard came from behind them. He walked around the line of Negroes to see what it was. Slumped down on the ground were about a dozen Indians. They were as miserable—looking a lot as ever came out of a slave ship, half-starved, sick-looking men whose bones seemed to be pushing through their gray-brown skins. The man at the other end of the line was dead. His fall had pulled down the man who was chained to him. The others were sitting down with their heads buried in their hands or kneeling. They were all moaning or sobbing.

The dealer appeared. He was angry because the man was dead and snarled at those who were still alive. They got to their feet and stood there unsteadily in the cold wind, with tears running down their thin cheeks and making paths through the dust and paint on them.

'I'll never bother with another lot of Indians,' the dealer said. 'There's no profit in them. It's always the way. They die and you lose your money.'

'That must be hard,' Peter said gravely. 'How much is one worth?'

The dealer told him, but added that if Peter wanted a good strong slave he had better buy a Negro at twice the price.

'There's value there,' he said.

'I have a fancy for an Indian,' Peter told him. 'The small one there looks healthy. The one with the parrot painted on his chest. I'll take him. Strike off his fetters.'

'Well, you can have him, Señor, and welcome, and the price is little enough, but I still think an African would suit you better.'

Peter's purse was light as he led the sobbing Indian away. So was his heart. He had paid a debt he had owed for a long time.

The Indian was Cacibi.

'There was something queer about that Indian you sold,' the slave dealer's servant said to him. 'He was whimpering and crying half across the Square. Then the man that bought him—the tall young man with the ugly dog—said something, not more than a word or two, and the Indian began to laugh and dance. I think he knew the man who bought him.'

'All right. And if he did, what then?'

'I thought you might have got a bigger price.'

The slave dealer grinned.

'I got double my price already. It never pays to be greedy. Besides, these Indians, I've said it to you often enough, you have to sell them as quick as you can. They'll break their necks or die of the measles. A Negro, a Moor, even a Jew will make a good slave, but no more Indians. I've had enough.'

So Peter came to England with an empty purse and two friends—one with four legs and one with two—and happiness in his heart.

'To help find a new world—to come back to the old one with two friends—people have done worse than that,' he thought.

GREEN GARDEN

IT WAS June when he came to England.

The Captain of the Spanish ship paid Peter his wages. He even tossed Cacibi a few maravedis. Cacibi had amused him during a flat calm by singing and dancing the *areytas* of the Green Valley.

'He is more fun than a monkey,' the Captain said. 'The only Indian I've ever seen who is good for anything. Ship for the voyage back, you and your dancing monkey and your dog. You'll only get lost in this gray city. Oh, it looks bright enough today, but they have fogs here that choke and blind you, and the first thing you know you walk into the river and drown.'

But Peter only thanked him and walked off into London with his friends at his heels. Cacibi was dressed in a sailor's shirt and breeches and had a red cap stuck on his black hair. He was very much pleased with the cap. He had shoes, too, but he wore them tied together around his neck. People stared at the queer-looking trio—the tall young sailor who strode ahead with such a serious, determined air, the big ugly fawn and black dog, the brown-skinned, smiling little man with the bare feet.

Peter did not notice the staring people. He walked fast. London had changed but he knew his way. There was the Abbey, and the Sign of the Red Pale, where Master Caxton had wondered whether to write 'eggs' or 'eyren.' The street where the lawyer lived was near by. Peter remembered the house and the pleasant garden behind it that stretched down to the river.

It was all there and hardly changed at all. Only the yews had grown a little thicker and the box smelled a little more fragrant and there were more roses. Some how the roses were redder and sweeter than roses ever had been before.

Master Studley was in his garden resting after his dinner, the housekeeper said. He could not be disturbed. Her look said that he could not be disturbed by sailors—either barefooted or with shoes—or by muddy-footed mastiffs.

'There is no hurry,' Peter said. 'I have waited a long time to see him. I can wait until he wakes.'

He smiled, and the housekeeper suddenly noticed that this big, soft-voiced young sailor was a fine-looking young man, not handsome exactly, but there was some thing about him... and he reminded her of someone... now, who was it? Not...? Of course not!

'My eyes are getting old. He died long ago,' she thought, and aloud she said crossly: 'Well, I can't have the dog's paws and that brown man's feet on my clean floors. The roads are muddy after the rain. And that man doesn't look English. You'd better go through the garden gate. You can wait there, but don't speak to the master till he wakes.'

Master Studley had been eating cherries. There was a bench under the cherry tree. He sat there now with his head against the trunk, listening to a blackbird. The blackbird was pretending he was several other birds and making up songs to show them how much better they could sing if they really tried. He was paying himself in advance for the concert by helping himself to cherries inbetween songs. He got better cherries than Master Studley did because he was nearer the top of the tree.

Master Studley's figure was better for sitting under trees than for climbing them. He was not dressed for climbing either. His old-fashioned long gown was of the finest silk. The shirt under it was of linen like a cobweb. A hat of soft velvet with a cord and tassels of gold shaded his round pink face from the sun. He dropped a bunch of cherries on the ground and dozed off comfortably. When he opened his eyes again there was someone standing there in the sunshine. For a moment he thought he was dreaming. He said, speaking with difficulty as people do in dreams: 'Don Luis Medina-Barrios—that is, my Lord Aubrey...' Then he rubbed his eyes and looked again. The figure was still there—a grave, dark-eyed, sunburned young man in clothes of a foreign cut.

'Not Louis Aubrey, Master Studley. I am Peter, his son,' the young man said.

Master Studley still stared at him, then: 'The boy was drowned,' he said.

'No, Master Studley, not drowned. Will you hear my story?'

It took a long time to tell it. Cacibi and Tiger slept on the sunny side of a box tree. The end of the June day came at last with its long pale twilight. The Abbey seemed to float in it. The river was cool green and silver under the first faint stars.

Cacibi shivered and woke up. He had been dreaming that he was chained on a ship that was tossed by a cold gale. He was glad to find himself in a green garden: a garden almost as green as his valley was before the Spaniards came. He thought about his father, and was glad that Guarion had been killed in the fighting around St. Thomas. Guarion was not a slave and he never knew what happened to his valley, so he was never sad. Cacibi took a great breath of the clean sweetness of box and roses and English air.

'This is a good place, Turey,' he said, strolling out from behind the box tree.

Master Studley's round blue eyes became rounder.

'What's that?' he gasped.

Cacibi had taken off his sailor's clothes so that he could sleep comfortably. He had on a few folds of cotton cloth—Turey had told him that he must not go without clothes—and of course his tattooed parrot.

'This is my friend from Española of whom I told you,' Peter said gravely. 'He says he likes your garden. It was Cacibi who saved my life.'

Master Studley said hastily that he was sure Cacibi must be an excellent young man, but if his housekeeper should see him...

'She is a fine woman, but easily upset. And then the dinner for the next three days—your dog would not touch it!'

'Put your clothes on, Cacibi,' Peter said.

'First,' Cacibi said, 'I must dance and sing. While I was asleep I was making an *areytas* for you, Turey. I will dance it for you and the fat pink man, What a good face he has, Turey! It is beautiful—like the face of a clean pig.'

'What is he saying?' Master Studley asked.

'He admires you. He wishes to dance and sing for you.'

'Not without his clothes,' said the lawyer hastily. 'Besides, we must make our plans.'

Cacibi was finally persuaded not to dance and to put on his clothes. He was told to eat all the cherries he liked and not to swallow the stones.

'You shall sing your ballad when we come to our own place,' Peter said, and Cacibi gave his attention to spitting cherry stones over a rosebush.

Master Studley paced up and down over the green turf and Peter walked with him.

'You have not told me yet whether you believe my story,' Peter said.

'It is a strange story, but I would have had you thrown out into the street long ago if I had not believed it,' the lawyer said. 'Your resemblance to your father, your knowledge of family affairs, your having still your mother's picture, the scar on your wrist—for I was there the day you were brought in bleeding from it and clenching your teeth not to cry when they burnt the wound with hot iron: all these things make me believe you. But your cousin is not going to believe you, you know. Neither is your uncle, although luckily he is in Spain. It seems he prefers your Spanish property. He left here soon after Esteban came back from the Indies. I cannot imagine why anyone should prefer Spain—hot, dusty place, full of Spaniards—what are you laughing at? Of course I never would think *you* were a Spaniard, Peter—that is, my lord. You're English, naturally.'

'I hope I am,' Peter said. 'And I care nothing about the Spanish property. Let him keep it. I want only Melcote.'

'That is all very well, but shall we be able to get the Court of Chancery to believe you? It will take a long time. Your cousin is in possession there by your father's orders. He and that Gonzalo Palma of whom you have told me.'

Peter said: 'Ah, so Gonzalo is there, is he? Good!'

'No violence, sir,' the lawyer said. 'No violence, I beg of you. It would hurt your case before the Court. The King is firm that there shall be no private vengeance, no parties of brawling men-at-arms enforcing their masters' will.'

Peter smiled.

'You have seen my man-at-arms,' he said. 'No, Master Studley, Cacibi shall not attack them—with cherry stones! I could have murdered both Esteban and Gonzalo on Española if that had been the course I thought right. You see I believe—because I have seen it—that murder breeds murder. I will not use violence, but I want what is mine, and I want it soon. I want to see my mother back in her own place. I have been patient, I think, long enough. Now would it not be clearer in the minds of the judges that Melcote is mine, that I am really Peter Aubrey, if my cousin should leave it? Leave it in some haste? And if he should admit in your presence that he knows that Gonzalo and my Uncle Diego plotted to kill me?'

'It might be so,' Master Studley said cautiously. 'If your cousin fled and left you in possession—yes, that might be a point.'

'Very well, be in the Great Hall at Melcote in three days' time at about this time of day. And contrive that my cousin and Gonzalo are there too. And notice all you see.'

'You have some mad scheme.'

'It is not mad,' Peter said, and explained it to him, ending, 'If nothing comes of it, we can still take the longer way.'

'I will do it,' Master Studley said. He turned a shade pinker and asked: 'Your—your cousin's wife—is she to be present, too?'

'Oh, he has a wife, has he? He has everything, my cousin Esteban. Who is the lady who had the great good fortune to be chosen by this gentleman?'

Master Studley stammered: 'Of—of course she thought—she thought you had died—died, my lord. It—it is Mistress Tallard.'

Peter's laugh made the lawyer's eyes pop open wider than ever.

'Hurray!' Peter gasped. 'I owe him something after all. So I don't have to marry Gwen. You know, sir, when I was cold and starving and had been beaten by Esteban's overseer, I used to think: "Well, at least I'm not married to Gwen." There's always a bright side to a cloud, you know. That was the bright cloud lining on Española. To have Melcote without Gwen. Why, it's paradise, Master Studley. I think Cacibi had better dance his *areytas* after all. This day should be celebrated.'

It was celebrated much to the displeasure of Master Studley's housekeeper—although Cacibi by special request wore his clothes—and greatly to the pleasure of the maids, the pageboy, the grooms, and the gardener.

'It's a disgrace,' the housekeeper said. 'Yowling heathen, man-eating savage dancing in a garden. It ought to be stopped.'

'He certainly yowls,' Peter said, smiling, 'but he's a Christian, and all he's eaten so far in England is a few cherries. Give us a crust of bread and a little ale, good dame, and we beggars will be gone.'

Master Studley snorted. 'Beggars! Dame, this gentleman is—'

But Peter said quickly: 'We must be beggars—for three days, Master Studley. It would be a pity if anything should spoil our surprise. In three days' time I shall be able to offer you some entertainment—I hope.'

Chapter 23

PORTRAIT OF A GENTLEMAN

IT WAS pleasant walking through England on those long June days. The lawyer had offered them horses, but Peter declined them.

'Cacibi,' he said, 'would as soon ride a wolf. As for myself, I like the feeling of English dirt under my feet. I have been a sailor, you know, and so I hate the sea. I will drink water and I will wash in it, but I will never willingly sail on it. If I ever look at the sea again, it will be to thank Heaven I am ashore.'

So they strolled down a wide road that led east from London, sometimes leaving it for a forest path or a lane between hedges full of the sweetness of roses and honeysuckle; sometimes plodding along in the dust raised by the feet of cantering horses. Great soft clouds rolled up close to soft green fields and spilled silver showers to lay the dust and keep the fields green. The sun dried the travellers and warmed them without burning them. The breeze was so gentle that it hardly moved the soft fans of the chestnut trees. The great oaks spread cool shade for them. Flocks of sheep lay in sun-flecked shade while the shepherds slept and the sheepdogs growled at Tiger.

Tiger did not growl back. He was a proud dog. He would have liked to stop and tell those lazy sheepdogs something about hunting wild sheep on Española, but it was his business to take care of Cacibi. His master had said so. Tiger gave up the investigation of a thousand attractive new smells and padded along with his short muzzle at Cacibi's bare heels.

It was that sleepy time of afternoon when they came to Melcote. They climbed an old oak at the edge of the wood and looked down on the quiet house. The ivy had begun to climb over the rosy walls, but otherwise there was little change. There was a soft murmur in the air—the sleepy voices of pigeons and hens, the droning of bees among the roses. There were men working in a distant hayfield. Everything else seemed asleep.

Peter gave Cacibi the last of the food he had bought.

'Stay here,' he said, 'you and Tiger, till I come. You stay in the tree, Cacibi. Take care of Cacibi, Tiger, and guard my cloak.'

He flung the cloak to the ground. The big dog lay down on it with a low growl that meant: 'Anyone who tries to touch this cloak had better take care. This is HIS cloak.'

From the tree Cacibi watched the tall figure with approval. Turey moved quietly. Hardly a leaf stirred as he passed. Even Caonabo's men were no better at making every bush and tree hide them. Cacibi soon lost sight of Peter. The only sign of his passing was the birds waking up as he went by. These birds had different voices from birds in the Green Valley, but Cacibi knew that they were saying: 'Who is this coming? Where is he going? Never mind. He means us no harm. Our nest is safe. He is going... going... gone.'

After a long time he saw Peter cross a little patch of sunlit turf and slip through a gate in the garden wall. Cacibi could not see into that corner of the garden, but he could tell by the chatter of sparrows that Peter must be moving among the dark green trees that showed above the wall. Their shapes looked like birds and beasts to Cacibi.

'What a place!' he thought. 'Even the trees grow like giant lizards! But what can you expect of a country full of horses?

His friend Turey had come out of the dark trees now. He was moving fast along the wall of the house. Then he stopped and felt among some green leaves that covered part of the wall. He seemed to be pulling at something. Next he took out his knife and cut the vines and tugged again. Something strange happened. A piece of the house moved. There was a dark crack in the wall. Then Turey slipped into the crack and in a minute the wall showed no sign that he had ever touched it.

Cacibi spent no time trying to think what might be going on behind the wall. He felt quite sure Turey would be all right— Turey, who could ride horses and make walls move. Cacibi curled up comfortably in the oak tree and went to sleep.

Peter's heart thumped as the door fell into place be hind him. He stood still until his own breathing was no longer the loudest thing in his ears. Melcote still held its sleeping silence as he moved slowly through the darkness, testing each remembered step, steadying himself with hands that groped along the wall.

It was cool in the passage after the hot sun outside, cool with a musty, dusty smell. He counted the stairs. Four. That was right. He was on a level with the Great Hall now. Two paces forward and here at his left hand was the knob that opened the panel. Farther along and above it was the cloth behind the face of the picture. He lifted it and looked into the Great Hall. He had to stoop now for the peephole instead of standing on tiptoe. Nothing else had changed. The Hall was empty, but he heard voices. He let the cloth fall back into place and moved along through the blackness. His glance into the Hall had made spots and streaks of light against the darkness for a moment.

Here was the roughness that was the brick chimney, and here was the narrow stair that twisted up to his room in the tower.

A woman's voice behind the panel said: 'My lady wants the floor swept clean before the new carpet is spread,'. and another, a man's, grumbled: 'I hate these new fashions. Now, at Tallard Castle we always had rushes on the floor. There was none of this sweeping there.'

'Yes, throw the bones down on the rushes for the dogs to gnaw, and when it smells too strong, move to another house and leave the old one to sweeten. With such good old fashions I've no patience, and neither has my mistress.'

There was more grumbling and the sound of a broom sweeping. Peter moved softly on up the twisting stairs. The peephole at the top showed him that his old room was empty. He had expected that, for the lawyer told him that Peter's mother had locked it when the news of Peter's death came, and he could see no reason to think it had ever been opened. There were plenty of other rooms in the house. The panel opened easily. He stepped in and looked around. The lawyer was right: it had never been used. It was so dusty that his feet made tracks across the floor. No one had touched his books. They were still on the shelf by his bed, thick with dust on top, but with the backs still showing faint gleams of red and gold. The coverlet that his mother had worked for him was still on the bed. Through the dust he could still make out the Aubrey arms and the border with birds and sheep and dogs and horses, all about the same size, dull gold among green leaves and red roses.

And—luckiest of all—the chest was still there. No one had disturbed it—the chest that had belonged to his father. The key was in the lock.

There were clothes of his own now, lying folded on top of the pile. Could he ever have been as small as that? The blue silk doublet—how grand he had felt the first day he had worn it! He lifted out the pile of his own clothes. His mother—it must have been she—had put lavender among them to keep the moths away. There was still a faint smell in the long dried bunches of it.

Underneath the blue doublet was the crimson velvet tunic with the gold embroidery and the soft brown fur around the bottom and at the neck and sleeves. It was there—just as his father had worn it when the King had first named him Baron Aubrey. Peter unfolded it carefully. It was wrinkled and creased, but it would serve his purpose.

'I can sleep awhile now,' he thought.

Melcote was beginning to wake up from its after dinner drowsiness, but in the hot, dusty room at the top of the tower, its master slept with his head resting on the dusty coverlet.

Stephen Aubrey—as Esteban liked to be called now—was not glad to see Master Studley come ambling up the road under the beeches on his fat white mare. The lawyer was always thinking of some excellent reason why there was less money to spend than Esteban wanted. Master Studley was much more likely to produce sermons than gold, and Esteban had no taste for sermons. One of his first acts when he began to manage Melcote was to send Father Patrick away. The chaplain, Esteban considered, was a tiresome old man who had an unpleasant way of talking about people's sins. The new chaplain also had this annoying habit, but not having known Esteban from boyhood, he had less material to work on.

Esteban received the lawyer politely enough according to his own standards of politeness: that is, Esteban shouted to the grooms to take care of the horse, made one or two lazy bows, and stood looking out under drooping eyelids while Master Studley got himself out of the saddle.

'I hope I am not disturbing you at your supper,' Master Studley panted as he thumped to the ground. He looked hot and dusty. He must have been riding hard, Esteban thought, and drawled: 'No bad news, I hope. Come into the Great Hall. Our supper is spread there.'

Master Studley said that what news he had—simply business about the estate—would keep until after supper. Really he had come chiefly to taste Melcote strawberries and cream again. Oh, it was pleasant to see a table like this again. His housekeeper had been—ah—troubled about something these last three days and his dinners had suffered strangely. Burnt pudding, scorched cabbage, soggy dumplings... but why talk about it? Here was real Melcote plenty! Where else did one ever see such a round of cold beef? Such roast young piglets? Such strong brown ale?

Esteban did not answer. He made another of his bows, kicked a dog out of the way, and flung himself into a chair at the head of the table. His wife, beautiful in silver and pale blue, sat at the other end of the long table. Esteban waved Gonzalo Palma and the lawyer to seats on a hard bench. They were facing the fire place with the first Baron Aubrey in his crimson velvet to the right of it, and to the left King Henry's thin face and black gown.

Tom the Jester in his second-best suit of scarlet and gold lay in front of the fireplace, using a big greyhound for a pillow. Tom stared up at the roof of the Hall and sang a ballad about a young girl whose wicked stepmother had her cut up and baked in a pie.

> *If you your daughter dear would see,*
> *My lord, cut up that pie,*

Tom sang by way of a cheerful supper-time song, and then stopped in the middle of the next line and said: 'Just as it might be in that pie at your elbow, Master Aubrey. No, don't throw your tankard at me, good master. No one thinks you ever had any of your kinsmen—cooked.'

'Quiet, fool,' Esteban said softly.

'Oh, yes. Fools should be quiet. Only wise men speak. I remember now, that is the way of the world—this merry, merry world. Men love dogs, and dogs love cats, and cats love rats. So men love rats. And so I am a friend of the rats that live behind this wainscot, though they do squeak and scratch most rudely.'

Gwendolen Aubrey said peevishly: 'Peace, Tom. There are no rats in this house.'

Master Studley stopped eating strawberries and said: 'No rats in this house? You are fortunate, my lady.'

Gwendolen yawned: 'No, nothing ever happens here. Even a rat hunt would be a change. Of course we can always go out and look at the pigs, but it will be better in London when we have our house there and go to Court.'

Seeing her husband's scowl turned on her she added hastily: 'Oh, it is only a dream, of course.'

Master Studley took a last strawberry, rinsed his fingers in a bowl of rosewater that a page brought him, wiped them on a bit of damask, put the tips of them together carefully, and looked through them at the portrait of the first Baron Aubrey.

When the page had left the room, the lawyer said: 'You wrote to me, Don Esteban, about selling Ashford. It seems a pity—one of our best farms—to have it go into strange hands. You say you have a letter from your father ordering the sale, but I think it would be better to wait until Don Diego returns. Selling the other property was Mistress Gwendolen's affair. It was hers to do as she liked with. Surely you do not need more money already.

Esteban said sulkily: 'The money of which you spoke went to pay—to pay a debt. As to having Ashford go into strange hands, you will be glad to know that the purchaser is Master Gonzalo Palma, to whom my father and I are both indebted for much faithful service. And call me Master Aubrey, please, as long as I own Melcote.'

'Certainly—Master Aubrey,' the lawyer said.

He put his fingertips together and added: 'And will Master Franco give all his attention to farming now?'

'Master Franco will stay here and attend to the wool business as usual—in case affairs should call me to London.'

'And you can count on him to shear the sheep closely,' the Jester murmured, getting up and kicking his long scarlet leg high in the air, and spinning around with a silvery tinkling of little bells.

Gonzalo's yellow face turned the color of a rotten orange.

'I shall not forget your praise,' he began, but something stopped him.

From somewhere in the wall came a loud thumping.

'What—what was that?' Gwen Aubrey stammered.

She got up from her seat and turned towards the fireplace. The sun had set. Only pale twilight came through the painted glass, yet in the dimness Gwen saw something, clutched at the lawyer's shoulder, and screamed: 'The portrait. Baron Aubrey. I saw his eyes move.'

Esteban had drunk a good deal of wine while the others were eating. He shouted roughly: 'What *is* this? Can't a man have supper in peace in his own Hall?

'In whose Hall, Esteban?' came a deep voice.

The painted panel swung back and a figure stepped into the shadowy room. It stopped near the fireplace and stood still, looking, in its deep crimson dress, so like Baron Aubrey's portrait that even Master Studley felt his breath come hard for a moment. The last of the twilight showed the portrait of Lady Aubrey in its frame of gold and pearls that hung around his neck, struck on the gold-embroidered purse that hung from his belt. The face in the shadow of the black velvet hat was the face of the portrait come alive.

No one in the Hall spoke and the grave, deep voice went on: 'Why did you kill my son, Gonzalo Palma? Why did you drown him? He had done you no harm. Why did you stone him into the sea?'

Gonzalo shrieked: 'I did not kill him. I tell you it was the other. It was young Alzate the stone hit. He was the one that was drowned. Don Esteban knows it. His father knows it... Keep off... Don't touch me... It was Don Diego told me to do it, but it was Alzate the stone hit...'

'Why did you kill my son?' came the voice out of the shadows, deeper than before.

'I did not kill him. He died on Española, the Indians killed him. He died at La Navidad.'

Esteban, who had hastily swallowed another cup of wine, now got to his feet and stood swaying and holding on to his chair.

'Yes, Peter died at La Navidad,' he said thickly. 'Everyone knows that.'

'Peter did not die at La Navidad, though I am grateful to you, Cousin Esteban, and to you, Gonzalo, for your kind interest,' Peter said in his natural voice. 'Gwen, I am sorry to have frightened you.'

Gwendolen moaned: 'Peter, Peter! You have come back.'

'Yes. I have come back, Gwen.'

'But too late.'

'Oh, I think not. Just in time, surely. Yes, Tom'—to the Jester, who was kneeling beside him crying—'I was the rat behind the wainscot!'

Esteban reeled forward shouting: 'The man's an impostor! Gonzalo, call the grooms. Have them throw him out. It's a plot. To take Melcote away from me. All lies. You know it's all lies, Studley.'

'I know there have been plenty of lies told, Don Esteban, but not by Baron Aubrey.'

Gonzalo was moving towards the door.

'Stop,' Peter said sharply. 'Don't move.'

He had been holding his right hand behind him all the time. Now he raised it. Martin Alzate's sling was in it.

Gonzalo shrieked: 'No! No!'

'Stand still,' Peter said, 'or there might be an accident. Now this stone, Gonzalo, is going to strike just to the right of your head'—there was a singing crack and the stone whizzed past Gonzalo's ear—'and this one to the left'—again that fierce singing noise—'and this one—'

'No, no!' Gonzalo shrieked. 'Mercy!'

'—and this one,' Peter said quietly, 'I will put back in my bag and keep it for you, in case you ever set foot in England again. Go back to Spain, Gonzalo, and you, Esteban. And take Gwen with you. I feel sure your father will be delighted to see you and to know that I am alive. I know the gentlemen at the Spanish Court will find Gwendolen beautiful. They like golden hair—and gold. Gonzalo will supply that. I am certain he has plenty of money. I remember well how he used to cheat you in the Valley of Pigs, Esteban.'

Esteban gasped: 'Valley of Pigs.'

'Yes, my dear cousin. When I was your slave and shod your horses, and was lashed on the back. Would you like to see your scars? And the Aubrey arms tattooed on my shoulder? Would you like to know how a little lashing feels? I might borrow a whip, I suppose, though I doubt if the lash will be pickled in salt.'

Esteban muttered something and Peter said: 'No, I thought not. You had better go, Esteban, before I change my mind.'

Master Studley said: 'You have decided not to give Gonzalo in charge for murder on the high seas, and your cousin for using his knowledge of the crime to get your property by fraud? There are men of the King's ready and waiting outside the gates if I give the signal.'

Gwendolen sobbed: 'No, Peter. Only let us go.'

'Out of respect for Don Esteban's wife, I will do nothing—except see that they are escorted to the ship. There is one sailing for Cadiz, the one on which I came. Go, Tom, and have the horses saddled. Say that Don Esteban and his wife and a friend, Master Gonzalo, are going on a journey.'

Tom turned a tinkling cartwheel and went out. They heard him singing as he went:

And as they ride along these three,
Happy the journey that will be!

CHAPTER 24

SAFE HARBOR

IN AN OLD gray house in the shadow of Lincoln Cathedral three people sat waiting. The old man in the coarse brown serge robe was Father Patrick. He had grown thin and the fringe of hair around his bald head was white. Dame Butts was no thinner, but she had begun to stoop, and she limped as she got up from the table to turn the spit so that the meat roasting in front of the fire would cook on the other side. Lady Aubrey, near the window, was surrounded by folds of green silk. Her needle moved quickly, but she looked out between stitches into the street and towards the new gray arch called the Stone Bow.

'I wish Meg would come,' she said. 'Only if she is late I may finish her dress before dinner. See, Dame, I have turned the silk, and I believe it will look better than ever it did with the new flowers I have embroidered on the girdle. See, I mended the torn place and I have embroidered a rose over it. It will never show now. Will you watch for her, Father, while I take my last stitches? When she comes through the gate, tell me and I will hide the dress. I would not like her to see it until it is finished.'

'I will watch gladly,' the old priest said. 'It's like sunshine when she comes.'

'She's more than sunshine,' snorted Dame Butts. 'She's meat and drink to us all. What should we have done all these years if she had not done a man's work managing the farm? We'd have starved, all three of us!'

'I wish she could live more gently,' Lady Aubrey sighed. 'This work is not womanly.'

Father Patrick chuckled: 'Which is why she likes it, my lady. Let's not pull long faces over Meg. She's happy with her horse and her dogs and telling the men what work to do: happy taking care of us, too. There's great pleasure in doing good every day—especially if you can hear the birds sing and see the flowers bloom while you're doing it. Did you know one of the best books ever written about hunting and fishing was written by a woman? And that she was a nun besides and a Lady Abbess? Master Wynken de Worde printed it. The Saint Albans book, I think it was called. There was a copy at Melcote.'

Seeing Lady Aubrey's needle stop he added hastily: 'Let us hope she comes soon, for that fowl is roasted to a turn, or my nose lies.'

He stood looking through the open casement in silence while Dame Butts lifted the lid of a pot that sent a warm steam of cabbage through the room, then looked at the fluffy white dumplings in the next kettle.

'Another minute and my dumplings will be spoiled,' she mourned.

'I hear horses surely,' Lady Aubrey murmured, sending her needle rapidly through the green silk.

'A horse—six horses, but not Meg,' Father Patrick said. 'It's—look out, my lady; is that not Master Studley?'

Lady Aubrey looked down the street towards the gray arched gate. There were men in gold and blue riding through it.

'It is Master Studley,' she said, turning pale and walking away from the window. 'And—and, those men wear the Aubrey colors. What can it mean? Some new danger? Can they—can Esteban and Diego take away the little we have left?'

'Master Studley has always been your friend, my lady. He would not see evil done to you,' Dame Butts said.

'There is a young man with him, but it is not Esteban,' the priest said slowly. 'It looks—it looks... but I am old... I see poorly.'

He put his hand over his eyes.

Horses came cantering up the soft road, thudded to a stop with creakings and clinkings and panting snorts. There was a knock at the door.

Master Studley walked stiffly into the room. His face was red and hot. The smile on it made it look like a full moon rising on a summer night.

'Lady Aubrey,' he panted, 'I bring you news.'

'Not—bad news?'

'I do not wonder you ask. I have brought it to you many times, though never willingly. I think the hardest time was on a day nine years ago. I came to tell you your son was dead.'

'Do not speak of it please.'

'I must speak of it. I lied to you, my lady. He is not dead. He is here. Come in, my lord.'

So Peter came into the hot little room where his black head nearly brushed against the black beams, where his mother ran through waves of green silk to meet him, where the old priest stood praying and blessing him, and where Dame Butts said crossly: 'Now my dumplings are burned,' and then cried into the cabbage so that it didn't need salting.

And in a few minutes Meg was there too and Peter said: 'Why, it can't be Meg—she's beautiful,' and everyone laughed at him. The dinner was spoiled, but no one minded, even Dame Butts. It was enough to see Peter, to hear his voice, to touch his sleeve. He had to tell his story again, and they all sat quiet and listened.

Tom the Jester was there and Cacibi. They had ridden all the way from Melcote together on an old gray mare and they were friends. Tiger was there. He took the fowl off the spit while Dame Butts was not looking and took it into the corner. He did not mind about its being burned. Hubert the Forester and the grooms crowded around the doorway and forgot where they were in hearing of that strange new world beyond the seas.

At last it was over. There was silence in the room. Then Father Patrick spoke.

'I am proud of you, my son. You were brave and patient in your time of trouble. You put aside vengeance in your time of triumph. You have done well.'

Peter said slowly: 'No, Father. I was not brave. I was frightened. I only wanted to live—to live and come home again. Whatever I did was for that. Perhaps I did not always judge well what was the best way. I might, I think, have come more quickly, if I had killed Esteban and Gonzalo there in the valley. I might have done it, but I would not come home to you with their blood on my hands. You had taught me better than that, Father, and mother. I would not repay cruelty with cruelty, murder with murder. There was enough of both on that island. And—I think they will not go unpunished.'

'But—Gwen,' Lady Aubrey said. 'You were betrothed to her. And Esteban married her.'

Peter looked across the room at Meg and smiled.

'Yes,' he said. 'Esteban has Gwen. And I have forgiven him.'

Meg wore the dress of green silk, turned so the best side was outside, when she and Peter were married. She would not have a new one, she said. She wanted to wear the roses Peter's mother had embroidered. There were roses, too, in the chapel at Melcote and in the Great Hall. Peter wore the tunic of crimson velvet that had been his father's, and looked so like the picture on the wall that everyone spoke of it.

'Good days have come again to Melcote,' people said. 'This young Baron Aubrey is like the first one. There'll be no more cheating us on our wool and gambling the money away. No more of that frog-faced Gonzalo Palma squeezing out every penny and never a new tile on the roof. The young master, he's all for England. They say he's sworn never to leave it again.'

Peter never did leave it again, but news of the land beyond the sunset came to him sometimes. One of the times was on a Christmas Eve. The year was 1510.

The Great Hall at Melcote looked as Peter had once on the *Santa Maria* dreamed that it might. The Yule log burned in the fireplace and threw a warm orange-red light on holly and mistletoe, and on the people around the long table: on Master Studley's pink face and Father Patrick's grown rosy and plump again now. It shone on Meg's bright hair—Peter would never let her cover it—and on Lady Aubrey's happy face; on Dame Butts scolding Tiger for snatching a bone and then giving it to him; on Cacibi and Tom, both magnificent in suits with silver bells wherever a bell could be; on two people Peter had never seen in any dream picture.

One was a solemn golden-haired boy of eight. The other was

a black-haired, black-eyed, dancing midget of a girl. Christopher was the boy's name. The girl was named Elizabeth, but her father, on whose chair she was climbing, called her by a dozen different names—My Pet Parrot, Melcote's Pride, Imp of Sunshine, were some of them.

She was demanding a story—the story of how the great ship went on the sandbank on a Christmas Eve long ago—when there was a knock at the door. The page who opened it came back saying that there were two men there who spoke so strangely that he could not tell whom they wanted. Foreigners, probably. They looked cold—should he take them to the kitchen?

But Peter already had one arm around a tall, shivering man and another around a short fat one with hair like a spaniel's and was dragging them towards the fire, saying: 'Juan! Pedro! So you have come at last. I wondered so many times about you both.'

So Elizabeth—that pet parrot—heard her story, but not from her father. It was about the man her father talked about, the man he called the Admiral. She heard it from the two foreigners. She liked them both. She liked Pedro de Salcedo because he took a pink-lined shell out of his pocket and told her she could hear how the waves sounded on the sandbar that Christmas Eve if she would put it to her ear. She liked Juan de Niebo best, though. He had such a funny nose and his teeth chattered.

Her father said: 'Tell me about the Admiral, Pedro, Juan.' And Pedro looked sadly at her father out of his soft eyes and said, 'Juan was there; he will tell.'

'He died in Valladolid,' Juan said. 'It is strange you had not heard, and yet it is not strange, because the world has forgotten him. They painted a great picture of explorers and they left him out. I do not understand. After his last voyage—'

'Tell me about that voyage, Juan.'

'I was with him, Martin—Lord Aubrey, I mean—my tongue forgets what my heart knows! We sailed along the mainland, found new islands, places where pearls grew as thick as peas. Great rivers we found, new tribes of Indians with much gold. But our ships were rotten and eaten by worms. They would not let him land at Española. Did you know that?'

Peter shook his head and stared at the fire.

'There was a hurricane coming. You know how it comes?'

Peter nodded, but his daughter said: 'What is that hurricane? Tell how it comes.'

'It is a great wind, my lady, but first comes a heavy stillness and it is hot, hot as if a thousand fires were lighted. After that comes the wind, and the trees are twisted out of the ground as I might twist the stem out of a ripe pear. The sea rises like a wall of gray stone and plays with ships as if they were walnut shells. Well, the Admiral anchored off Santo Domingo and told the Governor, Nicholas Ovando—may his name be forever written in letters of mud!—that there was a hurricane coming, and asked permission to take shelter in the harbor.

'"No," says Ovando. "It would be against the Queen's orders." "Well," says the Admiral, "at least do not let these ships sail that I see setting their sails, for this storm will surely wreck them." So they laughed at him and the fleet sailed. Bobadilla was on one of the ships. Tell them what happened to the ships, Pedro.'

'They were all lost,' Pedro de Salcedo said gravely, 'except one. It belonged to the Admiral. It had gold of his on it. It arrived safely in Spain. The others—I think there were fourteen—all carried gold too. The fishes have it now—and Bobadilla.'

Juan, who had been holding his trembling hands to the fire, went on:

'Well, the Admiral left the harbor and we anchored in a small cove farther along the coast and rode out the storm, but it did not do our ships any good. So after sailing, as I have told you, along the mainland, we went to Jamaica. The Admiral sent a message to Ovando that he had landed on Jamaica and that our ships would take us no farther and asked him to send ships to rescue us, but Ovando was busy. We had to wait a year.'

'A year!' Peter exclaimed. 'Had you food enough?'

'No. We traded with the natives at first. They refused to bring us food anymore after they had got enough beads and bells. The Admiral—he was ill but he could still do better than the fifty who were well—knew there was an eclipse coming. He told the Indians the face of the moon would be darkened that night if they did not bring food. The moon came up looking like a burnt-out coal, and then turned black like some thing dead floating in the blue. The next day we had enough food to make us sick for a week. He was too ill to walk without my shoulder to lean on, but he got out of bed and frightened them with a dark moon. His voice—you remember his voice, Martin—my lord, I mean—it almost frightened me.'

'Don't forget that Ovando sent you food,' Pedro said.

'I do not forget. After a year he sent us a side of bacon and a cask of wine.'

'For fifty of you?' Peter asked.

'Thereabouts. Some had died by then. I had a slice of bacon, I remember. It was good bacon.'

'Why did he do such a thing, this Ovando?' Peter asked.

'He wanted to see if the Admiral was dead,' Juan said calmly. 'The ship could have carried most of us to Española, but the Captain said Ovando had told him not to land.'

'What is it, Father, that cross noise you made?' Elizabeth said.

'Never mind, dear monkey. Go on, Juan.

'You remember a fat little man called Pedro de Salcedo?' Juan inquired.

'I remember a—a rather plump young man of that name, one of the best fellows that ever lived,' Peter said, laughing.

'Well, this stout fellow—don't blush, Pedro—hears at last about the Admiral. Ovando, of course, never mentioned that the Admiral of the Ocean Sea is shipwrecked on Jamaica—it's so much more interesting to talk about pigs, or about the weather. Still, Pedro hears about it accidentally, and he fits out a ship at his own expense and rescues us from that island. It is a very beautiful place, and if it sinks tomorrow, I shall not care.'

'What did you do then?' Peter asked.

'We sailed to Spain. We were greeted with the news that the Queen was dead.'

'That must have been a great sorrow to him.'

'Yes, it was so. He never, I think, forgot it. He followed the Court, but the King paid no attention to him. At Valladolid he took a room in the inn. He had not much money. All he had he spent to get the men who had been on Jamaica with him back to their homes and to pay their wages, although it was the Royal Treasury that owed the money. It was a poor room he had, over the stables. There was a trap door in the floor. He used to open it and look down at his mule eating his grain. He kept those chains—you remember?'

'Yes, I remember,' Peter said, shielding his eyes from the fire.

'He kept them hanging on the wall. He had very little else. He was very weak, but sometimes at night his hands would be steady enough so that he could write to his sons. They are very grand young men, his sons, well educated, splendidly dressed. The younger one, Don Ferdinand, went with us on the voyage. He is a gentle and courteous young man and a great lover of books.

'The older one was a little ashamed of his father, I think. You can see how he might seem. A crazy old man, ill, half-blind, dying, but planning to start out any day and win back the Holy Sepulchre from the infidels. It was not sensible, of course.'

'No,' Peter said. 'And it wasn't sensible to sail to the Indies in 1492. *But* we got there, Juan... Did the King do nothing at all for him?'

'Yes. When he thought the Admiral must be tired of poverty and neglect, he offered him an estate in Leon, if the Admiral would give up all the privileges of commerce and governorship in the Indies that the King and Queen had promised to him.'

'And he—?'

'Refused. And was left alone with his gout and his chains and his maps. He made his will. He had not much to leave except his claims on the Indies, but he left orders to pay small sums "to be given in such a way that those who receive them will not know from whom they come." They were to people who had helped him when he was unknown and trying to be heard at Court, I think.

'A man called Amerigo Vespucci, a pilot, came to see him. The Admiral received him kindly. Vespucci had not had the good fortune he deserved, the Admiral said. He wrote a letter to introduce Amerigo to his son Diego. Amerigo has had a piece of good fortune now.'

'What is that?'

'They call the mainland that Columbus discovered America.'

'What?' shouted Peter, getting up and stamping across the room.

'Peter, *darling*,' murmured his wife, 'would you like me to throw something at something for you?'

Peter groaned: 'Go on, Juan. You can't have anything worse to say.'

'He wrote to the young Princess Joanna, the heiress to the throne, but though she and her husband came to Valladolid she did not send for him. We heard the shouts of the people as she rode through the streets. I think it was the next day he died. It was the twentieth of May. Like our Queen when she died, he was wearing the robe of the Third Order of Saint Francis. We buried him in the monastery at Valladolid. It is a dusty town with bare mountains around it. No trees. He loved trees. Remember?'

'I remember,' Peter said.

'We buried his chains with him. It was his order.'

'I do not like this story,' said Elizabeth. 'It is too sad.'

'You must forgive me, my lady,' Juan said smiling.

'You must forgive her, sir,' said young Christopher gravely. 'She is too young to understand.

'I am as old as you, Chris Aubrey.'

'Half an hour younger,' her brother said.

'I will pull your red hair for that.'

'Not on Christmas Eve. Come here, little witch,' Peter said. 'Juan will tell another story.'

'About a ship?'

'No,' Juan said, 'about an egg.' He took one from a dish on the table. 'Is this one cooked, my lady?'

'Hard-boiled,' Meg said.

'Very well. Now I will show you something. I am the Admiral. I sit here at the table. I put my hat on my head. Everyone else has to take his off, because although I was once a poor man, I am now an Admiral of Spain. See what a fine scarlet and gold coat I have.'

'It's brown, really,' Elizabeth said.

'Be quiet,' said Christopher. 'You spoil the story.'

'So I sit here,' Juan went on, 'with many noble lords around me. They are all jealous of my fine clothes and because I have found the way to the Indies and because the Queen treats me kindly. So pretty soon one of these gentlemen leans forward and he says, lisping and in a voice like a girl: "Don Cristobal, don't you think that even if you had not made this famous voyage of yours, someone would have made it, sooner or later? We have plenty of fine sea-captains in Spain, you know."

'The Admiral bows to him very politely, "Probably you are right, sir," he says. Then he picks up an egg-like this one—and hands it to the fine gentleman. "Can you make this egg stand on end?" he says. Try it, my lady. See—it rolls over. Can you make it stand up, young Master Christopher? No. And neither can I. Pass it around the table. That's what the Admiral did. All those grand gentlemen tried it, but it always rolled over. Just like this.

'At last it came back to him. He taps one end of it on the table—like *this*—and then it stands up like that because the end is flat now, you see. Then the Admiral gets up.

'"You can all do it now, gentlemen, I am sure," he says, and walks off. So they could. When he'd shown them the way.'

'Is that a true story, Juan?' Peter asked.

'He only laughed when I asked him that, my lord. It may not be true, but there's truth in it. It's like him, is it not?'

'Yes, I can hear him say it.'

'Tell another story. Tell a story about a pig. My father knows a story about a pig,' said Elizabeth, yawning.

'No more stories tonight,' Meg Aubrey said.

'Juan will be here tomorrow and many more days. He will tell many more stories. So give me a kiss, my pet lizard,' Peter said.

'Here are five big ones. And will Cacibi sing tomorrow? Will he sing:

> *Turey was a strong man,*
> *He came to the Green Valley with a knife around his neck.*
> *He went with Caonabo in the moonlight.*
> *Dance Caonabo, white men coming.*
> *Dance Caonabo, white birds sailing.*
> *Dance Caonabo, chains are waiting!*

Will he sing that, tomorrow?'

'Yes, Cacibi will sing all you like, little wreath of parrot's feathers. Go to bed now.'

Meg carried her away still talking.

'They spoil that child,' said Dame Butts, who spoiled her too.

Young Christopher waited a moment.

'Thank you for your story,' he said to Juan. 'I am glad I am named for him. Good night, sir,' he said politely to Pedro. 'I am glad you came to Melcote to see us.' Then he turned back and spoke to Juan again: 'He was a great man, wasn't he?'

'What is a great man, young master?'

'One who is brave and patient and true. One who is kind. One who never gives up.'

'Tell me your whole name, young master.'

'Peter Christopher Columbus Aubrey.'

'Then,' Juan said gently, 'I think you were named for two great men.'